By Anna Quindlen

FICTION

After Annie

Alternate Side

Miller's Valley

Still Life with Bread Crumbs

Every Last One

Rise and Shine

Blessings

Black and Blue

One True Thing

Object Lessons

NONFICTION

Write for Your Life

Nanaville

Lots of Candles, Plenty of Cake

Good Dog, Stay

Being Perfect

Loud and Clear

A Short Guide to a Happy Life

How Reading Changed My Life

Thinking Out Loud

Living Out Loud

BOOKS FOR CHILDREN

Happily Ever After

The Tree That Came to Stay

AFTER ANNIE

AFTER ANNIE

A NOVEL

ANNA QUINDLEN

RANDOM HOUSE

NEW YORK

Published in the United States by Random House, an imprint and division of
Penguin Random House LLC, New York.

RANDOM HOUSE and the HOUSE colophon are registered trademarks of
Penguin Random House LLC.

Grateful acknowledgment is made to Copper Canyon Press and
The Wylie Agency LLC for permission to reprint "Separation" from
Migration: New and Selected Poems, copyright © 1963, 2005 by W. S. Merwin.
Digital and audio rights are controlled by The Wylie Agency LLC.
Reprinted by permission of The Permissions Company on behalf of
Copper Canyon Press (coppercanyonpress.org) and The Wylie Agency LLC.

LIBRARY OF CONGRESS CATALOGING-IN-PUBLICATION DATA
Names: Quindlen, Anna, author.
Title: After Annie: a novel / Anna Quindlen.
Description: First Edition. | New York: Random House, 2024.
Identifiers: LCCN 2023008069 (print) | LCCN 2023008070 (ebook) |
ISBN 9780593229804 (Hardback) | ISBN 9780593229811 (Ebook)
Subjects: LCGFT: Novels.
Classification: LCC PS3567.U336 A78 2024 (print) |
LCC PS3567.U336 (ebook) | DDC 813/.54—dc23/eng/20230221
LC record available at https://lccn.loc.gov/2023008069
LC ebook record available at https://lccn.loc.gov/2023008070

Printed in the United States of America on acid-free paper

randomhousebooks.com

2 4 6 8 9 7 5 3 1

First Edition

Book design by Sara Bereta

For P.M.Q.
One last time
Love never fails

Your absence has gone through me
Like thread through a needle.
Everything I do is stitched with its color.

—W. S. MERWIN

AFTER ANNIE

WINTER

Annie Brown died right before dinner. The mashed pota-toes were still in the pot on the stove, the dented pot with the loose handle, but the meatloaf and the peas were already on the table. Two of the children were in their usual seats. Jamie tried to pick a piece of bacon off the top of the meatloaf, and Ali elbowed him. "Mom!" he yelled.

"Bill, get me some Advil, my head is killing me," their mother said, turning from the stove to their father, her pony-tail waving at them, her hair more or less the same shade and texture as the Irish setter's down the street. She'd done the color herself, and she said she wasn't happy with it, too brassy, but she figured she'd just let it go. Her husband said it looked fine. Of course he did.

"Bill," she said again, looking at him with a wooden spoon raised in her hand, and then she went down, hard, the spoon skidding across the floor, leaving a thin trail of potatoes, stopping at the base of the stove. Ali didn't see it because she was still policing her little brother, but she heard it.

Ant and Benjy came running in from the back room when they heard their dad yelling, "Annie! Annie! Jesus Christ!" Her husband tripped over the spoon as he ran to her, lifted her like it was nothing, and carried her into the living room. He pushed the coffee table into the wall with his foot so he could lay her down flat in the middle of the floor.

"Call 911, Ali," he said to his daughter.

"What is your emergency?" said the woman, who had an accent that sounded like she was from somewhere else.

"My mother fell," Ali said. It didn't seem like enough, but she didn't know what else to say.

"Give me the phone," her father said. "Get out of the way."

The kids all went back and sat still at the kitchen table as though if they moved it might make things worse. It was so quiet that Ali could hear them all breathing, especially their father. After a few minutes there was the faint sound of a siren, the faraway sound the kids heard when they had been sent to bed and Annie and Bill were watching some cop show in the living room and had turned the volume down. The siren got louder until it was all around the five of them, in them, in their teeth and their skulls, and then it stopped, and *crash, crash, crash,* things moving outside, and then the crew was through the front door as their father held it open and their mother lay still. No one ever used the front door. If someone rang that bell, Annie always said, "Now who in the world can that be?" When the family came into the house, they came in through the kitchen. There was a mat there, bristly, brown, to wipe their feet on, and a bench inside to leave their shoes on. No outside shoes in the house—that was the rule. "Is she part Japanese?" Annie's mother-in-law once asked.

It was weird, the kitchen and the living room like two different places, two different stories, two different planets. Behind the big arch that separated the two rooms, the four children sat at the kitchen table frozen into something like a family photograph, meatloaf, peas, salt, pepper, the Brown kids gathered for a weekday dinner, Jamie, the youngest, with a smear of barbeque sauce on his fat pink cheek.

The EMTs made a wall of blue canvas backs around Annie so that all you could see were her slippers, like her feet were all that was left of her. Bill Brown bounced from side to side, adrenaline all over, his eyes big and then blinking, big and then blinking, like someone in a movie who was trying to send secret distress signals without giving anything away to the bad guys. Annie's slippers were purple and Bill had given them to her for Christmas even though she had told him she wanted a locket. They all heard her, a heart-shaped locket to put a picture in. "These are nice," she'd said when she opened the box and found the slippers. She'd prepared herself; you couldn't see a shoebox shape and think there was a locket inside unless your husband was the kind of man who would put a small box in a bigger one as a trick, and Bill wasn't that kind of guy.

When she came home from working at the nursing home in the evening or the morning, depending on her shift, she would take off her rubber clogs at the back door and put on the purple slippers. Sometimes Bill would smile when she did that, like he was thinking he'd done good. He said that when he was happy about something: "I done good."

There were the slippers, still, as if no one was wearing them, and there was Bill, bouncing up and down in the living room, his mouth open, panting. Hyperventilating, Ali said to herself, remembering Girl Scout training. She wondered if her father was going to faint, if there would be the two of them lying there on the rug, both their parents, their kids staring. "Stand back, Bill," one of the EMTs said, both men leaving wet, gray spots on the carpet from the old snow they'd picked up on their shoes outside. One of them was a man whose son used to be on Ali's Little League team. One of them was someone Bill and Annie had gone to high school with. They lived in that kind of place.

Jamie was still picking idly at the meatloaf so that one crispy corner of it was all picked out and most of the bacon was gone, but now Ali wasn't going to stop him. Ali was staring at her mother's feet. They hadn't moved once. She kept waiting for her mother to sit up and say "What happened?" or "I'm fine" or "Let me up." She kept waiting for the EMTs to do that thing with the paddles, to shock her mother's heart back to life. She figured that even if she couldn't see anything but the men's backs, she would hear that sound, *pop pop*, and her mother's feet would do a little jump. They had one of those machines in every hallway at the nursing home where her mother worked. Her mother had shown Ali when she'd visited once. "Do you know how to use that?" Ali had asked. "Of course," her mother said. "It wouldn't be much use to people if I didn't."

"Let's get her on the gurney," Ali heard one of the men say.

"What's a gurney?" Benjy whispered.

"I'm coming with you," their father said, and really fast they were out the door, him, her, the EMTs, and then there were all the hard metal sounds of things moving and slamming, the ambulance starting up and the siren wailing, then dwindling, as the ambulance moved off their street. The living room felt as empty as if there were no one home, the way Ali figured the house did in the mornings after they'd all gone to school and their parents had left for work and the only sound was the furnace in the basement clicking on and off, the hot air whooshing up through the vents, the occasional creak of the hamster wheel from Ali's room.

It was quiet now except for the sound of Jamie sucking barbeque sauce off his fingers and some murmurs from outside that were the sounds of neighbors, even in the cold, on their front steps trying to figure out what was going on over at the Brown house. A siren didn't sound on their street without everyone coming out to see. They'd done the same thing themselves. Chimney fire, their father might say, sending everyone back inside as the fire engine backed down the block.

"Where are they going?" said Benjy.

"The hospital, dumbass," said Ant.

"Shut up," Ali said. "Don't be mean to him."

"You're not the boss," said Ant, like he always did.

"What happened to Mommy?" said Benjy.

"I don't really know," Ali said.

Ant and Ali didn't eat anything, but the two little boys had meatloaf and even some potatoes, though they were cold, with ketchup on it all. They didn't eat the peas because there was nobody to make them do it. "We should go to bed," Ali said. "We have school tomorrow." Jamie and Benjy went to their room, and when Ali checked on them they were asleep, their clothes on the floor, no face washing, no tooth brushing, but she wasn't going to wake them up for that. Benjy had his thumb in his mouth, and in the quiet she could hear him sucking on it, just the way she'd heard him when he was a baby and couldn't be without a pacifier for even a minute.

The little boys had bunk beds up against the wall, but Ant had a twin bed up against the window. He was lying down flat and staring out.

"Is she going to die?" he said without turning his head.

"What are you talking about?" Ali said kind of meanly,

even though she was thinking the same thing. Her mother's feet, so still.

She went downstairs and sat on the living room couch. The house felt big all around her, even though it wasn't, like it had expanded without the grown-ups in it. It's not like they hadn't been left alone before with her in charge, like after school when their parents were both late from work, or when their mother and father went to the diner for dinner. But that was always planned. Ali, put the mac and cheese in the oven. Make sure Jamie does his eye exercises. One hour of TV, and that's it. They never just got left like this, like everyone had forgotten they were even there.

She turned on the television and turned the sound down low, but she kept getting shows that had people laughing on them, so she finally put some news show on mute, just for a kind of company. In the silence she heard a faint tap that she thought was a branch hitting the window, but then it got louder and she realized it was at the back door.

Mrs. Lankford, who had lived next door since her father was a little boy, was standing on the step, her arms wrapped around herself. In the light over the door Ali could see a thick white wreath of cold-weather breath surrounding her beret, the fuzzy one with jewels around the rim. "That doesn't look like it does much to keep your head warm, Sally," Ali's grandmother had said once.

"Are you okay, sweetheart?" Mrs. Lankford said. "Everything okay? We saw the ambulance."

"My mother fell," Ali said again. What else could she say? She didn't know anything. And she hated to think it, but she thought Mrs. Lankford was only there to spread the word, whatever the word was, and if she did, the next thing Ali knew, her grandmother would be in the living room asking her questions she couldn't answer.

"Do you want company?" Mrs. Lankford said, clapping her hands. Her gloves matched her hat.

"I'm good, thank you. My father will be home soon."

"Well, you have my number if you need anything. Or just come right over. Don't worry about waking us up. I'm sure everything will be fine."

"Me too," Ali lied.

She felt as though she should call someone, but she didn't know whom, and she didn't know what she would say. She didn't want to talk to her grandmother, and her friend Jenny couldn't get calls after eight, and her aunt Kathy was hours away. There was Annemarie, there was always Annemarie, but Ali remembered when she was much younger, her mother falling on the ice and thinking she might have broken her wrist, and saying to her father, "Don't tell Annemarie, I don't want to upset her. Whatever you do, don't upset her." Ali realized she only wanted to call someone to stop upsetting herself any further, to make this moment less scary, more real.

"It sounds like you got pretty dramatic about all this," her mother would say when she got home.

The dinner dishes were still on the table, and Ali started to clean up, just to have something to do. Two years ago Benjy had hit his head against the corner of one of the lower kitchen cabinets and bled all over the rag rug by the sink, and after fifteen minutes of struggling with a butterfly bandage, their mother had decided they needed to go to the ER. "While I'm getting him ready, you put some foil over that lasagna," she'd said to Ali. "We're all going to be hungry when we get home." Their father was out on a job, someone's toilet overflowing or the water heater broken, and it was before they'd decided Ali was old enough to look after the others, so they'd all gotten in the car and gone to the branch of the big hospital up on the highway. There was a little soundproof room for kids, with cartoons on the TV. It seemed like it was so the cartoons and the kids wouldn't disturb the people in the big waiting area, but it might have been so the kids didn't hear the noises coming from the examining rooms. Ant said that when he went to the bathroom he heard somebody yelling "oh my God" over and over again. When their mother came to get them she was carrying Benjy, even though he was so tall and she so short that his bony legs dangled past her knees. "I've never heard someone make such a fuss about a hair clipper," she said.

"Will he have a scar?" Ant said in the car.

"Probably," their mother said. "That doctor was so young she probably still gets carded in a bar. But when his hair grows back you won't even see it." She'd been right about that, wrong about the lasagna. They'd eaten so much junk from the vending machines that Ant threw up in the kitchen once they got home. "Motherhood is such a pleasure," Annie had said, mopping the floor, putting the lasagna in the fridge, dabbing at the blood on her shirt with cold water.

Ali was picturing her mother in one of those hospital examining rooms now. "I just had a monster headache," Annie would be telling the doctor. "Two Advil and I'll be fine. I need to get home." Ali tried to eat a piece of meatloaf. It tasted fine but felt bad, like gravel in her mouth, and she spit it into a napkin. Her mother had been on the morning-to-evening shift, six to six, so dinner had been a little late. The other shift, evening to morning, was better for everyone except maybe her mother. She'd make an early dinner, cover a plate with tinfoil if the two older ones had a sports practice or Bill was out on a late call, stick a chicken cutlet in a roll with a squirt of mayonnaise, and jump into the car, steering with one hand and holding what passed for her own dinner in the other. Back through the door just before sunup, and the kids would wake to the smell of coffee and maybe, if she was in the mood, pancakes or waffles.

Ali finished putting the dishes in the dishwasher and went and sat on the couch. She'd start to fall over a little bit, sleepy, but then would wake herself up. She had on the jeans she'd gotten for Christmas that had holes in the knees on purpose, and she picked at the scab from when she'd tripped on the steps outside the middle school. She hadn't thought of that when she saw the jeans on one of the high school girls and decided she wanted them. "I don't understand buying clothes already torn up," Grandma Dora had said at Christmas dinner, and her mother had just shrugged. She'd said more or less the same thing herself when Ali asked for the jeans, but she wasn't going to take her mother-in-law's side.

Ali had never stayed awake all night, even at slumber parties when everyone said they would. There were some stray pieces of plastic on the living room carpet that the EMTs had left. She looked at them to see if she could figure out what they'd been used for, but they were just like the things left in the box when her father would put some toy together and there were pieces that didn't seem to go anywhere. She was afraid to throw them away so she put them in the top drawer of the table next to the sofa. Inside there were two barrettes, a deck of cards, a knife with an orange handle that was supposed to be good for pumpkin carving but wasn't, and a couple of pictures from when people took pictures with cameras. They were a little curled at the edges, like the leaves on the ground in fall. One was of Annie and Annemarie, their arms around each other, both of them wearing flowered dresses and sandals. You could tell that no one had had to tell them to smile for the camera; they both looked as happy as could be. Ali's mom said she couldn't recall exactly what they'd been doing that day, although she did remember that she'd loved that dress. It wasn't just that day—a lot of the times Ali had seen her mother look really happy were the ones when she and Annemarie were sitting at the kitchen table splitting a bottle of rosé, eating junk snacks, talking about how the woman who invented Doritos was a genius because they both knew it had to be a woman, right?

"That's my mother and her best friend," Ali had told Jenny when they'd gone into the drawer looking for a pencil because they were playing Clue, and she had seen Jenny staring at the photograph.

"I don't think my mother has a friend like that," Jenny had said. "We move around a lot."

In the back of the drawer there was also a picture of her parents with Grandma Dora in front of the house. There was another picture of just her parents, same day, you could tell by the clothes, but that one was in an album her mother had in the bedroom. The next page of the album was a picture of the two of them at the restaurant the night they got engaged, then the wedding, then the two of them on the front lawn with baby Ali, then two kids, three. Annie told Annemarie once that it was like a flip book of her life, except that it had been so crazy the day she came home from the hospital with Jamie, Ali jumping up and down, Ant sulking, Benjy underfoot, that there was no picture of them all on the lawn with the new baby, who turned out to be the last baby. "The kitchen looked like a bomb hit it when I walked in that day," their mother always said.

The couch was up against the wall of the living room, facing the windows. Before, it had been under the windows, and before that it had been catty-corner to the arch to the kitchen. Every once in a while their mother liked to move the furniture around. "Come on, Bill," she would say, and together they would push an end table across the carpet, lift the sofa, drag the recliner, until Annie would say, "The room looks so much bigger." It wasn't that big a room, and it always looked the same to Ali no matter where they put the furniture. The couch still felt a little strange where it was now.

Around one o'clock she really started to drift off, but then she felt the whole house shake, the floor humming beneath her feet, the bowl on the coffee table vibrating so it made a faint buzzing sound like a wasp in the house. First her mother, then an earthquake, she thought, only half awake, but then it slowed and stopped and she realized that the furnace was right beneath the living room and it had rumbled on.

Ali moved the bowl back to the center of the table. Annemarie had given it to her mother for her birthday. Her mother said that if you bought it in a craft store it would be two hundred dollars, and Ali's father had said, "For a bowl?" It was one of those bowls you didn't use for anything. "A decorative item," said Annemarie, who was in the business of selling decorative items. This one was beautiful, deep blue turning to pale green as the sides sloped, with leaves etched into it.

You could scarcely tell it had been broken, although it was hard for Ali's eyes not to go right to the break, despite how well her father had mended it. Benjy and Ant had been playing Space Rangers on the sofa, jumping off the arm onto the cushions on the floor, Benjy so excited by the fact that Ant was even acknowledging his existence that he got a little wild and careened off the corner of the coffee table. The bowl had skidded across the wooden surface and landed on the thin carpet and broken into two almost equal pieces, as though it had been created for the day when this would happen. The silence had alerted their mother to trouble in the next room, and when she saw the bowl it seemed like the silence doubled, tripled, with her eyes big and her lips pressed together. She had lifted a piece in each hand and gone into her bedroom. "Sorry, sorry, sorry, Mommy," Benjy had said with his forehead against the door, and Ant put all the cushions back on the sofa.

"There's no point in even having nice things," Ali heard her mother say to her father that night when they were all in bed.

Ali went to the window and could see the irregular glitter of a few stray snowflakes spinning in the artificial glare and then falling out of sight. The rest of the street looked like one of the photographs in her grandmother's oldest albums—black, dark gray, light gray, the occasional spot or shaft or line of pure white. The snow moon shone down on it all, much brighter than any spotlight. Their mother had promised to look up why the full moon the month before, in January, was called the wolf moon, but then she got busy and forgot. Sometimes, when it was warmer weather and they'd been up late for the church fair or a barbeque, she would take them outside and make them look up. "It's the same moon over us all," she said, "no matter where we go."

"Where are we going?" Benjy had said, and their mother laughed and laid a hand on his head.

At one corner of the window frame there was some sort of break in the old wood, and Ali could feel the thin shaft of winter air like the steam whistling from the teapot, only cold, cold.

"This house needs new windows," her father said every year about this time.

"Good luck with that," her mother would reply.

Ali saw her own reflection in the window, but her face looked mostly like black holes—her eyes, the base of her nose, where her chin made the sharp turn into her neck. The flakes came down harder and she thought, Not a good night to drive. Her mother didn't like to drive in snow. Her father didn't care, although he always said the back end of the van fishtailed on the hills if they were packed down into ice and not gritted by the municipal trucks. If the snow came down harder, her father would have to be the one who drove home, Ali thought, and then as she looked beyond the spotlight she realized that the car and the van were there, that of course her parents both went in the ambulance. She hoped her grandmother wouldn't be the one to drive them home from the hospital, her purse string of a mouth tight, somehow blaming Ali's mother for what had happened. "Tripping over her own two feet, Bill, was that it?"

For some reason Ali started to think about what would happen if they got left, if her mother and father didn't come home by morning, if the ambulance had had an accident, which would be a weird thing, an ambulance having an accident instead of dealing with one, but it must happen sometimes. Annie always said that her daughter had a vivid imagination, but she didn't, not really. It was worry that made Ali think about things like this, not imagination at all. It was considering the worst things, like how she would do on her math exam if she didn't study or what would happen if she crashed into the wall of the gym chasing a loose basketball. She imagined the red F at the top of the paper, the sunburst of blood as her nose collided with the gym wall, even though she always studied, always stopped herself before she was out of bounds. Even if her mother was only in the hospital for a few days, like she had been with the new baby who was supposed to come after Jamie three years ago who didn't turn out to be a baby after all, Grandma Dora would move in and talk all the time about how hard it was to take care of four kids, and how great she was for doing it. "This better be the last one," she said to Bill when he'd said his wife was pregnant again. Which had turned out to be true.

It was cold in the house. The furnace hadn't stayed on for long. There was a new thermostat that had a timer so that they wouldn't waste fuel oil keeping the house warm while everyone was in bed. "It's freezing in here," her mother said almost every morning. "It'll warm up," her father said if he wasn't already at work. It seemed like they liked that, that they said the same things over and over again, back and forth. They did that a lot.

Ali looked at the clock on the cable box. 3:11 it said, when the sound of someone opening the back door woke her, and she sat up straight and wiped her mouth with its snail trail of spit down the side where her head had been on the arm of the couch. Her father saw her sitting there, her hands clasped, and he fell down on the floor, on his knees, and started to cry.

As far as she was concerned, that was the worst part of the night so far.

"Bill, get me some Advil, my head is killing me," her mother had said, and then she went down, just like that, one last wave goodbye from the thick, ragged ribbon of her ponytail. She hadn't even had time to take her hair down after work. "Like a ton of bricks," she used to say if someone fell at the nursing home where she was an aide. Ali remembered afterward what her mother had said in the kitchen word for word, because in books and movies, last words were special, something like "Look after my four wonderful children." But maybe just in books and movies.

Her father's hands had a lot of scars on them from work, and he was holding them in front of his face like he was trying to keep the tears in, but there were so many that the rug was turning from tan to brown in front of him, in front of the line of dirty footprints leading to where he knelt. In books and movies Ali would have hugged him and he would have hugged her and they would have both felt a little better. But he didn't get up from the floor, and Ali didn't get off the couch. They didn't move. They couldn't move.

"Oh my God," he said. "What the hell am I going to do?" He didn't say more, and Ali didn't ask, but she knew then that her mother was dead.

"Taken to heaven in the arms of the angels," it said in the newspaper. The Browns still got the paper every day because Bill didn't like to read the sports scores on the computer. Their grandmother brought a whole stack of copies that morning like they would be keepsakes, like everyone would want one to remind themselves of Brown, Anne Fonzheimer. There was a picture from the high school yearbook as though she'd never grown up or gotten older. Cherished wife of Willard J. Brown Jr. Survived by her adored children, Alexandra, Anthony, Benjamin, James, ages thirteen, eleven, eight, and six. The two older ones had looked at it and looked at each other. Alexandra, Anthony, Benjamin, James. Bill felt bad about it. Everyone had known them by their nicknames until now. If Ali had been called to the principal's office maybe they would have called her Alexandra. But she'd never been called to the principal's office. None of them had, even Ant, who all the adults agreed was what his grandmother called a tough nut. He'd probably been hoping no one would know that his real name was Anthony until the principal said it on the stage before handing over his high school diploma. Because of what had happened, no one at school would start in on him with the Anthony thing right away, but eventually.

Bill didn't know who had come up with the line about the arms of the angels. Probably his mother, or maybe just the staff at the funeral home. He knew someone had asked him what he wanted, but he didn't know what he'd said. It sure hadn't been him. He stayed in the bedroom with the door shut. Annie's phone kept coming to life on the bedside table, the picture of the kids on its screen brightening, then darkening, beating like a mechanical heart.

His mother tried to make him come out for meals, but mostly he didn't. "You have children!" she shouted, even though it had never seemed like she liked her grandchildren that much.

All he wanted was for things to slow down. When he had knelt across from Ali in the living room, ashamed that he was crying while his daughter sat there dry-eyed, her face as still as a school photograph, he kept thinking there were things to do. And there were so many things—decisions, arrangements— but all of them put you on an express train, the landscape passing so fast it was a blur. He guessed a blur would be comforting, but in his mind all he saw were the sharp edges of her hair spread across the kitchen floor, of her lying flat on the living room carpet, one hand palm up as though she were ready to wave. Hello, Billy. Goodbye, Billy. He needed things to slow down so he could be with Annie, wherever she was.

Annie's sister, Kathy, had driven down from Pittsburgh and

taken charge. That's what she always did. She was a certified public accountant. She was worried because it was close to tax season, but she said she had her computer with her and there was good wireless in the hotel. Annie said her sister had always been a very organized person, lining her dolls up on the shelf in a particular way, in particular poses. If Annie ever tried to play with them Kathy would know right away. When Annie was little she didn't dare, but as she got older she moved them sometimes just to make Kathy crazy. Annie always said her sister made April 15 sound like New Year's Eve. "Should we have her do our taxes?" Bill said once. "God, no," Annie said.

"I need to ask Bill where all the documents are kept," he had heard Kathy say to his mother, the kind of thing Annie would say was right up her sister's alley, and his mother had replied, "I'll find them. He'll have no idea," which Bill knew was an answer that was right up hers.

His life was being run by women. Even his daughter was getting in on the act. She carried in a meatloaf sandwich for him, just the way he liked it, plenty of ketchup and some bread-and-butter pickles on the side. "I'm not hungry," he said. "You need to eat," she said, like ventriloquism, a grown woman coming out of her thirteen-year-old mouth. "Also, you need to talk to the little boys. They're confused. Jamie wants to know when Mommy is coming home from the hospital." She'd stumbled on the last word.

"Jesus Christ," Bill said.

"Please eat the sandwich, Daddy," Ali said, sounding more like herself. "At least eat half. Please."

"I will," he said. After she left he wrapped the sandwich in the paper towel Ali had put on the plate and put it in the drawer of his bedside table beside the nail clippers. When he and Annie were younger they kept some porn in there, but now it was all on the computer. Nothing wild, pretty white-bread. "Oooh, I could do that," Annie said sometimes.

Kathy was staying at the Best Western two towns over so she could get work done. There was no place at the house, and Bill's mother had a guest room, but she didn't really like Kathy. Dora Brown always said Kathy thought she was all that and a bag of chips, but maybe she was really jealous because Kathy lived in a condo with a pool and went once a year on a river cruise. His mother resented Kathy. That's what Annie always said. Bill could hear his sister-in-law out in the kitchen clearing the cereal bowls.

"Get in the car," he heard her say to Ali.

It was a school day but none of the kids were going to school, not for the rest of the week. There was today, and tomorrow, and then the viewing, and then the next day what Mr. Grant at the funeral home called the internment. It felt like it would go on forever. Jamie wanted to make a snowman in what was left of the snow in the backyard, but Bill's mother said, "You don't want anyone seeing you playing outside today of all days."

"Maybe later, hon," Kathy said. Bill figured the two of them, his sister-in-law, his mother, were circling each other at the sink. "Who's the alpha?" Annie used to say to him when Kathy and Dora were sparring. "I am, babe, because I refuse to engage with either of them."

"Women are a mystery," he'd said one night at the bar, and the bartender had looked at him, laughed, and said, "Now there's a news flash." Nice guy, Bill thought, named Cyril of all things. He'd moved from Philadelphia and opened a sports bar on the block behind Front Street. He'd sent Bill a text: "Praying for you and your kids, man."

People were good. That's what Bill had always believed,

and nothing had ever really changed his mind. Well, almost nothing. He'd had to punt his emergency cases to Jack Bessemer for at least a few days. He didn't like doing it. Right out of high school Bill had gone to work for Ed Martin, who had taught him plumbing slowly and patiently—how to deal with a busted toilet seal, a furnace with a bad pilot light, a leaky pipe. Ed Martin didn't like Jack Bessemer, not because they were competitors, but because he said Jack did shoddy work at high prices and made comments to the women, who were the ones home most often when a plumber showed up. "Bessemer is never coming in this house," Annie said.

"You don't ever need to call a plumber, hon."

"Oh, plumber!" she'd called, putting her arms around his neck and grinding against him just a bit. He needed to stop thinking about things like that. He had to stop thinking about Annie soft and warm next to him, smelling like lemon and bread combined. It's why he couldn't sleep. He knew people said they didn't believe in ghosts, and he didn't either, not the woo-woo kind that made noise in the attic. But he couldn't stop feeling like she was there, there all the time, and then gone, like a song from the radio of a car flying by. Now that she was a ghost, would she know the things he'd tried to keep from her? Would she know that he'd never wanted to get married in the beginning, that he thought four was at least two kids too many, that sometimes his favorite place to be was in his van, alone?

He had to keep concentrating on the little things, like texting everyone on his list that for the next few days Bessemer Plumbing would be handling their emergencies. Mrs. McSorley had called him right away. Her furnace was out. "I'll wait," she said. "I've got a space heater and a fireplace and plenty of wood. You just take care of those children."

The women were taking care of the kids instead. It seemed to work best that way. Kathy had gone through the closets and decided that none of them had anything to wear to a funeral. The night before she'd come up with a plan to take Ali out for a dress. She said it could be navy blue if Ali wanted that instead of black. "I'll take her," he'd heard Kathy say on the phone with Annemarie. "Don't make yourself crazy. I've got this."

"Tell her it's just family here," his mother had said to Kathy when she hung up the phone, and he heard Annie clear as water: "Sometimes your mother is just mean." He knew Annemarie felt she was family; that sentence would level her for sure. But Kathy wouldn't say that. She'd known her sister, and loved her, and so she knew what Annemarie had meant to Annie, even when things were bad, hard, almost impossible, when Bill didn't want to hear Annemarie's name or see her face.

Kathy had come to him after the phone call with Annemarie and said, "I need to get something for Annie to wear, too." And for just a moment his mind did a stutter stop and he heard his wife as though she were sitting next to him on the couch say, "I can choose my own dress, thank you very much, sister dear." But then the room had gone silent with the kind of silence that fills it up until it's likely to burst, and Bill had just nodded.

"Do you have an opinion?" his sister-in-law had asked, and he shook his head. His opinion was that if he tried to look through his wife's closet he might go out of his mind.

Kathy had gone into the bedroom and stood in front of a row of the kinds of things she never wore herself—flowered blouses, red capri pants—while Bill waited outside in the hall. She'd pushed the hangers aside as quietly as she could, hoping that the kids wouldn't hear, but Bill had, and through the half-open door he'd seen her lean in and put her arms around the clothes and inhale and weep. Then she shook herself, took a dress off a hanger, folded it neatly into a tote bag, bent down for a pair of shoes, and straightened up again. Bill thought she'd realized that Annie wouldn't need shoes, and he struggled for a moment to catch his breath. He didn't know if they were doing the right thing, having an old-fashioned wake and funeral with a viewing and a burial. But when Kathy and his mother had tried to talk to him about it, he'd just walked away. Later his mother had cornered him in the kitchen and asked about a eulogy. "Do you want to say something?" she'd said. "Just think about it."

Here's what he thought, lying in bed that night, staring at the popcorn ceiling with moonlight raking it as though it were trying to make it less ugly: All the general things people said, about how the person was a good friend and a good wife and a good mother, were useless, almost insulting in their lack of specificity. But all the specific things he could say about Annie, the girl he'd picked up at the party, picked up and knocked up, married, made a life with, were too intimate. It wasn't just that Bill was uncomfortable standing up and speaking in front of a lot of people. It was that what he had he didn't want to share. He needed to hold it all now like a life preserver.

The Lord is my shepherd. He'd heard it so many times, at so many gravesides. That's all he wanted, although there was a part about restoring your soul that he wasn't sure he'd be able to hear without rage.

His mother thought the boys should have suits, but he said white shirts and ties were good enough. He hated wearing a suit himself; he liked his work clothes, Carhartt pants with reinforced knees and a T-shirt laundered until it was as soft as the skin on his wife's belly, skin that was puckered and pleated from pregnancies. Since Ali was thirteen, she was apparently obliged to wear a dress. "I think it's respectful," Kathy had said.

The last few years, Annie had said the one good thing about having a small house was that you could eavesdrop on your kids. Bill was an eavesdropper now on what was left of his life. "They think your mother had an aneurysm," Kathy had told Ali, sitting on the edge of Ali's bed. She had said the word the way the principal said words at the middle school spelling bee, broken up into syllables. An-eu-ry-sm.

"Was your wife complaining of headaches in the last few months?" the doctor had said at the hospital in the small waiting area, the one they took you to for really bad news.

"I don't think so?" Bill had said. "Maybe? Everybody gets headaches, right?"

"Stop complaining," he'd heard Annie say to the kids more than once. A paper cut, a stomachache. "Nobody's dying here," she would sometimes say.

"That's why your mother told your father she had a headache," he heard Kathy say in the bedroom.

"I know," Ali said.

"Stop picking your cuticles," Kathy said. "Who told you?"

"You've all been talking about it on the phone." So Ali was eavesdropping too. He wondered from behind the bedroom door if the rest of his life he'd be hearing things he needed to know said by other people in other rooms.

"She sees things," Annie had said once of Ali, and not entirely happily.

"An aneurysm is when an artery bursts in your brain," he

heard Kathy say. "There was absolutely nothing anyone could have done to stop it. It wasn't anyone's fault." He heard nothing from Ali.

"I suppose I should get checked out myself," Kathy added.

"For what?" he heard Ali say.

"If it's congenital. That means it runs in families. Don't worry. Not you. By the time you're my age they will have cured everything."

The dress they'd found for Ali to wear to the funeral looked like a black bag made out of T-shirt stuff. It was the best they could do on short notice. Ali was at the in-between age, when little-girl dresses looked stupid but grown-up clothes had darts in the front and she had nothing much to fill out the darts. Kathy told Bill she felt like Annie would have come up with something better, but she'd done the best she could. "Ali didn't seem to care what we got," Kathy told her brother-in-law. "She said okay to everything."

"That's a nice dress," Bill said when Ali came out of her bedroom to show her grandmother, who insisted on seeing, and Ali and Kathy looked at each other. He tried hard to keep his voice even. He didn't know why, but he had always been touched somehow by his children's collarbones. Touched, and fearful, too. Somehow they made children look that much more vulnerable, breakable. Ali's collarbones looked like a knobby necklace at the slack top of the dress. The fact that she had been made to look, suddenly, almost like an adult woman made him sad. When he had come home from the hospital and seen her sitting on the couch, still dressed in her school clothes, her hands clenched, he had suddenly seen that all their lives had changed in one night, seen it in a kind of hardening of her mouth and eyes, a look that was still there. That he thought might be there always.

"Well, no one expects you to look like a fashion plate at a funeral," his mother said.

"She looks fine," Bill said. "She looks good. You look good, honey."

"Did you eat your sandwich?" Ali asked.

"It was great," Bill lied.

Annemarie was sitting in her car in the funeral home's back lot and staring out the windshield, seeing nothing. Jesus God, do I want a pill, or three, or ten, something to take the edge off, she thought, even though she knew there was no taking the edge off this. "Don't you dare start taking that crap again," she heard Annie say in her head. "I'm not around to pull you out of the hole this time."

February, way past nightfall, but the funeral home was lit up like a Hollywood premiere, spotlights on either side of the big redbrick building trained on the sign on the lawn. She'd driven down past the circle with the fountain at its center, halfway down the back drive that led to the part they didn't want you to see, you didn't really want to think about, the windowless cube of matching brick, the garages with the hearses. Business in the front, party in the back, she and Annie used to say about mullet cuts, only here it was reversed.

She'd turned her lights off so that no one could see her sitting there in the car talking to herself. Only she wasn't talking to herself, she was talking to that little girl with the too-short bangs who had wound up in the desk next to hers in first grade, who irritated the hell out of her in the beginning, who later had turned out to be the only thing standing between her and disaster.

"Shotgun!" she heard Annie yell while skipping through the high school parking lot to the car, and that had irritated the hell out of her too, because who else was going to sit in Annemarie's passenger seat but Annie, pulling lip gloss out of her cheesy leather bucket bag that she loved so much for some reason, tapping Tic Tacs into her own palm and then into Annemarie's like they might be kissing someone any minute and needed fresh breath. "Lezzies," one of the Ballmer brothers, who liked Annemarie—which was a waste of his time for sure—had once called them, because the Ballmer brothers were well-known jerks. Annemarie and Annie talked about how in high school they'd just missed the time when it was finally safe to be gay, about how much easier that would have made everything for some of the people they knew. Next county over, the year before, two girls had been named prom queen and queen. "Here's what I don't understand," Annie had said at the time, sitting at the picnic table in the backyard eating chips and dip. "Where is it written that one woman in the gay couple has to wear pants? Why can't they both wear dresses?"

Annemarie had looked at the prom picture on Annie's phone. "Come on," she said. "That's a great suit she has on."

"What are you two talking about?" Ali had said through the sliding screen door.

"Pantsuits," her mother said.

"Boring," Ali said.

"She's jealous of me," Annemarie had said after Ali was gone.

"What? No. Are you nuts?" But Annemarie could tell that Annie knew it was true. There was so much history between them, so much that Ali could sense was there but unspoken, or at least unexplained. Every once in a while, when they'd cracked the second bottle of wine, they'd hold up their glasses and Annemarie would say, "To the year we turned twenty-three. You peed on a stick, and I got my wisdom teeth out. You had a baby, and I had a problem."

"And we both managed to survive," Annie would say.

"Sort of," Annemarie would reply. "So far. I think."

"What are you two talking about?" Ali had asked again that one time.

"Nothing," they said in tandem, and then they laughed, and Annie said, "Owe me a coke," and Ali rolled her eyes.

The car they drove around in together when they were young was the one Annemarie's parents let her have on her sixteenth birthday, with a fancy key ring—a crown with pink sparkly stones that said "Princess" at the bottom, as though the car was a gift. It was the same old Toyota her two older brothers had driven; on a rainy day you could still sometimes smell pot rising like a memory from the seat cushions. It was a beater of a car, and the speakers made a noise like a wood-pecker on a dead tree when you turned them up to where they needed to be, which was loud. She bet that if she found that car now, in some really used car lot, instead of pot it would smell like the two of them. Back then Annie wore a perfume called Happy, Annemarie Opium. Every time Annemarie thought of that she shook her head. Happy and Opium. There it all was, the story of their lives in two words.

Now she had a car like the inside of an expensive purse, with high-end speakers front and back.

Annemarie had met Tom at a trade show, where he was doing a presentation. Your automobile, he told the small-business wannabes, the ones who knew that his small stationery business was now a very big paper and party supplies business, your automobile—not your car, your *automobile*—is as important as your suit and tie. Afterward she went up to him and said, "I don't wear a suit and tie." He'd looked at her patterned wrap dress, what Annie called her get-a-load-of-this dress, and said, "Nor should you."

He was a smooth guy, and she loved him, but it had turned out that he wasn't a whole lot of fun. Stable. That's what he was. She had needed stable, would always need it, especially now. "I wish I could give you something to help you sleep," he'd said last night. Instead he'd given her a foot massage. It was a nice gesture, even though she hated it when anyone messed with her feet. "Just sit in the next chair so we can talk without any interruptions," Annie always said when she could get away and have a pedicure.

Annemarie watched through her windshield as Bill and his children went in. Ali had that bedraggled look she'd noticed kids have when they're dressed up for special occasions, the way little girls always looked at Easter, winter coat over flimsy spring dress, nothing matching. Ali was wearing some kind of dress, shorter in the front but not intentionally, Annemarie thought, with a down jacket instead of a dress coat. She was holding the hands of Jamie and Benjy. Already. Already. A grown-up in an instant, which would make her mother so, so sad. Bill was in front, Ant trailing behind in pants that were too short. "He's only eleven and he's already started to get fuzz on his upper lip," Annie had said sadly at Christmas.

Annemarie was Ant's godmother, something neither one of

them talked about or even thought about much. Annie had asked her sister Kathy the first time, for Ali. "I had to," she'd said. "You'll get to be godmother for the next one."

Annemarie could still remember walking into the kitchen that one Sunday wearing a dress, heels, and pearls, and being surprised to see Annie in a pair of old jeans and a T-shirt. It was a warmish day just this side of spring, and she was a little fried but not too bad, not so you'd notice. Except that it turned out the christening—church service, buffet, sheet cake, presents—had been the day before, on Saturday. "I just don't know how anyone could reasonably expect you to know that something in church wasn't on a Sunday," she'd said, looking from Annie to Bill and back again. "I mean, right?"

Bill had left the room, shaking his head.

"Bye-bye," Ali said, waving from her high chair, a mess of something orange around her mouth.

"What she said," Annie said to Annemarie, and turned her back on her at the sink.

"You showed up a day late for my son's christening," Annie had shouted at her two years later, when they had both stopped pretending that Annemarie wasn't coming around because she was just busy at work, on a weekend trip, tied up with friends. "And you were his godmother. Where's the godmother, the minister said, and I almost said, She's a train wreck. She's a train wreck and the idea that she would be a good godmother for anyone is a joke. For a year, I'd been making excuses for you, pretending that everything was fine, that you were just tired, stressed, overworked. Nothing's wrong, I kept saying to my husband, even though I knew it was a lie. But that was the last straw. I could have killed you when you didn't show, and then that next day, when you came waltzing in. And you didn't even bring a present."

Annemarie had taken second place with Annie from the

time Ali was born. Second, then third, fourth, and fifth. From the time Annie had first discovered she was pregnant and decided after seeing the sonogram in a city clinic, with Annemarie by her side, that she was going to say to hell with everyone and everything and have a baby instead of an abortion, Annie had been a natural mother the way she'd been a natural shortstop on the softball team. It had just been in her, waiting to come out. The saddest Annemarie had ever seen her was when she was in the hospital that last time, pregnant again three years after Jamie, this one ending early with blood and surgery. "The doctors say I'm done," Annie had said.

She didn't imagine Annie would have wanted all this—the wake, the burial, all these people crowding around a casket like she was a table centerpiece. But she didn't really know. It sure wasn't anything they'd discussed when they were talking about what was really good for stretch marks and whether cashmere was worth the money and if Annemarie and Tom should try IVF and whether Annie needed a boob job and a tummy tuck after five pregnancies, four deliveries, and years of breastfeeding. "Why are we even discussing this?" Annie had said. "I can't afford it."

"I'll buy you new tits and a flat stomach," Annemarie had said.

"Yeah, I think I'll just settle for a push-up bra and tight jeans. Besides, Bill doesn't care. I complain about sag, and he says, Where?" Sitting here now Annemarie thought they'd talked about everything but this. They were young; dying happened to old people.

You didn't really talk about the big things because nothing started big. Everything big in their lives had started small. Annie leaning against the wall at that one party, saying, "Do you think Bill Brown is cute?" It was like a seed, and now there was a tree. "He's a plumber," Annemarie had said, and "Don't be a snot," Annie had replied, playing with the necklace she always wore, with the gold A hanging from a chain. Now the necklace had four letters, AABJ. Life got made that way, bit by bit, at the party, the doctor's office, the stop sign, the grocery.

The lawn around the slate walk to the door of the funeral home was pocked with little hillocks of old crusty snow, so that when a bigger group arrived you heard a crunching sound. The slate on the walk itself was clear as July—no snow, ice, salt, grit, nothing—and she wondered whether, when the Grant family had traded in the old Victorian house that had been their funeral home on Front Street for this faux colonial outside town, they had put in a heated walkway. The driveway at her house was heated; the snow magically disappeared, which she always found a little sad. "The rest of the world plows while we melt," Tom had said triumphantly.

Annemarie thought that making the move had been smart for the Grants, although the dignified old Victorian in town was shabby and neglected now, with a sandwich shop on the first floor and an insurance broker above. A front walk that wouldn't freeze would have been smart, too. "They're calling for snow tomorrow," Annemarie's father had said that morning at breakfast. "Let's not talk about that now," her mother had said, as though snow would just make this terrible thing worse.

Annemarie had gone through the heavy double doors of the funeral home thirty minutes before. "The Brown wake begins at six," a man she didn't know had said, carrying a wooden podium with a guest book under one arm. But then Mr. Grant had come out of a side door and said, "It's all right, Robbie." Mrs. Grant had been in Annemarie's mother's bridge group.

Annemarie had been at Mrs. Grant's wake. She'd seen Mr. Grant in Target once wearing a polo shirt and sweatpants, and it had been so strange, like when they were younger and ran into one of their teachers at the pizza parlor. But tonight Mr. Grant was in context, a source of solace as he guided her into the room. The big room, she was glad to see. When one of the old people died in the nursing home tucked behind the mall or the assisted living facility with its rows of arborvitae to make it seem less institutional, the services were usually in a small room near the back. Empty chairs, the ghosts of the friends and family who had gone before them. Annemarie knew that Mr. Grant knew his business, knew that the big room would be full for this wake.

She'd thought maybe she'd have to squelch some primitive impulse to hug Annie, to climb in with her, to pull that shoddy quilted satin blanket over the both of them so they were side by side the way they'd been so many times before, staring at the ceiling:

Are you asleep?
Are you?
I was until you started to talk.
No you weren't.
Yes I was.
Go back to sleep then.
Now I can't.

A hundred times. A thousand. Maybe more. Jesus, the voices in her head. The voices, clear as that slate sidewalk.

But it hadn't happened. It wasn't Annie. It was like one of those things you heard the police did with witnesses, building a picture of a person from spare parts. Yes, that nose. Yes, that hair. When you finally saw a picture of the real person you usually thought, Well, I guess they were sort of in the ballpark. Inside the oak casket Annemarie could see a very conventional version of a certain sort of pretty youngish woman, with russet hair a little garish, curled up at the ends on her shoulders. It made you think of how much of a person lived in their eyes. Without Annie's glittery gleeful eyes, there was no one home. She was wearing the necklace. Annemarie was pretty sure someone had glued it into place, so that the letters were spread a little apart, each one distinct. AABJ.

On an easel to one side, past the kinds of arrangements of flowers that Annemarie only ever saw at funerals, was an enlarged photograph that made a mockery of that tableau in the casket. Annie held Jamie in one of her arms and snaked the other around Benjy, with Ali and Ant sitting on either side. "The End of a Long, Hot Day," the picture would be called if it had a name, everyone's hair glossy with perspiration, plates and cups here and there on the picnic table, faces a little grubby, even Annie's. Exhausted, rumpled, with that smile that said, Look, world, look what I made.

Maybe taken five years before, Annemarie figured, doing the math in her head, because Jamie was still a baby, all thighs and cheeks, wearing a diaper and a tired T-shirt. "I'm the Big Brother," the shirt said, and she knew that it had been passed down from Ant to Benjy and then to Jamie, in the failed expectation that someday the baby would be a big brother, too. Annemarie wondered where that shirt was now. Knowing Annie, it was folded in one of her drawers, to be treasured forever.

Annemarie suddenly realized she was shaking.

"Sit down, honey," Mr. Grant said, leading her to a chair. "This is probably worse for you than for anyone."

"I wouldn't say that. It has to be worse for the kids, and for Bill."

"You knew her longer than any of them," he said, patting her arm, and she was grateful, because it was true. Her parents had folded the newspaper back to the obituary page and left it on the kitchen table next to the sugar bowl, and when she read it—"Oh my God, angels?" she had muttered to herself—she felt irrationally aggrieved that she was not listed among the survivors.

"Too young," he added, rubbing his hands together. "Far, far too young. We had a young man a couple of months ago, just thirty-two, but that was because of the opioids, you know? That was different."

Annemarie looked at his face for any sign of an undercurrent to the remark, any sign that there'd been a time when he'd heard that Annemarie wasn't doing so well, had a problem, the kind of problem the women talked about in whispers, or code. But there was nothing, just his eyes cast down. She reached into her bag and pulled out a half bottle of rosé. "Mr. Grant, please don't think I'm crazy, but could that go in there somewhere?"

He took the bottle in both hands, almost reverentially, and with his back to her did some rearranging of the satin blanket, then sat back down. "No one will know it's there except you," he said.

"I can't believe I asked you to do that."

"Oh, Annemarie, the things I've put inside caskets. Letters, books, photographs. I put in a hammer once, a hairbrush. Teddy bears, of course, when we've had a child, which thank God isn't often. I had one mother, wanted some video game in there, what could I do, I did it. Then there are the ones who want things taken out. I had a big fight one night, one son who wanted his father buried with his wristwatch, another who said they could sell it on eBay. We had to make the mourners wait in the parking lot."

"I think I heard about that from my mother. What did you finally do?"

"The one brother stomped off and the other told us to keep the watch on. At the end he wouldn't leave until we closed and locked the lid because he thought his brother was still going to try to take the watch."

"There's a lock?" she said, looking over, and that's when she lost it. Mr. Grant handed her a wad of tissues and patted her shoulder. Finally she took a deep breath, checked the tissues for smeared makeup, and pushed them into her pocket. "My wine bottle seems pretty benign," she finally said.

"Exactly," Mr. Grant said, patting her one more time.

She kept thinking about it as she went back outside and sat in the car, watching, thinking about the bottle glowing pink as though it were keeping Annie warm. "It's barbaric," she'd told Tom the night before. "Wakes, burials. Why couldn't they just have her cremated?" But then she'd thought about the kids. She'd never been sure what they were thinking, especially the older ones, especially about her. But she tried to imagine herself at that age. Would it be better to have your mother buried or burned?

God, she wanted something to take the edge off, she thought as she sat in the car in the dark.

There was a crowd going in for the wake, *crunch, crunch, crunch,* guys in heavy dress shoes letting wives and girlfriends in heels take the walkway. As she looked through the windshield she saw Dr. Finley, their family doctor, his black dress coat reaching almost to his polished shoes. She'd made a mistake there, waking up the Friday of one Thanksgiving weekend ten years ago and reaching for a prescription vial as empty as a busted baby rattle. "Horrible periods," she'd told Dr. Finley, putting on her saddest face. "So debilitating." She'd watched him write the scrip with that adrenaline surge she always got, but instead of a refill he wrote the name of a gynecologist. "Pain medication isn't something to fool around with, Annemarie," he'd said, and it was all she could do not to spit out, "I'm not fooling around, Doc."

"You tried to score with Dr. Finley?" she heard Annie say in her head. "My God, you used to be such a sad case." Used to be, Annemarie said to herself, wrapping herself around the words. Used to be, used to be, please, please.

She was relieved to see him come back down the walkway only a few minutes later, threading his way through the growing crowd. Some of it had a high school reunion vibe, the girls who had been on the softball team, the guys who had hung around the convenience store parking lot, all twenty years older now. There were women she knew were friends of Bill's mother and some very old people with walkers or wheelchairs who must have been from the nursing home where Annie had worked, first to pay for community college, then to pay for diapers and shoes and day camps. She couldn't think of a job she would want less than the one her best friend had had. But unlike most people she knew, Annie seemed to have the life she wanted, except that she wanted it with more money, better cars, and more bedrooms and bathrooms. There were lots and lots of women from that life, too, women who were more or less the same age she was, Annie's friends, the mothers in the kids' classes, the ones she met when they were trying to get the basketball courts refinished or the dead trees replaced along the perimeter of the park. Annie would drop an unfamiliar name into the conversation from time to time, but not too often, because she could read the look on Annemarie's face. Annie had always been good at reading people. She had friends, friendly acquaintances, people she knew and who knew her, who said hello at the diner or in the supermarket. Annemarie mainly had Annie. Had had.

This is the worst day of my life, she thought, and then said aloud, and she knew Annie would say, Oh, babe, come on, I was there for the worst day of your life, remember? But she would be wrong about that.

B y the time they all got to the funeral home Jamie had taken off his tie and Benjy wanted to know if he had to keep his on. Ali could tell that Ant liked wearing his. It wasn't a clip-on. He had never worn a tie before, and it made him feel important. He was fine until they went inside Grant's Home for Funerals.

Ali had been inside before, for the wake of the husband of her fifth-grade teacher. "Who thought that was a good idea, to take a bunch of ten-year-olds to a viewing?" Annie had asked Bill. Two kids got notes from their parents saying they didn't have to go. The rest of the class filed in in height order and walked by Mrs. Pensky and handed her letters they'd written. Ali's mother had said Ali's was sweet. It said, "We are all sorry for your terrible loss." One of the boys wrote, "I wish Mr. Pensky wasn't dead."

Her father looked terrible, like the few times he'd been sick in bed. He hadn't done a good job shaving, and his eyes were red. At first Ali thought he was sucking on something, a mint or a piece of candy, and then she figured out that he was doing something with his teeth to keep his mouth from shaking. He had on a dark-blue suit jacket and dark-blue pants, but they didn't match and you could tell they weren't a suit. The last time Ali had seen her father in a suit was when she was a little girl. Maybe that suit didn't fit anymore. The two little boys had never seen him in a suit at all.

"Mr. Brown," said Mr. Grant, sticking out his hand like he hadn't seen their father a million times before, like Bill Brown the plumber who came when the home's drainage system conked out and Bill Brown whose wife was dead were two different people. Then Mr. Grant shook the kids' hands, too. Jamie kept his hands in his pocket, where he'd put his clip-on tie. Mr. Grant called them by the names in the paper: "So very sorry, Anthony. My condolences, Alexandra."

Mr. Grant's grandson was a class ahead of Ali. He was there, too, wearing a black suit, a white shirt, and a black tie. At school the other kids made fun of him all the time, calling him Coffin Boy and the Undertaker. Ali had no idea how her life was going to turn out, where she would live if not here in town, what kind of job she wanted or would have. Sometimes she thought of being a teacher, sometimes she thought of being a nurse, sometimes she thought about being someone who just ran a business, she didn't know what. "Dream big!" said a little plaque she got for Christmas from Santa, because Benjy and Jamie still believed, so she and Ant had to pretend they did, too. Big dreams seemed like movie star or president, both of which seemed unlikely to her.

But she thought Chris Grant was kind of stuck. His grandfather was a funeral director. His father and his uncle were funeral directors. Ali didn't know how he could get out of being a funeral director unless he ran away from home. He didn't seem like the kind of person who would do that. Ali seemed more likely to run away from home than Chris Grant did, but she wouldn't because she liked it there okay most of the time. Or had, before.

"Daddy," Ali said. "I don't think the little boys should do this." Every time she tried to talk to their father it was like he was lost somewhere inside his head and had to drag himself back. He'd look at Ali the way the boys did when she had to get them up for school, like they were part awake and part not. "Go wake your brothers up," her mother would say, taking juice glasses down from the cabinet.

Her father narrowed his eyes like he was trying to focus. Then he nodded. "Jamie and Benjy," he said, and took them by the hands. Chris Grant followed them like a little funeral director.

There was a room near the back that was a kind of living room. Ashley had fainted at Mr. Pensky's wake and Ali had walked her back there. One of the other teachers said it was because Ashley hadn't had any breakfast, but Ali was pretty sure it was because Mr. Pensky had looked like he was made of wax. The back room had a TV, and Mrs. Pensky's brother had been watching baseball. "Whoops," he'd said when Ashley came in and lay down on the couch, but he never left or changed the channel. There was a bowl of butterscotch candies on the coffee table and Ashley had two and said she felt better. Jamie and Benjy would eat a lot of butterscotch candies for sure. Maybe somebody would put on *Teen Titans Go!* for them.

Nobody was in the main room yet except their family. Their

father came back in, and this time he held on to Ali's and Ant's hands. Ant looked surprised when he did, and then he looked scared when they walked up to the coffin. Their mother looked like a doll of herself. Her cheeks and mouth were too pink, and her eyebrows were too brown. She was wearing a flowered dress that she'd gotten for her thirtieth birthday party seven years ago. It had been a surprise party but Ali knew that her mother knew, because she bought the dress to go out to dinner, and she wouldn't have done that if she hadn't known it was more than dinner. Their grandmother always said their mother was tight with a buck, which was kind of true. Ali wanted hundred-dollar sneakers for school this year and her mother said, "Are you crazy?" but really matter-of-factly, as though they could both agree that it was never going to happen.

Their father was crying again, and breathing like he'd been breathing in the living room when he got home from the hospital—*uh, uh, uh*—like one of the kids at school having an asthma attack. "Why don't you take a seat?" Mr. Grant said, coming up behind him and putting his hands on their father's shoulders. "The children will be more comfortable." Ali thought Chris was going to have to learn all these ways to talk to people. That was a good one. Their father would sit if he thought it would make them feel better.

"It's all right to cry," their aunt Kathy said, sitting next to Ali and handing her a tissue. That isn't my mother, she wanted to say. She balled the tissue up in her fist. It made Ali feel bad that she didn't feel like crying. All she wanted to do was leave, but she knew she couldn't.

Ant kept shaking. He sat in a chair the whole time, even when some kids in his class came in. A bunch of kids from Ali's class came, too. Her best friend, Jenny, came with her mother. Jenny looked scared, her blue eyes big in her pointed face. Then she saw Ali and put her arms around her neck, which wasn't like Jenny at all, and then, finally, Ali did start to cry. She was a little surprised to realize it was for the first time, which made her cry even harder. Chris Grant came over to them with a box of tissues.

The problem with crying was that it made her believe it was all true, what was happening. "She's not a crier," her mother had said once, when the doctor was checking whether Ali's ankle was sprained or broken after a soccer scrimmage. For Ali to cry meant that something really horrible had happened. Her mother had been on the kitchen floor, then she'd been gone, then she'd been nothing but other people's talk about her. It hadn't seemed real until now, and even now she kept thinking about what her mother would say about all this.

"We should say a prayer," Jenny's mother said, which meant she thought they should go and stand by the coffin.

When they came back, Jenny's mother said, "She looks beautiful. They did a beautiful job." She went over to where Ali's father was sitting and bent at the waist, her hair making a curtain over her face. "I'm so sorry for your loss," she said. He had that half-asleep look again. "Thank you," he said slowly. He probably didn't know who Jenny's mother was. They were new, and they didn't go out a lot. Annie had told Annemarie that Jenny's mother wasn't easy to know. "I gave it my best shot," she had said to Annemarie. "You can't make people like you."

"I'm coming tomorrow, too," Jenny said.

"You don't have to," Ali said.

"I want to," Jenny said. "Your mom was really, really nice to me. Like, about so many things."

There were a lot of people going in and out, whispering to

Ali and Ant and then moving on to their father, so that after a while it was like a chant: so sorry, wonderful woman, loved you so, too young, better place. Over and over. Some of the people who came were people Kathy had known in high school and hadn't seen since then, so there was some hugging and kissing and catching up. She was telling everybody why her parents couldn't be there. It was just a bunch of excuses. Annie and Kathy's parents had gotten divorced right after Annie finished her second year at the community college. Annie sometimes said that it was the worst thing that had ever happened to her. She never said why it happened, but she and Kathy also never talked about their father, who was in Colorado somewhere, so Ali figured it was his fault. Their mother, the children's other grandmother, lived in California but was afraid to fly. "That says it all," Kathy had said once. "A woman who won't get on a plane but moves clear across the country from her daughters."

"People can't be better than they are, sis," Annie had said.

"Your tolerance irritates me," Kathy said back. Annie wasn't really that tolerant when Kathy wasn't around, but when the two of them were together Annie was definitely the tolerant one.

There was something going on out in the hall, the kind of to-do you had at school when there was going to be a classroom visitor and they'd arrived, and then Annemarie came in. Ali was surprised she hadn't been there right at the beginning. Aunt Annemarie, the kids had always called her. Apparently in first grade their teacher said, "We have two Annes in this class." "Glare and stare, and then we were a pair," Annemarie said at the not-really-surprise birthday party for their mother. Annie had started to laugh and cry at the same time when Annemarie said that.

Their father saw Annemarie and he stood up, his face really still and a little scary, like it was a mask. Annemarie blew by Ali and put her arms around him and they just stood there and all the other people moved back, like in Ali's parents' wedding video when they were having their first dance. Their father was patting Annemarie's back, she was shaking so hard. Then he took her by the hand and led her over to where their mother was.

"I still can't believe this is happening," Annemarie said, pretty loud, and then, "Annie, I can't even," she cried. Everybody in the room was quiet. Most of them knew Annemarie. Most of them knew Annie and Annemarie together. She stood silent for a minute more, and then she shook her head and said, "Jesus God, Bill. She really loved you."

"I know," he said. "I know. You too."

Ant was crying, and Annemarie walked over to his chair and put her hand on his head. She looked around for Ali, didn't hug her, but got right in front of her and stared into her eyes as though she were searching for something. Then she leaned in and put her forehead against Ali's.

"Your mother was the best person I ever knew," she said. "She saved my life. I don't know where I would be now if it wasn't for her. I will be there for you. All of you. You and the boys and your father. That's what she would want me to do. Don't you worry. Don't you worry."

Ali said, "I'm really sorry for you," and Annemarie pulled back and stared at her, and then her face fell apart in stages: chin first, mouth, eyes, and Ali put out both her hands. Someone that night had said that having your mother die was the worst thing that could happen to a person, which Ali thought was stupid to say where Ant could hear it. But having your best friend die must be pretty bad too, especially if you were as close as the two Annes were, glare and stare and then a pair. For years Bill complained about how his wife slept with her phone under her pillow because she couldn't miss a call from Annemarie. Sometimes when she was little Ali would wake up in the night and hear her mother talking, mainly saying uh-huh, uh-huh. Then after a while the phone stayed on the night-stand, near but not emergency near. It was there now. Ali knew because she'd called it last night. "Hi, you've reached Annie Brown," a light, bright message-machine voice said. "If you need to speak to me, leave a message here." Ali had called it a few times, and once she even thought of leaving a message, but she didn't know what she would say. Wake up? Come back? What do we do now?

Ali's father came over and said to Annemarie, "Is Tom coming?" Annemarie's husband always showed up at the house with things like colored pencils and notebooks with stars or superheroes from his stationery business. Their grandmother said that Annemarie had lucked out with him. "And vice versa," Annie always said. Annie wasn't having any of what she called her mother-in-law's negativity. "When Jesus rose from the dead she'd say that three days was too long to wait," she said once to her husband, and instead of getting mad he'd started to laugh.

"Tom will be here tomorrow," Annemarie said. "I wanted to be closer, so I'm staying with my parents. They're both a mess. She was as much their daughter as I am. My mother said not a week went by when she didn't drop over pumpkin bread or muffins or something for them." When Annie went grocery shopping, she made her daughter push one cart and she pushed another. Ali's cart was for Annemarie's parents. Annie did their grocery shopping every other week. "It's easier for me," her mother had told Ali. "Annemarie's an hour away, and she's always traveling for work."

"You two were sisters for sure," Bill said.

Ali kept drinking bottled water, mainly so she would have something to do with her hands, and every time she would finish one Mr. Grant would hand her another, so that after two hours she really had to use the bathroom. She went down a hall to what looked like the right door, even though it wasn't marked. Maybe at a funeral home it didn't feel right to advertise that there was a toilet behind a door.

But when she stepped through, she was outside on a little pad of cement at the back of the building looking down on the park-and-ride lot. The ramp to the interstate curled like a comma and fell below so that cars sped by and then disappeared with a *whoosh*. When you took your driving test you had to take that ramp, drive a couple miles on the highway, exit, and circle back. People said it was the hardest part of the test, but Ali looked down and thought she could do it.

She hugged herself to keep warm and then pulled at the front of her dress. It didn't fit right—she had to keep rearranging the neckline so no one would see that she was wearing a sports bra, which was the only black thing she'd had. She was at that stage where she was all nipples but no breasts yet, like the tips of fingers pointing at whoever was standing in front of her. The neckline of the dress slipped off her shoulder, and she yanked it back and wondered how she would get through tomorrow, twisting it here and there when she needed to be paying attention. Or maybe that was the point. She could concentrate on how terrible she looked. She for sure would never wear the dress again.

She was tired of having people tell her things she already knew about her mother, the people she worked with at the nursing home saying what a hard worker she was and how much the residents loved her, the people she had gone to high school with talking about how much fun she had always been and what a good dancer she was, the new people in town talking about how she brought over a basket of cookies to welcome them and told them where the best farm stands were. No one said, I wouldn't want to get on Annie's bad side, although that was true, and no one said, Boy, did she look tired some days, although that was true, too. It made Ali wonder whether anyone ever said true things about people after they were dead, or whether dead people were always perfect, or at least very, very good. She wanted someone to say that word, so she said it herself, quietly. "Dead." It didn't make things any more real.

The stars were silver pinpoints in a clear black sky, even with the sulfur lights from the parking lot burning dull yellow below. The snow moon was past its prime. In a month there would be the worm moon. Their mother had promised to figure out that moon name, too. Ali would look it up.

Maybe tomorrow there would be clouds. Maybe tomorrow there would be snow. Ali's toes were starting to go numb but she didn't want to go back inside. Back inside and through the double front door of Grant's Home for Funerals, doors with a sheen so glossy you could see yourself approaching, led to one place, and this cement area behind maybe led someplace else—a better place, a place where the real Annie Brown was, not that pink-lipsticked doll lying so quiet inside, halfway to being a mannequin, her hair the wrong color, one her mother would never have a chance to get right.

Ali heard someone breathing behind her, and she knew it was her brother because she'd heard him breathing behind her her whole life—in the car, in the line for the matinee at the movies, on the school bus. She wondered if he'd made the same mistake she had, and she realized that she definitely needed to find the real bathroom.

"What comes next?" Ant asked.

"In the morning the minister says some prayers in there, and then we all go to the cemetery and he says some more, and then everyone comes to our house to eat."

"I know that," Ant said. "But after that. What happens after that? Like, who takes care of us now?"

"I don't know," said Ali. "Dad, I guess."

"Dad by himself?"

"I don't know," she repeated.

The viewing was supposed to end at nine o'clock, but there were so many people that a lot of them stayed longer, and two guys their father sometimes worked with on construction projects got there late and seemed as though they were drunk, which Kathy said was not that unusual for a viewing. "Man, Annie was such a cutie when she worked at the Tastee-Freez," one of them kept saying. "That uniform."

Finally Mr. Grant told them it was time for the family to gather, and they left. Their grandmother had been sitting in a corner for a while, but she got up then and put her arm around her son's waist as he stood staring down at his wife. "Now, Bill, that's enough," she said. "They need to close it up."

"After you all have left," Mr. Grant said.

In the little room in the back, Benjy was still staring at the TV, and the dish with the butterscotch candies was empty. Jamie was asleep on the couch with his head in the lap of some woman Ali didn't know. She was wearing office clothes, a black skirt and a jacket made out of different colors all woven together, with fringe down the front and on the cuffs. She had on makeup and black heels. She looked a lot like the woman who read the news on Channel 6. When she saw Ali at the door she put her finger to her lips and looked down at Jamie.

"We have to go now," Ali said, wondering who she was and why she was here. When Jamie sat up, a butterscotch candy fell out of the corner of his mouth and onto the black skirt. The woman picked it off her lap, then smoothed his hair and smiled at him.

"I was keeping your little ones company, Billy," she said when she got out to the hall and saw their father, and Ali started wondering again, because the only person she had ever heard call her father Billy was her mother.

In the car their father started to talk. Just like Kathy explaining about an aneurysm, it sounded like something the adults had decided he ought to say. "I need you all to understand something really important," he said. It was dark in the car and his knuckles on the steering wheel were shining white in the light through the windshield like a string of pop beads. "You know how, when you have a bird in a cage, and you open the door, what's left is an empty cage? That's like your mother now. The thing that made her her, like how nice and sweet and funny she was with all of you, and how she took care of you and loved you, is still there. It's just inside of you now instead of inside of her body. It's still alive inside the four of you."

"So she's not dead?" said Benjy.

"Dumbass," Ant said really quietly.

"Just close your eyes," their father said, "and think about your mom, and how she used to help you get dressed and give you a hug and touch your hair when she put food on the dinner table and play Chutes and Ladders. I bet you can hear her saying your name. Can you hear her talking?"

Their father was starting to lose it a little bit again. His voice was shaking and he was moving his jaw around, that way you try to hold your mouth so you won't cry. Maybe the boys could tell, because the two little ones said, "Yes, yes," they could hear it. Ant said, "I guess I can."

Ali closed her eyes. "If you need to speak to me," she heard. "If you need to speak to me, leave a message here." She would call again when they got home.

Just like that, Annemarie thought as she drove west, the world spins forward. The kids go back to school. The adults go back to work. The open rectangle of earth is filled in. People begin the work of forgetting. But not me, she thought.

Her phone rang and the caller ID lit up on her dashboard. The Sophisticated Closet in Langhorne. She didn't answer, her mind elsewhere, in the blessed past, the terrible future, the days that she'd just managed to survive, although she wasn't sure she had survived at all.

"Keep it together," Kathy had said as Annemarie was leaving the Browns' house. "Keep it together," Annemarie said in her head.

She didn't know if she could keep it together. "Strategies," they gave you at the rehab place, to get through "challenges" and "setbacks." Exercise. Breathing. Meditation. But none of the strategies could help with a challenge or setback like this. None of the meditation sessions anticipated trying to quiet your mind and, in the quiet, hearing only the vast silence of eternal absence where your bestie forever had once been. Forever was so much shorter than she'd always thought. Quiet was soothing. Silence was terrible.

At least she'd gotten through the day of the funeral without taking anything, maybe because she'd felt all afternoon like Annie was right there with her. After the funeral the women had all been in the kitchen at the house. It had always been that way. Holidays, parties, birthdays, tragedies. The kitchen full of women, and the men in the living room. One of the men would come in to get a beer from the refrigerator, and the room would freeze a little bit, like everyone was just waiting for the normal order to reassert itself.

She had lingered right outside the kitchen door, listening. She and Annie had figured out to do that years ago. When they were Ali's age they would step into the room of adults, and the room would go silent. No secrets, gossip, bile, in front of the girls. So they'd learned to lurk. They actually liked lurking better than being in the room. That way they were never required to contribute to the conversation, never had to give away little pieces of themselves to those older women, and they also learned more. Pregnancies, bankruptcies, lost jobs, bounced checks—over the years they'd heard it all. They'd lurked at bridal and baby showers, holiday dinners, graduation parties. Annemarie never forgot the Fourth of July when they'd heard Annie's mother talking about that cheating, lying son of a bitch and realized she was talking about her husband, Annie's father. They'd both gotten drunk that night, Annie because of her parents, Annemarie because of Annie.

They'd lurked at the repasts after funerals, too. "There's no mourning," Annie had said once. "All they talk about is ailments and recipes."

The kitchen had been crowded, with women and casserole dishes and bakery boxes. Bill's mother, Dora; her friend Betty; Mrs. Lankford from next door, whose name was Sally; Sally's sister, who lived with her since her husband died; her sister's home health aide; another home health aide who was a friend of the first one; the last three nameless, at least to Annemarie.

Annemarie had leaned against the dining room wall at the Browns' house and listened to the voices. Annie would want her to do it, would expect her to do it. The truth was, she had felt someone in the doorway, to one side of her shoulder, that faint force field you got when a person was behind you almost close enough to touch but not quite. She kept feeling Annie standing where she always had. She felt her sitting in the passenger seat now as she drove. "Eyes on the road," Annie said. If this is haunting, Annemarie said to herself, bring it on.

Alone in the car, Annemarie's phone rang again. Tom this time. He'd held her hand in bed the night before. "I'm worried about you," he'd said softly. He was a good man. For a moment she thought that he was of no more use than all those strategies, but she was ashamed of that, although she thought it was probably true. She'd squeezed his hand in the dark. There was no moon, clouds thick and black, edged with gray, and the dark outside the big windows of their bedroom had felt baleful.

Baleful was how she thought of Annie's mother-in-law. As Annemarie had stood just outside the kitchen doorway it occurred to her that Bill's mother seemed to be enjoying herself. "Your mother just loves to be the center of attention," Annemarie had once heard Annie say to Bill, and he had shrugged, marital agreement without words. At the cemetery Dora kept telling people, "I gave them my house and now I've given them my plot." "They didn't have a plot?" the older people kept saying in disbelief at the funeral home, as though the very thought beggared the imagination. "Why in the world would they have a cemetery plot at their age?" said Kathy. There was a spot next to Bill's father that was supposed to be for Bill's mother, but she let Bill have it for Annie. Bill's father's gravestone said "Beloved husband and father." Annemarie assumed Annie's would say "Beloved wife and mother." She didn't figure she could get them to add "partner in crime." Maybe she'd get a little stone of her own, drop it into the dirt. Mr. Grant had said it at the funeral home: She was here first.

"'I gave them my house,'" Kathy had whispered in disbelief. She was angry because it was more or less a lie. Annie and Bill and the kids all lived in the house where Bill had grown up. The boys slept in Bill's old room. Annie and Bill slept where his parents had slept. Ali's room was the room where Dora's mother-in-law had slept until she had to go to a nursing home. Annie said Dora Brown didn't like her mother-in-law and made her go. Bill had loved his grandmother, Annie said. She once showed Annemarie the card Bill's grandmother had given him when he graduated, which her husband kept in a dresser drawer. "Billy boy," it said, "you are a dear person."

Annemarie and Annie had both thought it was such a funny, old-fashioned thing to say but nice, too, and true. People pretty much agreed that Bill Brown was a dear person, even if they didn't say it quite that way. Annemarie had once heard two women at the Giant supermarket talking about having him fix a garbage disposal, and how you didn't even have to stay home, just leave the key on top of the doorframe because he was as honest as the day was long and didn't try to charge you an arm and a leg like some people did. She couldn't argue. He hadn't been the guy she would have chosen for her best friend, but he'd been good to her, and probably that was all you could ask for. Annemarie had been crazy about Greg Isley in high school, and last she'd heard he was on wife number three—cheated on one with two, on two with three. She figured three was probably looking over her shoulder for four. She was sure Greg was.

Dora Brown turned the house over to her son and daughter-in-law after her husband died, and she picked out a garden apartment for herself. "Someone else takes care of the roof and the lawn," she liked to say. But she charged her son and his wife rent. She said you shouldn't mix business and family.

Bill and Annie had saved their money and decided they wanted to buy the house. Bill had said they could put an extension on the back, two more bedrooms, a bathroom, a den. They asked his mother over coffee after the kids had left the table, but when Annie told Annemarie the story, trying to make it funny the way she did when she talked about the things she didn't like but had to live with, she said Ali had been in the little pantry at the back of the kitchen, a closet really, and she'd heard. Ali had learned to lurk, too, from watching Annemarie and her mother.

"Buy it? Buy it?" Annie said Dora Brown kept repeating, like she was shocked at the idea of homeownership. "Whose idea was that?" She'd gotten up and knocked over her chair when she took her handbag strap off the back. That's what she called it, a handbag, just like she called the refrigerator an icebox. "I don't see why you're getting so upset," Bill had said. "Sure, of course you don't, why would you, it's not your idea anyhow, is it?" she said. "Don't worry, Annie, you'll have it when I'm dead."

"Can't come soon enough," Annie told Annemarie she had said when the door closed.

"Maybe she'll charge Bill rent for the cemetery plot," Kathy had muttered to Annemarie. "My poor sister couldn't even do a kitchen renovation in this house. Or paint. She couldn't paint, for God's sake."

It had been lonely lurking alone, but Annemarie felt that if she didn't do it she would have given up somehow, and she was just waiting for Annie's mother-in-law to say something nasty about her dead friend so she could come around the corner and tell her off. It was a welcome distraction, like watching a television show while you were sick so that for a few minutes you'd forget the high fever and the congestion. She and Annie had had strep throat at the same time, and they'd bedded down on the sectional in Annemarie's den and watched the soaps all day long. "You girls are having way too much fun," Annemarie's mother had said.

"I can't believe her mother isn't here," Sally Lankford's sister had said, and Annemarie knew she meant Annie's mother.

"I can't explain it," said Dora Brown. "If anything ever happened to Bill—"

"Bite your tongue," said Sally Lankford.

"They're all lucky to have you," the aide had said to Bill's mother, and Annemarie rolled her eyes. It was the kind of thing people always said, but in this case it didn't come close to being true.

In the car, turning off the highway, she said it aloud for some reason. "They're all lucky to have you." Maybe she was trying to convince herself about herself, about the future, about her role. Annie, Annie, I will take care of them all, they will be lucky to have me. Bill loved you so much that he's not quite all there. I think he's in shock.

That's what Dora's friend Betty had said in the kitchen while taking a tray of something out of the oven. "I think Bill is in shock. He looks like he's in shock."

"He has to be strong for the children," Sally Lankford had said.

"Look at all this food," Bill's mother had said, and Annemarie had almost laughed. Trust Dora to pivot away from the kids, the emotion, from Annie, from her own son.

"Bill is a nice man," said Betty.

"With four young children," said Dora. "I don't know that they'll eat half this stuff. The two little ones are picky eaters. I told Bill, I said, don't give them anything else and they'll eat what's on their plate. Don't cater to them."

"People just want to show they're thinking of Bill," said Betty. "Everybody loves him. And Annie. Everybody loved Annie."

"I've never heard a bad word about Bill Brown," said Sally Lankford. "Never."

"Bill was a good husband," said Betty.

"Did you see Liz Donahue at the funeral home?" Bill's mother said, and it was all Annemarie could do not to pop out and whack her with a dish towel.

"She sold the last house where I worked," said the home health aide. "I like the way she dresses."

"She's really kept her figure," Dora Brown said. "She was Bill's girlfriend in high school. Everyone was surprised when they broke up."

"You heinous bitch," Annemarie had whispered.

"She owns that stone house over the mountain," said Betty. "The one where Ruth Bissell's grandparents used to live. I wouldn't want to live out there all alone. Especially if I was young and single. It's hard to figure, why she isn't married yet." Annemarie leaned in closer.

"Every single woman in town will be all over Bill Brown like a bad rash," Betty added.

"Oh my goodness, that's a terrible thing to say," said Sally Lankford, and Annemarie had thought, Yep, it's terrible, and it's true. The world was full of bad men who didn't know how to settle down, and Bill Brown was a good man who'd proven he knew how to do it, and gladly. The downside being, of course, the four kids. She kept thinking of watching the soaps with Annie, because she was feeling now like she was in one. Liz Donahue was a plot point for sure.

Why did the phone keep on ringing in the car? Had it always been this busy, her work life, and she hadn't found it irritating until now? She reached into her bag to turn it off and felt a plastic container at the bottom. She pulled her hand away like it was a live thing, because it felt like a live thing. "Keep chugging the mints, babe," she heard Annie say, and the phone ringing through the dash seemed to drown out that voice in her head, and she thought that was when she would really be in trouble, when she couldn't hear Annie clearly anymore. Silence, not quiet. She started to cry, and a deer ran across the road, and she swerved to avoid it and pulled onto the shoulder.

She hadn't been able to really distract herself with the talk in the kitchen, not when those women got to talking about a future for Bill that didn't include Annie, so she had gone into the bathroom and locked the door and run the water. The morning had been just about as terrible as it could have been, all of it designed to make it seem as though what had happened hadn't—the Annie doll in the box, the unseen hole covered with its cheap blanket of fake grass, the minister talking about eternal life. She hadn't been sure, but she thought the minister was the same one who had married Annie and Bill.

Maybe the limousine the family emerged from was the same limousine that had driven the bride and groom that day. There weren't that many limos in the town of Greengrass.

The winter grass at the cemetery had been tipped with white, its stems yellow, awaiting better days. It had snapped under their feet. It seemed that the moment was frozen too, as though time had stopped. "We consign our sister Anne to the earth," the minister finally said, and Tom had reached for her hand and squeezed. "The good Lord receives her into his loving arms." The sound of sobbing was everywhere except closest to the grave; they were all still stunned by the improbability of the truth—the children, the husband, the best friend. Later they would weep in bathrooms, in bedrooms. Out here in the world they faced the no-hole with a no-face.

"The family would welcome you at their home now," the minister had said, closing his Bible, and Annemarie had thought, The family with its heart gone. Bill had put his hand on the pale oak of the casket, beside the spray of pink roses, and each of the children did the same, and then they had walked away. Only after they were all gone would the two men in institutional green jackets waiting and watching at the side of a mausoleum lower the casket. A not-burial, Annemarie thought, but she told Tom not to pull away, and she sat in the car and watched out the window until there was nothing to see but an enormous mound of flowers atop the dirt, looking terribly joyful in their assorted colors and shapes, like a crazy quilt that would be sodden and brown by day's end. A light snow had begun to fall, gilding the edges of the petals silver.

"Are you all right?" Tom had said, putting a gloved hand on her knee, and before she could turn to look at him, he said, "That was a dumb question."

When they had gotten to the house for the repast, Tom had squeezed her hand, and then gone to sit in the living room with Bill, Mr. Lankford, and Mr. Bessemer. Whenever there was a blocked toilet Mr. Bessemer accused women of flushing what he called "those damn things." When Annie and Kathy were teenagers and their toilet got plugged up, they left the house because they didn't want to hear about tampons from Mr. Bessemer or have him say, "Look at the fanny on her," when one of them walked past. If someone called the Brown house and said the furnace was out on a freezing night, Bill would take his heavy Brown Plumbing jacket off the hook by the back door and go out no matter how much Annie huffed and said everyone took advantage. Mr. Bessemer told people to put on a sweater and he'd see them at nine the next morning.

Jamie and Benjy were sent down the street to the Murphys' house after the funeral to play with the two Murphy boys. Annemarie had found Ant in the back room on the computer. His skin looked transparent in the light from the monitor as he leaned toward the screen. His mother had been concerned about his vision and made an appointment with the eye doctor at the nursing home. That way, she had told Annemarie, she wouldn't have to worry about the insurance. Annemarie was always offering to pay for things, and Annie was always saying, "Now, there's a good way to wreck a friendship." "Nothing could," Annemarie always said, although she had surely come close.

"There's food," Annemarie said to Ant. She looked at the desk. "Is that a beer?"

"Mr. Bessemer gave it to me," Ant said. "It tastes really bad."

"Who gives an eleven-year-old boy beer?"

"He's weird. He has kids, right?"

"Three, but they left and never came back."

Annemarie had picked up the beer and gone back to the living room. Ali's friend Jenny was standing right inside the front door, with what Annemarie thought seemed like a fearful look in her eyes, as though she didn't know whether she should stay. "Come have something to eat," Ali said to her. "There's brownies with chocolate chips in them. Are your parents coming?"

Jenny shook her head. Annie had told Annemarie the parents were unfriendly, that Ali had told her that when she went to Jenny's house, the father always said, "Leave the bedroom door open," as though he suspected them of something. He was one of those people who worked at the industrial park, an executive who traveled and always wore a suit and tie to work. They lived in a big new house with a two-story front hall and what Jenny's mother called the master suite at one end and Jenny's room at the other. Ali said Jenny had a canopy bed and a TV in her room. "Good for Jenny," Annie had said, which was her way of saying, Dream on, my daughter.

"Why are you holding a bottle of beer?" Jenny had said to Ali.

"That's a good question," Annemarie said, coming up behind them and taking the beer from Ali's hand.

"Mr. Bessemer gave it to me."

Annemarie shook her head. "He gave Ant one, too," Annemarie had said. "He probably would have given one to the little boys if he saw them. What a creep. You can quote me." Jenny giggled.

"I wonder how the coven is doing," Annemarie said, looking toward the coven in the kitchen.

"What's a coven?" Ali said.

"Never mind. That's just me being mean. I'm a cynic. Do you know what a cynic is?"

"I'm not stupid."

Annemarie put her arm around Ali. "You're the best. Don't pay any attention to me. Have some food. You need to eat. One of the baked zitis is really good and one is kind of eh."

"My mom said you're a successful entrepreneur," Jenny said.

"She did, did she?"

"She created a supply line from the Amish and Mennonite communities to craft shops and boutiques all over the country," Ali said.

"That is absolutely correct," said Annemarie. It should be: Annie had said it a hundred times. "Annemarie made something out of nothing," she would say sometimes, so proudly, "and look at her now." Annie, Annemarie had thought at the graveside, looking at the four children, You were the one who made something out of nothing. I cart bowls and baskets and quilts and sweaters around from shop to shop so that women can buy things to try to fill the holes in their hearts. But you had no hole in yours because you made a family. No hole except for this horrible one we are hovering over now without you.

Here in the car, the back filled with boxes of all those things she sold, Annemarie wondered if there was anything on earth to fill the hole in her heart now. She had given Annie some of those things: the bowl with the leaves embossed in it, some baskets, and a quilt that Annemarie had given her for some ridiculously low price when Annie insisted on paying. It was beautiful, that quilt, the bright green and soft purple of Granny Smith apples and lilac bushes against a tea-colored background. Annie kept it folded carefully at the bottom of the bed, took it off every night and laid it over the rocking chair in the corner. "Someday, somebody is going to explain to me why anyone would have a quilt that's too nice to actually use as a quilt," Bill had said, and Annemarie and Annie had both lifted their eyes heavenward and started to laugh. "Bill, Bill, Bill," Annemarie had said. "You are such a guy." "That's the truth," he'd said.

"A glass of bad wine?" Kathy had said as the gathering after the funeral was winding down, coming up to Annemarie, Jenny, and Ali. "I can't finish it, I'm driving."

"Can't," said Annemarie with a shrug, and Kathy lifted her brows and looked down at Annemarie's belly.

"Not that," Annemarie said. "Sadly. The other thing."

"Got it," said Kathy.

"Don't go in the kitchen, whatever you do," Annemarie said.

"I was just in there. They're having a long discussion about how to heat up a ham without drying it out." The two girls had drifted away, and Kathy pulled Annemarie into a corner. They had never been close: Kathy had been a plain, pragmatic girl who shelved books at the library on weekends and played the French horn in the marching band. "Don't be mean," Annemarie's mother had told her and Annie once. "Just because you two are spark plugs, there's no cause to have an attitude about Kathy."

"I'm going to try to help Bill with logistics," Kathy had said.

"Logistics are right up your alley," Annemarie said.

"Don't be a bitch," Kathy said, and then she hugged her. "We need to step up for those children, and you need to keep it together. You need to keep on keeping it together for my sister. If anything happened to you it would break her heart.

Are you listening to me? Don't screw up." She took the beers out of Annemarie's hands and looked from one bottle to the other.

"Bessemer gave them to the kids," Annemarie said. "I took them away."

"This place. Nothing changes."

"I called her phone last night," Annemarie had said. "Am I crazy? Tell me I'm not crazy."

"Bill says it keeps vibrating. He had to turn the ring tones off so he could try to get some sleep." That made sense. When Annemarie called Annie, her phone played the chorus of "Little Miss Can't Be Wrong." That would wake anybody up, although Annemarie didn't think Bill was sleeping much. She had come by the morning of the funeral to help make sure the kids were dressed and had seen his bed. It looked like one of those before-and-after split screens they had on the morning shows when they did makeovers. "That looks really good," Annie would say when the screen switched from the half-and-half view, before and after, of someone with dark crescents under her eyes and no-color hair to the same person with blonde streaks and a blowout and eyeliner and usually some little leather jacket that that kind of woman would never wear otherwise. "I wish someone would make me over," Annie would add.

"Way too much makeup," Bill, glancing up at the TV, would always say.

Now he was sleeping in a before-and-after bed. One half looked like someone had slept in it, and the other half was made, like there was a line down the middle Bill couldn't cross. Annemarie had caught Ali making his half so they matched.

"Keep it together," Kathy had said, and hugged Annemarie.

"Keep it together," Annemarie whispered to herself in the

car, her forehead on the steering wheel. She pulled down the sun visor and looked at her face in the mirror, her eyes red, her skin blotchy. She had three stops to make before she could go home. "How the hell am I going to keep it together?" she said to herself.

"You can do this," said that familiar voice. "Oh, honey, I don't think I can," Annemarie said, pulling off the shoulder of the road.

SPRING

The house he was looking for was a nice little Cape on a back road a few miles out of town. He'd never been before, but he'd driven past and could tell it had fresh paint, white with blue shutters, and some shrubs around the foundation that hadn't been there a year ago. They were twiggy, with just the tiny tight nubs of buds along their length, but they looked like azaleas, and they'd be pretty later on in the spring. Some of their branches were still encased in ice, dripping onto the soil beneath, a slow watering.

Young families from Philadelphia and New York were buying these kinds of houses all over the area, ordinary old places that would become a new kind of old, with ceiling beams and kitchen islands and hand-painted tiles. Houses that were bargains until you figured out what was wrong with them. He bet some people were sucked in by the name of the town. Greengrass: What could be better? Of course it didn't refer to the area, although it was green enough, with its bands of forested game lands around the newer developments and their golf course lawns. It was called Greengrass after a man from the bigger town of Belmont who had opened a pharmacy a hundred years before that had stayed in business until the chain pharmacy opened at the mall. Then it had become a vintage store, although it still had the old name over the door in leaded glass. "Vintage," his mother said every single time she drove past. "They called that secondhand when I was growing up."

He pulled into the gravel drive of the house. "Thank you so much for coming this early," said the woman who opened the side door. Karen Feeney, the message had said. He didn't know the name, which was a bit of a relief. She probably wouldn't know about Annie. His crazy mother had made him suspicious of every woman who said she needed a plumber. Susan Tyler had stopped at the house and left cupcakes last week, and he'd made the mistake of mentioning it to her. "There will be more where those cupcakes came from, mark my words," Dora Brown had said. "She's been divorced for, what is it, five years now? You just be careful. Her boys are a handful."

"Sometimes I can't believe the things you come up with," he'd said.

"Patsy McCutcheon, too," his mother had said. "If she asks for a service call and there's nothing wrong with the plumbing, I won't be a bit surprised." Or Ramona Sandford. Or Lori Williams. Sometimes it felt like his mother had thrown the name of every single woman in town at him. Although Lori had asked him if she could make him dinner some night. Picturing sitting across the table from Lori was like watching a movie. The man in the chair was not him, not Annie Brown's husband. He was still Annie Brown's husband.

It had been almost two months and he still waited for her to walk in the back door every morning. That morning he had leaned over Ali's bed, and when his daughter opened her eyes and he saw the look in them, he knew she did, too. They were all floating in some in-between where nothing seemed real and nothing seemed right. Waiting for the rest of life, whatever that was, a future that felt like a betrayal. He kept her phone charged.

"Can you get the boys up and out to school?" he had whispered to Ali. "There's a pregnant lady over in Tompkinsville who's got no heat, and I told her I would be there by seven. Maybe give the boys some cereal?" If there was milk. Was there milk?

Every day he looked in the refrigerator as though it would somehow be different, the way his mother always complained he had done as a teenager. That is, once he'd actually managed to step into the kitchen. The little boys didn't seem to notice anything different about it, but every time he stood in the doorway he saw her splayed on the floor, still in her work smock, the one with flowers on it, the one they'd cut off at the hospital. He knew Ali could see her, too. There was something about the way she moved around the kitchen that told him. Maybe he should lay new vinyl tile.

The day of the funeral the countertop had been crowded with Tupperware, chafing dishes, and cake plates. Baked ziti, lasagna, pineapple upside-down cake, bran muffins, chicken enchiladas, beef stew, chocolate layer cake, angel food cake. The refrigerator had been full. The freezer, too.

It seemed as though there were only four or five options in the funeral meals cookbook, all of them involving pasta or cheese, or pasta and cheese. Most of them were gone now. But it turned out one of the foil baking dishes had had a casserole that was mainly French toast, which got them all through breakfast for a week. The bread had those tiny sesame seeds along the crust, and he had watched, dead-eyed, as Benjy insisted on picking them all out, even once there was syrup, so that there was syrup under his fingernails and later lint from his gloves on his fingertips because of it. Then he'd sucked on his fingers and gotten the lint in his mouth, so that all during dinnertime he was picking red fuzz off his tongue. "You're disgusting," Ant had said, shoveling in lasagna.

"There's bread for toast," Bill had said, putting his hand on Ali's shoulder as he woke her.

"I'll take care of it," she muttered, throwing back the comforter, a shiver moving through her narrow body as her feet hit the cold floor.

"The heat will come up in a little while," he said.

He had a good business and he didn't want to mess it up, didn't want people whispering that Bill Brown was falling apart. People liked him and trusted him. They knew that if he put a seal on the toilet and there was still water on the tile floor, he would be back the same day to double-check. That had only happened once. Come to think of it, it was at Susan Tyler's house. "It's just a trickle," she had said, pointing, and when he got down there he laughed and said, "That's not water and it didn't come from inside the toilet."

"Travis!" she'd yelled for her son. "Oh my God, Bill, I'm mortified."

The calendar said that it was spring, but you couldn't prove it by the temperatures some nights, or the early mornings. Spring messed with you, stepped up, rolled back, gave you hope of better days to come, snatched it away. One beautiful sunny day, with everyone taking off their jackets and smiling up at the sky as though it were a friend they hadn't seen in a while, and then it was for sure that two days later there would be a sleet storm. Daylight, daytime, still seemed to Bill to come hard—black to dark gray, an ashy color that was dawn but didn't feel like it. It was still a dim strip outside the windows when he sat on the edge of Ali's bed and smoothed her hair from her forehead. She had smiled in her half-sleep, and he felt bad because he figured she must think it was her mother, back from the overnight shift, still smelling of rubbing alcohol and hand lotion. She'd always been the one to do this. His hands were hard and tough, but even as hard as she'd worked, Annie's were soft and smooth from putting lotion on her patients. One of the old men at the wake had said, "I hope you don't take this the wrong way, son, but your wife had a good set of hands on her."

Bill knew he had always been one of those guys who couldn't say no to anyone. Annie had complained about it all the time. "They could hire a U-Haul," she would say, or, "He could get his own posthole digger." Things like that. He couldn't say no to her, either. That's why they had four kids, would have had five if she hadn't wound up bleeding out onto that same floor she'd died on. That's why their kids had the names they had. He said since Annie did all the labor she should get to choose. "Just because you're stuck with the last name Brown, you don't have to make the kids sound like they're members of the royal family," Kathy had said one night when Annie thought she might be pregnant again and was mulling Arthur or Elizabeth. Annie said her sister could be spiteful sometimes. "What about Jasper?" Annie had said later, lying next to him in the dark.

It was funny he'd turned out that way, so agreeable, because his mother was someone who couldn't say yes to anything. She'd been county clerk as long as anyone could remember, and she made it sound like she was a whisper away from running everything, when the truth was it was mainly paperwork. But it offered a lot of chances to say no to all kinds of permits and licenses. Even when it was certain that something was permissible, she would find a problem with a signature, a statement, a survey, a stamp. He'd heard there were people who waited until she was on vacation to submit anything to her office.

Do the math, and you could tell that she'd been childless for years before her only child was born. She had once told Annie, early on, when she still told Annie things, that she had thought she was going through the change and was flabbergasted to discover that she was pregnant instead. Most of the mothers in their neighborhood stayed home, at least for a while, but his mother had moved her mother-in-law in to her house and gone right back to the municipal building. Occasionally she'd get angry—at spilled milk or a messy room—and she'd wallop him, but he didn't really remember much about that until the week of his tenth birthday, when she'd pushed him and his father had said, "He's bigger than you now, Dora," said it like a warning.

"You will never lay a hand on our children," Annie had said when he told her that story, and he sat back in the diner booth, hard. "If you think that would ever happen then you don't know me at all," he'd said. It had been early days, before he'd realized that no one would ever know him the way Annie did.

He had friends who had it worse, whose mothers were drunk by the time the kids got home from school, and one whose mother got caught half naked with the track coach in the locker room. "How's your mom?" team members would say to that poor guy afterward, and what could he do but fight them? Bill hadn't really realized what he was missing until he saw Annie dancing around the living room with Ali, singing, "I love you, you love me, we're a happy family." She'd looked over, laughing, as tired as she was, wet spots on her T-shirt where her milk had let down, it seemed out of sheer joy sometimes, and she had looped her arm around Bill's neck and pulled him in. It was amazing, being part of that, but it made him understand that it was something he'd been missing without even knowing it.

He'd thought of that moment the other day, he wasn't sure why, and he'd felt a pain so crippling that he'd stopped halfway out of the drugstore lot, thinking he was having a heart attack. He wasn't a dramatic guy in any way, but he had put his hand on his chest and thought, My heart is broken, that's the problem. He'd heard a horn behind him, looked in the rearview, and seen Pat Murphy from Murphy's Towing walk up to his window and say, "Your van okay, Bill?" And he'd pulled himself together. He kept using that turn of phrase to describe what he needed to do because it felt like he was leaving pieces of himself wherever he went, in every room, like he was dismembered by loss. Pull yourself together, Bill, he would think.

His mother had told him her job made it impossible to pick the kids up at school, and anyhow, she said, they could always stay for afterschool and take the late bus. Ali was plenty old enough to take it from there. Or maybe he could hire one of the girls from the college. He'd lost half his income, which he tried not to think of, because thinking of Annie in terms of lost wages made him feel sick. "Did you apply for the Social Security survivor's benefits?" his mother had said the day after the funeral. "Back off, Mom," he'd replied. The one good thing he could say about the terrible thing that had happened was that it seemed like Annie's gift for going at it with Dora Brown had been magically passed to him.

Grief was like spring, maybe. You thought you were getting out from under it and then it came roaring back. And getting out from under it felt like forgetting, and forgetting felt like treason. Sometimes when he reached in the closet for a shirt, a sleeve or two from her side would touch his arm, like it was reaching for him, and there would be a faint smell, lemon and hand cream and something else, maybe her shampoo.

His mother had shown up a few days ago, pulled him into the bedroom, shut the door, and opened the one to the closet.

"I know you don't want to handle this, and I understand that," she said, "so I've cleared my schedule Friday. You'll come home, and everything in the closet and the bureau will be boxed and gone."

Gone where, he almost said, as he had a crazy vision of his mother showing up for a Sunday dinner in one of Annie's silky blouses. But saying "gone where" would have assumed consent.

"No," he said.

"It's time, son."

"No. It can stay as it is for now. Don't move anything. You hear me? Don't move anything."

"Whatever you say. But a little gratitude would be nice."

"What's wrong with Grandma?" Ali had said as his mother slammed the back door.

He pictured the big empty closet space his mother wanted, and he was not having it, not now, maybe not ever. Everybody wanted you to move on, but moving on felt like just another way of saying "turn your back."

He had on long underwear beneath his work pants and shirt, his padded jacket, too, but he could still feel the cold in the cab of the van as he'd headed down the block first thing that morning. A man walking a dachshund raised a hand. His van was easy for people to spot, white with a picture of a fireplace with logs burning inside, orange and red. It had been Annie's idea. "It doesn't really make any sense," he'd said. "It's about heat," she said. "What's the thing people count on you for most? Heat."

"Water," he'd said, so on the other side of the truck there was a picture of an old-fashioned well, with a bucket and a crank. No matter what he said she was always a couple of steps ahead of him.

The kids kept saying they wanted a dog. Maybe he'd get the kids a dog. Or maybe not. He couldn't even manage the kids, let alone a puppy. There were still hamsters, weren't there? He was pretty sure he'd smelled them when he'd gone into Ali's room.

He'd always been so proud of himself, sitting at the bar with a Yuengling glistening in a mug in front of him, listening to guys talk in turn, about how they only saw their kids the odd weekend, how they didn't have kids because who needed the hassle, how the wife was home with the kids and good thing because one of them had been puking all night long. He'd always been so proud that he and Annie shared the burden so it didn't feel like a burden. Now he knew he'd been kidding himself. He couldn't remember the names of the teachers, the doctors, the kids' friends, without checking her phone. She had ninety-one messages. He hadn't listened to any of them.

Bill had thought he was better than those guys, the ones who had a shot and a beer, a shot and a beer, until Cyril the bartender took their keys and called a cab. "His wife split," the bartender might say. "He's in pretty bad shape." Now he wasn't so sure. He'd been to the bar twice in the last week, just for an hour, but an hour when he knew the kids thought he had a late-night call. The place had had a pull on him for years, not because of the drinks, but because of how it made him feel, like he was a different guy, the guy he might have been.

Was his life a choice or an accident? He'd tried not to ask himself that over the years, but sometimes he'd be at the bar, staring at the big-screen TV, bitching about how the coaches didn't know what they were doing anymore, hearing about a new development outside town that looked promising in terms of work, and he'd look down at the chilly mist on the beer, the pressed paper coaster, the cheap bamboo bowls they put the peanuts in, and imagine that he didn't have life insurance premiums, utility bills, four sets of shoes to buy and buy and buy again. He'd look at a table of younger guys in the corner, taking their time over nachos, getting a little loud, and think, That could have been me. He knew exactly the moment when it all changed, the night at Greco's that Annie said, pushing a slice of pizza away with a shudder, "Billy, I'm going to have this baby, with or without you. But I sure hope it's with." She'd pulled together a wedding in three weeks. The money he'd been saving for a new truck he used for a ring.

"Man, you got married young," the best man had said when he'd stumbled upon a bachelor party one night. There was a fifty-pack box of condoms on the bar, and one of the other guys said, "Give Bill here some of those, he needs them bad!" And he laughed and put one in his pocket, and two days later, when Annie was separating the darks and the lights for the laundry, she'd said, "What the hell is this?"

There had always been something about sitting there with a beer in front of him that gave him a window, just for an hour, into another life, and it would be like a little itch, a tickle in his mind. And then he'd put a ten down on the bar and go back out to his van and his house, and he'd see the back of Annie's neck as she bent over a stew pot on the stove, and he'd think to himself, This is what those younger guys at that table are looking for. You just don't know you're looking for it until you have it, until you drive to the jewelry store in Belmont and buy the biggest solitaire you can manage, and circle back and kneel down and say, "This is me, on board."

"What happened to her engagement ring?" his mother had asked when everyone left the house after the funeral, all that food, the sight of it making him feel slightly sick, still on the counters. He hadn't answered because he knew she would give him hell for tucking it into the casket before they closed and locked it at the funeral home. He'd gone in there alone, everyone else in the limousine.

He tried not to cry in front of the kids, not since Benjy had patted his leg one day when they were watching cartoons and said, "Mommy will be sad that you're sad." The shower was a good place to cry, although you couldn't take a long shower in a house with four kids and just one bathroom, and if he cried in the van on the way to a job he just had to make sure that he stopped and mopped up before he got to wherever he was going. He'd checked out his eyes in the visor mirror before he got out of the van at Karen Feeney's house. They were red, but she would probably put that down to how early it was.

"I'm really grateful you could get here first thing," she said as she led him inside, and he was almost relieved to see that she was wearing a heavy sweater with a vest over it, and the vest wasn't zipped because of the swell of her belly. He figured her for maybe six or seven months along. No dinner invitation.

"No problem," he said. "It sounded like you needed me fast." In the living room he could see his breath, like pale cotton candy. Hers, too. She had her hands wrapped around a mug like she was using it for warmth.

"Can I give you some coffee?" she asked.

"Maybe after," he said. "I don't want your pipes to freeze."

She came down the steep basement stairs behind him, holding tight to the banister the way he'd seen Annie do when she was pregnant. Bill took off the front of the furnace, and three mice ran across the floor and disappeared into cracks in the masonry. Karen shrieked, then said, "It's ridiculous. They're tiny little things. Why am I screaming?"

"That's your problem, I bet. They build nests inside the furnace and chew on the wires. They get cold in this weather, too."

He went out to the van to get what he needed. Karen Feeney followed him back up the stairs, no matter how tiny the mice were. A wire replaced here, another there, the removal of a little pillow of old insulation and bits of straw and cardboard that someone was planning to use as a nest for mouse babies, and when he lit the pilot there was a soft exhale and the sound of air moving through the ducts. He put a block of poison bait inside the back of the furnace to take care of the mice. She didn't need to know about that.

"You're all good," he said, coming into what had once been a kitchen and was now messier and more slapdash than the mouse nest, a coffee maker and toaster oven on a scarred pine table, big chunks of plaster missing where the old cabinets had been removed, dead spots in the faded linoleum where the refrigerator and the stove once stood.

"At least the baby's room is done," she said, handing him a mug of coffee. "It's just all taking so much longer than we expected. We have lots of plans."

He smiled. So many plans. Annie had planned to become a nurse, to go to the community college to save money so that she could go to State, where she and Annemarie would share an apartment. Then her father left, and her mother fell apart. Her sister had only one semester of college to go, but there was no tuition money left for Annie, and she took the job at the nursing home to make some, and waved as Annemarie packed up her old junker of a car to go back to her dorm. Annie had turned into one of those girls who hung around town, and he became one of the guys who did the same, a little like high school, but with work instead of the school part.

He took criminal justice classes at the university satellite campus so that when the test came around for the state police he would be ready, but only one class at a time so he could work, too, because as his mother liked to say, she wasn't made of money. But there was a law enforcement hiring freeze, and in the meantime he worked at AAA Plumbing as an apprentice, and when the doctors told Mr. Martin he had COPD and that his working days were done and he ought to buy that place in the Carolinas he'd been talking Bill's ear off about forever, Bill found himself with a business on his hands.

Liz Donahue was away at college, full of stories about people he didn't know and things he hadn't done, and neither of them seemed sure whether she was his girlfriend anymore. But Annie Fonzheimer was around, at the diner, at the parties. Things with Liz had worked the way they sometimes did in high school—sex in stages, starting with French kisses, maybe ending someday in the real deal. The guys pushed, condoms in their wallets, and the girls gave in, telling themselves it was more than it was. Annie was different. "Are you and Liz still together?" she'd asked in the car on the way to her house. "Not really," he said, and she'd put her hand on the inside of his leg, high up. The first night he kissed her was the first night he had sex with her, and when the two of them were lying on the living room rug she had grinned at him and said, "Wow!" He'd never had a higher opinion of himself than he did that night.

By the time the state police exam came around again, he was married with a baby who slept between the two of them or never slept at all.

"Your first?" he said now, sipping his coffee, nodding at Karen's belly, and her face changed, got hard and set in a way that made him understand that what seemed like a simple question somehow wasn't. "Sort of," she said. "It's been complicated, I guess you'd say. Not easy. What about you?"

"I have four."

"Oh my God," she said, "your wife must be a superwoman."

"Yep," he said. Her "complicated" and his "yep" were first cousins, were two answers designed to keep the jack in the box, because who knew what might pop out, everyone has a whole universe of trouble inside and no one wants the world to know.

"Yep," he repeated, "she sure is."

G oing back to school after your mother dies was worse than Ali could have imagined. Jenny stuck close to her without saying much, which was her way. But some of the other girls just looked at her as though they were going to cry, and one or two actually did. A few of the boys said sorry with their heads down, and then stumbled away. The worst was when Melinda Buxbaum, who had been at war with Ali since fourth grade, when Ali won the spelling bee and Melinda came in second, made a big show of sympathy on their way into school the first day Ali was back. "It's, like, the worst thing I can imagine," she said with a catch in her voice, her hand on her chest, which was a real chest now, not like Ali's.

"I hate her," Jenny had said.

"Even her friends hate her," Ali replied.

"That doesn't really make sense," Jenny said, and Ali

remembered how her mother had said once that Jenny seemed literal-minded. Ali hadn't said that that was one of the things she liked about Jenny, that you didn't have to figure out what she meant when she spoke.

But the sympathy cloud finally dissipated and died, and then, right after spring break, Ali was in math class and the principal came to the door and whispered to Mr. Horton, their math teacher. "I don't think I have an Alexandra in this class," Mr. Horton had said. The thing about Mr. Horton was, he was clueless about everything but math.

On the Monday she'd gone back to school, when everyone else had acted as though Ali could basically go into some kind of suspended animation—her English teacher saying she could hand in last week's work whenever, even though Ali had it with her, the basketball coach saying he knew she wouldn't be at practice, even though she really wanted to go to practice—Mr. Horton had said, frowning, "Brown, you missed class last week." He called them all by their last names and never read the notices he got from the front office; there was a story that he had come in twice on snow days because he didn't know snow days had been called. Jenny said her mother said he was gay and shouldn't be allowed to teach in public schools. "I don't think so," Ali had said.

One of the girls in the front row had whispered something to him. "You have something to say, McIntyre?" He'd leaned toward her. "Oh," he said. "Brown, I'm sorry. I'll give you the worksheets from last week at the end of class." Ali was glad he hadn't acted as though falling behind in math was a natural part of having your mother die.

What was a natural part was the principal whispering at the door six weeks later, when people had finally stopped looking at her with that sad look on their faces, and Mr. Horton saying, "I'll tell her." She had to see the counselor, who was at the middle school on Thursdays and the high school two other days during the week. "Lunch period," Mr. Horton said as she was leaving. "Apparently you can bring a sandwich." Jenny passed her a package of cookies in a plastic wrapper and shook her head, hard. "Don't tell her anything," she mouthed.

That was Jenny all over, Ali thought. Ali's mother had once said someone she knew was a locked door, and Jenny seemed like a series of locked doors. Their homeroom teacher the year before had pulled Ali aside and asked her to look after the new student, and in the beginning that's all it had been, looking after, because Jenny was so quiet. The open doors came later, and they were all doors into Ali's life, not Jenny's. Jenny was always interested—in Ali's brothers, her parents, the things they all did together or said to one another, as though Ali's life were a book Jenny was reading. "I think she's living through you a little bit, hon," Ali's mother had said. Ali had to admit, it was flattering. It made Ali's life seem interesting in a way it never had to her. Jenny had stopped doing it for the last few weeks, as though she had mostly wanted a look into Ali's life when it was soothing, not when it was scary, and it had left long silences between them. If the counselor was supposed to talk to you about what you were thinking and feeling, Jenny was a terrible candidate for a session. She hardly even talked to Ali about those things. No wonder Jenny had only seen the counselor once—the old counselor, who everyone said wasn't very good. He must have really felt like he'd hit a locked door with Jenny.

"Come in," the new counselor said, sitting at one end of the table in a little room off the teacher's lunchroom. It had a big glass window, and Ali could see the soccer coach and the social studies teacher hunched over bag lunches.

"I know," the counselor said, watching Ali watch the teachers. "Let's try to sit with our backs to them so we have at least the illusion of privacy."

It wasn't just Jenny. The word in school about talking to the counselor was: Don't. Just don't. There were times when they made you, when there'd been a fight at recess, when you'd talked back to a teacher. But the word was that you'd get sent to see the counselor, and the next thing you knew they might say you had ADHD or some kind of depression, and your parents would freak out and ask how you were every single morning, like you were a grenade with the pin pulled and they were just waiting for you to blow. Then the counselor would be built into your schedule and you'd never get lunch or play practice or basketball. The counselor would become your extracurricular activity, and you would become that kid. Oh, Ali Brown? Yeah, she's the one whose mother died.

Maybe the counselor would have gotten better traction if the parents had been more on board, but lots of them weren't. Some of the parents who had kids with problems didn't really want them to talk about them, and some of the parents who had kids without problems, or thought they did, didn't see the point. Ali's parents were about as good as it got, and even her mother had said she thought it was fine for the high school, but she wasn't sure middle school children had the kinds of problems that made it necessary. "We could have used one when I was in high school," she'd said one night to their father when he was saying that someone who had just gotten his tax bill was complaining about the added expense of what the guy was calling a headshrinker. "I mean, there was a lot going on behind the scenes, right?"

She'd started to rattle off names, but some of them were people who still lived in town, and their father had put his hand around her upper arm and just nodded, which meant,

"The kids will hear." Actually it usually meant, "Ali will hear." Ant didn't seem to notice, or if he did he didn't say anything, whereas her parents knew that Ali might ask what they meant by saying Mr. and Mrs. Richter should have given up trying a long time ago. "What exactly does 'light in the loafers' mean?" she'd asked her mother once, and her mother had lowered her head and looked under her bangs at her husband and said, "I wonder where she heard that." Because of course Ali had heard it from her grandmother, about Mr. Horton.

"They think you'll talk more because it's a woman," Jenny had said. She'd been sent to see the counselor that one time last year, and when Ali asked why, Jenny had said, "Some stupid thing," and started to work on a math sheet. Ali knew that was the end of the discussion, door slam. There were things Jenny just wouldn't discuss, like what her old school had been like and whether her parents would let her do sleepovers when she got a little older. There were no pictures in her bedroom of friends from before, or even grandparents; everything in it looked brand-new—the hairbrush and the little ceramic tray on the bureau, the pens in a pink mug on her desk. She had a computer that looked new, too, but she was only allowed to use it for schoolwork, and a walk-in closet filled with dresses: flowered, ruffled, full skirts, lace, velvet. But the funeral was the first time Ali had seen Jenny in a dress since a birthday party they'd gone to a year before, and the dress she wore to the funeral might be the same one she'd worn then, tan and shapeless. "I hate dresses," Jenny had said when Ali asked about the ones in her closet.

The first time Jenny had stayed for dinner at Ali's house she acted as though she might get in trouble. "My mother is picking me up at six-thirty sharp," she said. "You'll be done by then," Ali's mother had said. "It might even give you time to help with the dishes." She'd winked, but Ali could tell that Jenny thought she was serious. There were all these things Jenny did as though they had to be hidden, the way some of the eighth graders would go out behind the bleachers to smoke and then spray air freshener around themselves, as though that would stop the smell from leaching into their sweatshirts. Jenny acted as though getting ice cream on Front Street or hanging around the practice field while Ali played soccer were forbidden. She lied to her mother all the time about having to stay after school for tutoring. She'd been to Ali's house three times, and all three times it was because she said she and Ali were working on a project for the science fair. Ali figured that when the science fair came around, if Jenny's mother showed up at school, she would just put Jenny's name alongside hers on her submission card. Jenny's father never showed up, even for parent–teacher conferences.

Jenny's bedroom was enormous, bigger than Ali's living room, but Jenny said she liked Ali's bedroom, that it was cozy. She had been so excited to see the hamsters that it made Ali realize how seldom Jenny got excited about anything. When they had gotten the hamsters last Christmas, her parents had decided they should live in Ali's room because there was more space in there, which was something Ant complained about all the time. "How come she gets her own room and I have to share with those two babies?" Even Jenny had said, "I don't really understand why your brothers are all smushed up together and you have a room to yourself." Jenny was an only child, which Ali used to think sounded great, but not so much now, when she would have been alone in the house at night while her father was out on a call or crying in his room with the door shut. The boys weren't much help, but at least she could hear them breathing when she couldn't sleep.

"I got stuck with the hamsters," she had told Jenny that first time she came for dinner.

"I like hamsters. I think white mice are creepy, with those pink eyes, and guinea pigs are too big. Hamsters are just the right size." Jenny held the hamsters in her cupped hands under her chin, and they wiggled their whiskers. It reminded Ali of how her mother would hold a buttercup under her chin when Ali was younger to see if she liked butter. "Who doesn't like butter?" Ali said once, and her mother had stopped doing it. Ali wondered whether she'd gotten too big for her mother to do it anymore, or whether she'd spoiled it that day.

"So why don't you get some hamsters?" she'd asked Jenny.

"My father won't let me," she said.

"Your house is big," Ali said. "You could put the cage on the sun porch. Then they wouldn't smell up your bedroom."

Jenny put the hamster in its cage and stroked its back. "I can't," she had said.

Ali's mother had made cheeseburgers and french fries, which she thought of as a fun dinner, and Jenny broke her burger into tiny pieces and ate them one at a time. It was the way she ate at school, but somehow Ali had never paid that much attention to it before. "You can pick it up," Benjy said, holding his burger in both hands, and Ali's mother said, "People have different ways of eating different things. Look at corn. You eat around the cob. Ali eats side to side."

"I eat side to side too," Jenny said quietly.

"I rest my case," Ali's mother said. "And it's after six, so maybe Jenny wants to wash her hands and have a chocolate chip cookie before she goes."

"Me too," said Benjy.

"When that plate is clean," Ali's mother had said.

"She doesn't exactly seem like a happy girl," she had said

after walking Jenny to the car and telling Jenny's mother how much they liked having her and how she was welcome to come anytime. "She's happy," Ali had insisted. "If you say so," her mother said.

"They try to make you tell them stuff," Jenny had told Ali once about the counselor.

"What kind of stuff?" Ali had asked, but Jenny just frowned and shook her head.

The old counselor had been fired over winter break because a girl in the high school who had seen him three times had had to go to the hospital. She'd gotten so thin that she kept fainting and finally had what was rumored to be a heart attack. "I mean, what's the point of having a counselor at the high school if he misses something like anorexia," Ali's mother said at Christmas dinner. "I don't understand this nonsense where they starve themselves," their grandmother had said. "That's obvious," Ali had heard her mother whisper in the kitchen, where she was cutting more turkey because their grandmother had taken the last two pieces on the platter.

The new counselor was a woman with a round face, broad across the cheeks, with a smile that made a long straight line above a rounded chin. Ali thought she would be easy to draw, even if you were as young as Jamie: big circle, small circles, curves, lines. She had brown skin, black eyes, black hair. Jenny said she had heard she was Filipina. "From the Philippines," she'd added. Her name was Miss Cruz.

"Do you know why you're here, Alexandra?" she said.

"My name is Ali. I mean, technically it's Alexandra, but nobody calls me that."

Miss Cruz made a note. She used an old-fashioned copybook, black-and-white marble cover, like the one Ali had used in grade school.

"Ali. I try to see every student who has lost a parent."

"I didn't lose my mother. I hate it that people say that. I didn't lose her, and she's not gone, and she didn't pass away. She's dead." Even to her own ears that sounded harsh, and angry in a way that had stayed safely inside until just this minute. Plus she'd broken the first rule of talking to the counselor: don't. Let her talk, ask questions, say what she thinks. Just nod or make some comment that means nothing. But don't get mad about the stupid way everyone talked when your mother died. Don't tell her that the thing about people saying you've lost her is that deep down it makes you think that if you tried hard enough you could find her. Don't tell her that there was a part of your brain that hadn't gotten the message that your mother was never coming back, that you'd seen someone in scrubs outside school the other day and almost run to her, that you hid the dish towel with the smell of her hand lotion so no one would wash it although the only person doing any laundry was you, and really badly, so that Jamie's underwear was pink because of a red polo shirt. Don't tell her that you're not allowed to have a cellphone until you're fourteen so you use the landline at home to call your mother's cell and listen to her message voice. That alone would probably mean you would have to see the counselor all year, maybe longer. The woman had a pen in her hand. Who knew who might read what she wrote?

Miss Cruz tilted her head. "You're absolutely right," she said. "Why do you think people do that?"

"Do what?"

"Talk about someone dying as though it's something different. Something less final, maybe? I hadn't really focused on that before."

"Have you ever counseled someone whose mother died? Or father?"

Beneath her broad brown cheeks Miss Cruz's face turned a copper color. "Let's talk about you," she said, but that copper color gave her away. This was her first dead-mother student. Ali narrowed her eyes. Miss Cruz looked young. Maybe she hadn't been a counselor long.

"I'm fine," Ali said.

"That would be surprising to me," said Miss Cruz.

"Why?"

"You seem like a thoughtful person. You must know that it is an important event, perhaps the most important event of your entire life, to lose—to have your mother die."

For some reason Ali thought of her mother's little feet in their purple slippers. "It's cold in here," Ali said, pulling her hands into the sleeves of her sweatshirt. She realized that her hands were in fists.

"It's early yet, though, isn't it? It takes a while to process a change that enormous. How are your brothers?"

How were her brothers? Jamie had wet the bed the night of the funeral, and nine times since. Benjy had told some kids at school that his father said his mother was still alive in his head, and the biggest bully in his grade said he was mental, and "What did he mean by that, Ali?" Ant was Ant. He was a fortress, always had been. "I know who's really in there," his mother had said once, tapping him on the head. If she did, the secret had died with her. Ali wondered whether Ant ever thought about that.

"They're fine," Ali said.

"And your father?"

"Where are your mother's work shoes?" he'd asked last week.

"I put them in the closet," Ali said. She didn't want to tell him that she'd put them there because when they came home from school one afternoon Benjy saw them and said, "Mommy's home early!"

"Put them back by the door," her father said. He was still sleeping in half the bed. Maybe he was mental, too. Maybe they all were. Ali could barely walk across the kitchen floor without shivering. Her mother had once said that that feeling was someone walking over your grave. Thinking about that expression had only made her shiver again.

"He's okay," said Ali. She figured another "fine" would be stretching it.

"Tell me about your mother," Miss Cruz said with a smile, leaning in a little bit.

Ali was silent, and stunned. Don't talk to the counselor. That was the deal. But don't talk about her mother? That seemed cruel, to her mother especially—who wasn't in a position to care, and yet somehow that made the cruelty of refusing to talk about her seem worse. Words were all Ali had to make her mother alive again, words and stories. Ali wondered if Miss Cruz had seen that she was trying to channel Jenny, trying to keep her door locked, and the question the counselor finally came up with was the key. That kind of thing was probably something they taught in counseling classes.

"My mother's name is Anne, but everyone calls her Annie," Ali said, letting her fists poke from the sweatshirt sleeves. "She works as an aide at the Green View Nursing Home in Bentonville. She went to nursing school for a while but then she had me and she didn't have the chance to go back, so she's an aide, not a registered nurse, but all the patients say she's better than the nurses. She crochets a lot. She doesn't even have to look at what she's doing when she crochets. Like, she watches TV, but at the same time she's making an afghan. Most of the people at the nursing home have afghans my mother made. Sometimes she makes little afghans as baby gifts for people."

Ali could remember four years ago, when her mother had

started making a little afghan for Annemarie, yellow and pale green and light blue. Her mother had been in the kitchen, looking at her phone, and she showed Ali a picture in shades of gray of what looked at first like a thunderstorm but was apparently the beginning of a baby. Once her mother had pointed out what went where in the picture, Ali thought it looked like a monster with an outsize domed head and tiny flipper limbs. "The best news," her mother had said over and over again, her voice quivering, tears in her eyes. "The best news in the whole wide world." There were tears in her mother's eyes again, two weeks later, when she told Ali that Annemarie's baby had died, and Ali thought for a minute that she had been right, that the odd look of it meant there had been something wrong with it. But her mother told her this happened a lot, a baby started and then was gone, and that people didn't talk about it enough. "Don't mention it to Annemarie, though," she'd added. "She's having a hard time coping." There'd been another one, two years later. That one died too. "I can read her mind," she'd heard her mother say to her father. "It's killing her, that I did this without even trying." For a while her mother had had a baby every couple of years. "Like congressional elections," her aunt Kathy had said once.

"This could send her over the edge again," Ali's father had said.

"I'm on it," Ali's mother said. "Don't you think I've thought of that? I'm on it."

"Your mother sounds lovely," Miss Cruz said. "What kinds of things did the two of you do together?"

"When you have a lot of kids it's not really like that," Ali said. "Like, there's not that much time to do things with one person."

"I know all about that," Miss Cruz said. "I'm the youngest of nine." She looked down at her notes.

"The youngest," Ali said. "That's an easy job."

Miss Cruz laughed. "Most people say that's a lot of kids."

"Well, it is, but at least you didn't have to take care of any younger ones, right?"

"Oldest children always think being the youngest is easy," Miss Cruz said. "And there's no doubt that being the oldest can be hard." She looked down at her notes. "I know you're the oldest of four. You must have a lot of responsibility now."

Another key to a locked door. For a moment Ali could hear herself that morning saying "I'm sorry" to the hamsters, giving them Ritz Crackers because there was no lettuce or carrots or apples. They had seemed happy; they snatched the crackers up in their little paw hands and started to buzzsaw the edges with teeth the same color as the crackers, both of them making a purring sound as Ali left for school.

"You probably have a lot on your plate," Miss Cruz added.

You have no idea, Ali thought. It's not just the meals and the homework and the sharpened pencils. It's listening to the little boys say, "That's not how Mommy does it." It's having to forge my father's signature on permission slips because he forgets. It's Ant complaining that his basketball clothes smell like feet. "Learn to use the washing machine," Ali had said, knowing as she said it that she'd wind up washing them herself. She almost said to the counselor, What gets washed in hot and what gets washed in warm?

Instead she sat silent, not even nodding.

"Do you have good support at home?" the counselor added. She looked down at her notes again. "I see your grandmother lives nearby."

Ali nodded. Her grandmother had stopped by twice for a

half hour that week. She'd left with a Tupperware of chicken tetrazzini she'd found in the very back of the freezer, left over from the funeral, "before it's past its sell-by date."

"So, good support," Miss Cruz had said, making a note in her copybook, and it was the closest Ali came to saying what she was really thinking, which was, Not really. Not really good support. It was harder getting the boys up by herself than Ali would have thought, and she wound up having to do it more and more often. "December to March your father is MIA," her mother had said once. "Frozen pipes are no joke." But MIA seemed to be slopping over into April, too. When she looked in the fridge she wished instead of mac and cheese Sally Lankford had shown up with some milk, because there wasn't a whole lot left. That morning she'd sniffed at the milk container. Maybe, maybe not. At least a few people were bringing a second round of food. There was banana bread that Mrs. Tyler had dropped by when she came to get her cupcake plate. "Your father at home?" she'd asked, and Ali wanted to say, Hardly ever, but instead said, "Not right now." The banana bread had been warm through the tinfoil, and Ali put it on the breakfast table with the butter dish and cut off some thick slices.

"Are there nuts in there?" Benjy had asked.

She guessed her father had forgotten that the elementary school was five blocks away but her bus stop for the middle school was a block up in the opposite direction. She kept thinking of having Ant take the little boys, but she could almost hear her mother say, There are upsides and downsides to being the oldest. The first day she'd walked the three boys to the elementary school, she'd circled back and seen her bus pulling away, the big red eyes of the taillights turning to amber and growing faint in the dim morning. "No, no, no!" she shouted as she ran, her backpack bouncing between her shoulder blades, just the way it felt when she gave Jamie a piggy-back ride. "Faster, Ali," he always yelled. "No," she wailed, and then the red lights came on again, and the bus door opened with that sharp pneumatic slap.

"You're late," said the driver. "Don't be late again."

"My aunt Kathy is coming next weekend," Ali said to Miss Cruz. "My aunt Annemarie is coming, too. She's not really my aunt, she's my mother's best friend."

"That sounds helpful. How about your friends? Have they been supportive? You're friends with Jenny Mason, correct? How is she doing?"

"She's fine."

"It's hard being a new student sometimes."

"She's not that new," Ali said.

"It's good that she has you as support," Miss Cruz said. "Does she spend a lot of time at your house?"

"I guess."

"That's good," said Miss Cruz, making another note.

"Do you need to talk to my father? Because he's kind of busy with everything. Really busy."

"Your father knows that we're meeting. I'm not allowed to meet with a student your age without parental permission, so I called and spoke with him. He sounded very nice. He said that your mother would have wanted you to have this sort of resource." That was probably true, Ali thought. She could almost hear her mother arguing back and forth with their grandmother:

Oh, for pity's sake, she doesn't need a counselor, this happens to people every day.

That doesn't mean you shouldn't make it easier.

She'll just wind up raking everything over the coals.

She'll do that anyhow.

Sometimes I don't understand you.

You can say that again, Dora.

Ali thought maybe her grandmother would miss having their mother around to oppose. She fought with a lot of other people as part of her job, but no one so consistently or with so much obvious enjoyment.

"The plan," the counselor was saying, "is that you and I will have three more sessions unless you want to continue after that, but your father has agreed that what passes between us will be confidential. Except for certain parameters the state sets about reporting."

"Like if I wasn't eating or I was cutting myself."

The counselor smiled. "I can tell you all talk about these sessions, even those of you who have never participated."

Ali got to the lunchroom with ten minutes to go, so she had a chance to eat half a peanut butter and jelly, even though she still wasn't hungry and felt nauseous most of the time. She didn't want the counselor to have to tell her father that she wasn't eating. Next time she would wear short sleeves so the counselor could see that she wasn't cutting herself. Although, Melinda Buxbaum said there was a girl on the cheer squad at the high school who always wore tights under her skirt because she cut herself on her legs instead of her arms.

"Did you talk to her?" Jenny said when Ali sat down.

"Not really," Ali said. "She mainly wanted to know how my brothers were doing. I said fine."

"Did she ask about me?"

"Why would she ask about you?"

"Because you and I are friends."

"So when she asked about you I just said that. That we're friends. That we're best friends." Though sometimes now, thinking about her mother and Annemarie, Ali wondered if that was true. She didn't know if Jenny would ever be able to say that Ali had saved her life, and Ali was sure she wouldn't be able to say that she and Jenny could read each other's minds. Sometimes she wondered if you needed a different kind of friend when you didn't have a mother anymore.

"Don't tell her anything," Jenny said. "My mother says it's none of her business. She says counselors just stir up all kinds of trouble. Besides, she can't fix anything. What's the point if she can't fix things? It's just to make adults feel better."

"I thought she seemed pretty nice," Ali said.

"Yeah, that's what they want you to think," Jenny said. "That's how they get you to talk."

Annemarie arrived Saturday morning. "It's all you, babe," she said to Ali. "What do you want to do? Movies? Mall? Paris? Rome?"

"I need to go to the supermarket," Ali said.

"What? Bill, have you done any grocery shopping?"

"I've been working fourteen-hour days, Annemarie," he said. "Frozen pipes, furnaces, you name it, I'm fixing it. I barely have time to sleep. There's plenty of food in the refrigerator." He opened the door to the fridge and looked inside as though to make the point. Annemarie looked inside too. Bill straightened up and gave her a long look, squinting and sniffing the air. She put her hands on her hips and looked right back. Annemarie was slender but she had the stance of a big person. Mints on her breath, coconut oil in her hair, and she wasn't taking any attitude from Bill Brown after driving an hour when she could have been doing the books on her business or having the color done on her hair or drinking rosé by the fire pit and quietly crying.

It was true that she'd made an appointment with a back doctor one of the boutique owners had recommended, someone who would gladly write a prescription if you said your sciatica was bad. But she'd already canceled it. Or would, when she got home, knowing by the look on his face that Bill Brown was just waiting for her to fall.

He was waiting for her to fall and she was waiting for him to fail and to forget. Two scorpions in a jar, Annie had once said about a pair of roommates they'd had to separate at the nursing home. That's what they'd become, both of them made poisonous by grief. Annemarie could feel her relationship with Bill curdling without Annie as an interlocutor between them. Maybe they'd always quietly circled each other but couldn't see it with Annie smiling in the middle.

"Should we take the boys with us?" she said to Ali.

"The little boys are going to DayPlay at the Y," Ali said.

"What time is that again?" her father said.

"It starts at eleven," Ali said, her tight little adult-person voice making Annemarie sad.

The two of them went to Giant Food and spent a lot of money, filled two carts, but Annemarie said Ali shouldn't worry about how much it cost, it was the least she could do. Annemarie said she would get one of Tom's whiteboards, and Ali could put it on the fridge, and they could all write down what was needed at the store and what the day's schedule of meals was. But when she saw Ali's face she said, "You're going to wind up doing everything, aren't you?"

Then they went to Olive Garden for lunch, and Ali got ravioli and only ate two of them. "I had a big breakfast," she said to Annemarie, which Annemarie could tell was a lie, but she couldn't complain because she didn't eat much either. "I'm waiting for someone to open a decent restaurant in this town," she said.

"You said that to Mommy all the time," Ali said.

"I know," Annemarie said, and she smiled, and then her smile crinkled up and collapsed, like someone had grabbed and crushed it so it could be thrown away like foil or wrapping paper. She kept wondering when it would stop, when she would get control of herself anytime she talked about Annie, or thought about her, or heard a song on the radio they'd listened to together when they were young. Good song, bad song, didn't matter. She'd almost started to cry in front of the Doritos rack at the supermarket.

"Sorry, honey," Annemarie said, wiping her eyes with one of those big-checked Olive Garden napkins that were made out of some fabric that seemed to be water-repellent. "This is so not about me. How are you holding up?"

"Is everything all right, ladies?" said their waiter.

"We're fine," Annemarie said. "We want to take this food with us, and I'll have coffee and we'll split the Italian cheesecake." Annemarie looked at her face in the flat of the butter knife. "I guess this mascara really is waterproof," she said.

"You look fine," Ali said, the adult voice again.

If only I felt fine, Annemarie thought, scrabbling in her purse for some Tic Tacs. Sometimes at night she tried to imagine that Annie was just away, tried to imagine her in London, or the Caribbean, or someplace where she would send postcards, buy gifts. "My treat this time," she would say to Annemarie, handing over the package. She had tried to get Annie to go on one of those trips when Ali and Ant were toddlers, called her from her office, her eyes back then glittering the way they did, her voice a little wild: "Three girl days in the Bahamas. I know you want to."

"I do," Annie had said, laughing, "but you know I can't."

"Oh my Lord, when did you turn into such a grown-up? Come on. Leave the kids with Bill. I have to get you when you're not pregnant." And in the silence that followed Annemarie could hear herself breathing, hard. Then she had groaned and said, "Again? Really? Really? I mean, it's only been two years since the last one. Cut yourself a break, girl-friend."

"I know what I'm supposed to want," Annie had said coldly, "and I know what I want, and I know what I have. Now leave me alone."

Annemarie could still hear the sharp click that had fol-lowed, a finger snap, done. "Babe?" she said into the silence. They had not spoken again until two weeks later, when her moment of reckoning had come, when the Mennonites called and Annie came to pick her up off the front porch of their farmhouse. Pick her up and hide her away and get her clean and deliver the bottom line of their friendship: this far, Annemarie, and no further.

"At least you talk about her," Ali said. "My father never talks about her. Neither does Ant. The little boys talk about her like nothing happened."

"I guess that all makes sense, but it's not easy for you."

"So, like, you must have other friends, right?" Ali said. "The counselor gave me this pamphlet, and it said when peo-ple's friends die they have other friends, but everybody only has one mother."

"Not the same kind of friends," Annemarie said. "Not like that. Not from the beginning, through everything. Through thick and thin. We were practically twins." Annemarie saw the look on Ali's face and realized she was making it worse, like she was playing competitive grief. She was also lying. She didn't really have other friends, just acquaintances, which had seemed fine, before.

"Never mind about me," she said. "I'm glad that you're seeing someone, that you're going to a counselor. I told your father I thought you should, but I wasn't sure how he felt about it."

"It's the counselor at school," Ali said, drawing lines on the cheesecake with her fork. "Once a week. They make you go. She's okay. She seems pretty nice."

"So maybe that's a good idea. Someone you can really talk to who isn't so involved, right? Kind of an outside observer. Talking to someone like that can be a good thing." Because, Annemarie thought, when you tell them you're fine they can tell you you're not. She knew that from past experience. But Annemarie wanted Ali to be fine, so that when Annemarie felt Annie looking over her shoulder she wouldn't hear her best friend whisper, "I was counting on you to help. Like I helped you, babe."

"The school counselor told my father about somebody he could talk to," Ali said. "I don't know if he will. I could ask if she has someone for you."

"I already have a whole group of people I talk to," Annemarie said. "All the time, whenever I want. I have to say, sometimes I get sick of talking to them." A rotating group of familiar strangers, all introducing themselves in the same way: My name is Annemarie, and I'm an addict.

"Does she know about my problem?" Annemarie had asked Annie last year as they sat in the backyard, out of earshot of the kids, a full moon beaming down on them, a spotlight. Annie had always loved the moon, was always forcing the kids outside to look up: thumbnail moon, half-moon, new moon, full moon. She had a telescope that her father had left behind when he ditched his family. "At least he knew how much I liked that," she'd said once, years ago, and Kathy had said, "Or he just forgot it, or didn't care about it."

"Your former problem," Annie had said, narrowing her eyes to dark darts. "Your past problem. And to answer your question, I don't think so, but that girl always hears more than you imagine. We did too, right? She did ask me the last time we were at the orthodontist about getting her wisdom teeth out, and when I said that wouldn't happen until she was much older, she said, 'Like Aunt Annemarie.'"

"Shit," Annemarie had said, snapping the elastic she always wore on her wrist. It was Annie who had first put one on her, and she'd worn it ever since. "To keep you from self-destructing," Annie had said. Evening clothes, swimsuit, and Annemarie still had an elastic band on her wrist to remind her of what she never managed to forget, to remind her what not to do. "Whenever you feel like you're going to relapse, snap it hard," Annie said, and she'd reached out and pulled back on the rubber band and let it go. "Stop! That hurts!" Annemarie had said. "Good," Annie had said.

Standing on the slope of that cemetery two months ago she had snapped it nonstop, so that when she got home that night her wrist was bright red and hurt to the touch, and she was glad, glad that it hurt. It needed to hurt.

Sitting in the restaurant now, her hands beneath the table, she looked at Ali, who had Annie's cocoa-brown eyes beneath Annie's full brows, and thought of the back doctor and her appointment a week from Thursday, and snapped it again. Cancel, cancel, cancel, she said to herself, or was it Annie talking to her again?

A woman came over to their table from across the room. She had the kind of bleached spiky hair and big jangly earrings that Annie had always said were the marks of someone living in the past. "And not the best past, either," she'd said once.

"Annemarie?" the woman said. "Oh my God, it is you. Oh my God, you look great."

"Hey," said Annemarie, pretending to know who the woman was. That's the kind of place they had grown up in. Some people had been born and stayed there, like Annemarie's parents, like Annie and Bill. Some people moved away and never came back, or only for holidays to see their family. The ones who stayed would run into the ones who'd left at the Wawa or the Presbyterian Church at Christmas or Easter and say, "Hey," like a long musical note, like Annemarie just had, her mind flipping through the Greengrass Rolodex. JV soccer? School play? Sister of? Secretary to? At least she knew it was someone she hadn't gotten pills from. She'd only made a mistake in Greengrass that one time, with Dr. Finley.

Not one of the newcomers for sure, although there were plenty of those, but Annemarie didn't know any of them, even though Annie had. Some people moved in for jobs at the industrial park and the office complex that had been built where there used to be a big dairy farm. They bought newish houses and stayed for a while and then moved on to other places with industrial parks and office complexes and better jobs. Annie said Jenny's parents were those kinds of people, that she hoped it didn't break Ali's heart when they left.

"It's good to see you again," Annemarie said to the woman standing at their table, because that was usually a safe bet.

"Wow, it's great how great you look. Is this your daughter?"

"She's my mother's best friend," Ali said, and the woman sucked in her breath so sharply that it sounded as though her tongue was going to retract. "Annie and Bill's little girl, am I right? Oh, sweetheart, I'm so sorry about your mother. She was such a lovely person. You must miss her so much."

"They're doing okay," Annemarie said, putting her hand on Ali's. "Annie was such a good mother, and that's a big help. That stays with you." Annemarie wondered if there was a book somewhere that told you what to say that was useful. If there was, she was going to buy one tomorrow. "Thanks for stopping by to say hello," she said, closing the door on anymore conversation with whoever that was.

Ant ate the ravioli right out of the Styrofoam container when they got home, and then he looked at Annemarie's leftovers and said, "What is this stuff?" But he was already forking it in before Annemarie had the chance to tell him it was chicken francese. She and Ali unloaded the groceries, and as soon as they had, Ali went into her room with a carrot and broke it into pieces for the hamsters. Annemarie stood behind Ali and watched as they came out of the Band-Aid box, put their little splayed paws against the glass as though they were saying "Feed me, feed me," and then grabbed the carrot pieces like they were afraid that if they didn't they would vanish. Maybe they were smarter than they seemed.

"Did we just buy three hundred dollars' worth of groceries because the hamsters were hungry?" Annemarie said. And she looked at Ali's face and added, "Just kidding, hon," because she knew Ali knew she wasn't, that it was part of the reason they had gone to the supermarket instead of the mall. She could almost picture Ali looking into the empty crisper drawers, maybe finding only half an onion that was soft and curling around the edges, which meant that it had been there for weeks and weeks, which meant that maybe Annie was the one who had cut it up. She could almost see Ali leaving that onion there, unwilling to throw it away.

"I remember when you first got those hamsters," Annemarie said. She remembered the exact date, and how she had felt that day, the throbbing in her lower abdomen, the warmth of the blood below, her shaking hands, and then later Annie's arms around her.

She and Tom had been so happy the first time she got pregnant, crying onto each other's cheeks as, heads together, they'd heard the *thumpa-thumpa* of that racing heartbeat. Then the next time, nothing, the empty sound like a seashell to your ear. The wand traveling from one side of her still, flat belly to the other, the technician crooning, "Come out, come out, wherever you are," and then, frowning, going to fetch the doctor. "This is very sad and very common," the doctor had said.

She'd tried not to get her hopes up that second time, but she hadn't needed some machine to tell her what had happened when she woke up with blood all over the white sheets. "I'm in a lot of pain," she told the doctor, and the doctor gave her a prescription—not as many as she'd been given a decade before for her wisdom teeth, but some. She'd gotten in the car after Tom dropped her at home to rest, and driven to Annie's. The smell of stew was strong in the house, and Ali had said, "Come see our new hamsters!" Annie had put an empty paper towel roll in the cage, and the fluffy little things ran in and out, in and out, and then stopped to gnaw first on one end of the cardboard roll, then the other. "If they have babies, I'm going to kill those pet shop people," Annie said, and Annemarie hadn't meant to but she made a sound, and Annie looked up and said, "Oh no, honey," and put her arms around her. Over Annie's shoulder she could see Ali staring. Annemarie reached into her pocket and pulled out the doctor's prescription and handed it to Annie.

"Oh my dear God, when will these people wise up?" Annie had said. "You don't need this. I have Advil in the medicine cabinet. And a heating pad." She had looked down at the scrip. "Vicodin? Are they crazy? I could kill them, every one of them."

"What people?" Ali said.

"Let's eat," Annie had said, ignoring the question. "Your father is going to be late again." Stew over buttered noodles and a big bowl of green beans, Annemarie could almost taste it, although that day she'd eaten very little of it, still cursed with the nausea that now was for nothing. Before she left Annie's house that evening Ali had made her look into the hamster cage one more time, and as she did she watched Annie put the folded prescription in next to the tissue box in which the hamsters slept. Annie had stared at Annemarie and said, "That'll disappear and be dust by morning."

Annemarie looked down now at the hamsters, their noses quivering. The carrot was already gone, and Ali went to get another. Annemarie came back into the kitchen. "Where's your dad?" she asked Ant, who had finished the chicken and was eating the Oreos they'd bought, taking the two halves apart and lining them up on the table like he was playing checkers.

Ant stuffed a cookie into his mouth and said, "Some lady called because she's selling a house and one of the toilets won't flush."

"People won't buy a house they want to buy because the toilet won't flush? It's really easy to fix that," Ali said.

Annemarie knew she had what Annie always called her death stare on her face, her arms crossed so hard across her chest she was pushing what the two of them liked to call boobage up into the V of her sweater. "What was the lady's name?" she said, even though she thought she already knew the answer.

Ant shrugged and licked cream filling from the Oreo.

"It wasn't her house?" Annemarie said. "She was the real estate agent?"

Ant shrugged again.

"How long ago did your father leave?"

Ant shrugged a third time. "Like blood from a stone," their grandmother always said about Ant.

Annie had said you just had to look at Annemarie to tell when she was in a temper, that she didn't hold anything back. Hurricane Annemarie, she said. When Annie told Annemarie that Ali said she had a hard time figuring out what Jenny was thinking a lot of the time, they'd both started laughing. They didn't have that problem. Ali had realized a long time ago that they didn't even speak in full sentences. Her mother would say, "Remember that time with the car?" and Annemarie would interrupt and say, "And the bottle broke?" They'd been talking like that one night in the kitchen and Ali had said, "Like, you guys talk in some kind of weird code."

"That's for damn sure," her father had said.

Annemarie took the pad of paper near the phone and wrote a note and stuck it to the refrigerator with the magnet that said "Nurses Do It Better." The note said that she was going to hire someone to clean the house once a week. The boys' room smelled like a hamster cage when no one had cleaned it for a while, and Annemarie could tell when she was in Ali's room that no one had cleaned the actual hamster cage for a while, either. Even Bill smelled a little musty, like an old man, when she'd hugged him that morning. She'd always thought old people just got to smelling different, but now she wondered whether it was because they bathed less. Annie had spent a lot of time at the nursing home giving people sponge baths. "Better you than me, babe," Annemarie had said once.

They had gotten two rotisserie chickens, a family-sized pan of mashed potatoes, and some jars of applesauce from the supermarket, so after Ali and Annemarie did some laundry and vacuuming, the boys all got fed and were happy to be done with funeral food. Ali said her mother had taught her to make Toll House cookies, grilled cheese sandwiches, and salad dressing, but that was about it, and the little boys wouldn't eat salad. Annemarie got ready to sit down, and then she realized she was sitting in Annie's chair, and she moved. It stayed empty.

"You did good cooking, Ali," Jamie said, holding a drumstick in his fist.

"Stupid," Ant said, rolling his eyes.

"What?" Benjy said.

"Your sister's a very dependable person," Annemarie said, and Ant rolled his eyes again.

Bill came in while they were already eating ice cream for dessert, but Ali had covered a plate with foil and he sat down and ate with all of them for a change.

"Out on a big job, Bill?" Annemarie said.

He didn't reply, just got up and went to the refrigerator for a beer, even though there were none in there and they hadn't bought any. "I don't think we need it," Ali had said, which made Annemarie wonder.

He read Annemarie's note and sat back down.

"I can take care of my family, Annemarie. I appreciate the thought, but I've got this. How much do I owe you for the groceries?"

"Oh, for Christ's sake, Bill," she said, standing up. "At least clean the bathroom."

B ill Brown drove due east away from the warehouse where he stored parts and equipment. His mother was always saying it was a waste of money to pay for storage, that he should just use the garage, but the garage was full of bikes, scooters, and sleds, and he wanted it to stay that way.

"These kids are spoiled," Dora had said just the other day when he announced he was sending Ant to sports camp for three weeks.

"They're all having a hard time," he said.

His mother made that dismissive noise she made, like she was blowing out a candle. "Life isn't a carnival," she said.

The day was a sliver of silver along the horizon, dividing the ash of the sky from the slate of the highway. Some days now he forced himself to stay home until the kids had left for school, even made a production of stacking the dishes in the sink after they'd gone. Other people's sinks will still be there later, he tried to tell himself—the waste line, the wellhead, the toilet, the tub. It was a convincing voice but it was Annie's voice, and most of the time he tried to shut it down. He couldn't figure out why what he mostly heard from her now was complaining. At night he would close his eyes and wait for the whispers and throaty chuckles, but they didn't come. Only the complaints had survived the last three months. There was plenty to complain about. Life wasn't a carnival.

The grief counselor he'd gone to see once, her name provided by the counselor Ali was seeing at the middle school, told him that research showed people only dreamed when they were in deep sleep for a decent period of time. That explained why the dreams he feared and also longed for never seemed to arrive. The best Bill did was to slip around on the surface of sleep. The digital clock told him the story: 11:07, 1:12, 2:42, 3:05. That was another reason he left for work early. People with no hot water were happy to see you at six-thirty in the morning, and you were happy to be there if you'd scarcely slept all night. "Coffee, Bill?" they'd ask, and you'd say, "Love some." Ali didn't seem to mind getting the younger kids to school, or at least if she did she didn't show it. At this point she seemed to expect it. So did the kids. Annemarie said he was piling too much responsibility on Ali, but he'd be damned if Annemarie was going to tell him what to do. Everything about her reminded him of who Annemarie wasn't. She could move on to other friends.

He still felt like he was stepping on shadows every time he moved from the stove to the refrigerator, like one of those crime scene chalk outlines was on the floor: my wife. Those precious moments when he thought she'd fainted and wondered in passing what the hell smelling salts were and whether they had any. If they did, it was because Annie had bought them.

The sun was starting to sidle up and he yanked the visor down as he made the curve onto the off-ramp to Shadyside Estates, where there apparently were a bunch of slow toilets in one house, which probably meant he would have to call Ron Jeslow, who did septic pumping. When he first got out of high school and was working as an apprentice, waiting to take the test for the state police, he'd watched the light die in the eyes of certain girls at the bar when he said what he did. Plumbing had no allure. Another reason to be a statie; they said that women loved a man in uniform. "You got no clue," Ron had said when he complained one day during a pick-up basketball game, and Bill felt bad. It would take some visionary woman to look past the profession of a guy who pumped septic tanks all day. They could call them "honey dippers" all they wanted, with a bee on the side of the tank, but everyone knew what it really came down to. And yet here Ron was, married five years to a woman he met at an all-inclusive singles resort in Jamaica, with year-old twins and a constant smile on his face.

"You never know," Bill thought, and then realized he'd said it out loud, his voice a little throaty because it was the first time all day he'd used it. There was no harm in talking to yourself in the car, but he tried not to do it in the house.

He turned up the radio, old Top 40s, that U2 song that they'd blasted in the inn during their wedding reception. "It's a Beautiful Day." That was mostly what he knew of the lyrics. It's a beautiful day. There was some Faith Hill song, too, that Annie had sung all whispery in his ear, so that even though he could feel the hard little lump of her baby belly against his crotch, she could feel the hard bump of his crotch against her. "Easy, tiger," she'd said.

He guessed that's what he had instead of dreams, memories, trying to retrieve pieces of Annie to fit together into a memory person he could talk to in his mind at night. A jigsaw Annie made of the look on her face when one of the kids finally broke loose of her body and lay on her sweaty chest still attached by the cord, made of the times when she danced with her arms held high over her head and her face all pink and dewy, even made of those mornings when she sighed in the kitchen and said, "Is there some law that says you can't replace the paper towels?" He had to make a memory person because he was never, ever again going to see, speak with, hold, the real one. It seemed so obvious that that would be the case when someone died, but he couldn't seem to wrap his mind around it, that he would never see Annie again, that they were in the kitchen together one winter evening and then she was gone for good. The foreverness of it shocked him every single day.

He had a little notebook in the center console of the truck, and he made lists on it of equipment he was running low on: clamps, pipe fittings, the guts of a toilet—you always had to have those on hand. He sat outside the Shadyside house and added some electrical tape to his list. Then he went to the second list. "Haircuts," he wrote. "Shoes Jamie." He stopped for a second and squinted, then wrote, "Shoes Benjy." Ant and Ali had new sneakers from the sporting goods store. The people who owned the place were nice, said, "Just send them in," and then charged his card, and when he looked at the amount he thought they'd given him a discount. You could tell people thought he was running on empty. He needed a haircut, too, and he had that blurry look you get when you haven't slept. The grief counselor said she could recommend some meds, but he said he'd pass. He knew what meds could do.

"I'm thirty-eight years old and I've never lived alone until now," he'd told the counselor.

"But you have four children at home, don't you?" she'd replied, head tilted to the side. Dr. Goodfriend was her name, but she didn't feel friendly at that moment. Bad dad, he thought she must be thinking. Bad dad, he thought all the time. Or not so much bad dad, as not Mom. And no idea how to make things better. Ant was mean and getting meaner and getting in trouble because of it, Benjy was being tutored after school because he didn't seem to be able to read, Jamie still thought that his mother was being patched up at the hospital no matter how many ways he was told different, until sometimes Bill wanted to yell, "She is never coming back." Only Ali seemed more or less the same, although he had noticed the other day that her cuticles were tattered and bloody.

He'd given in and hired a woman to come clean the house once a week, set up her hours so he never even saw her, because having a stranger clean his house felt like some kind of a defeat. He'd just walk in the door and think, Oh, I guess it's Wednesday, because he could smell Lysol and bleach. He'd found her through the church, and she kept leaving pamphlets about finding the Lord and the wonders of eternal life in heaven, and he kept throwing them out.

"New sheets," he wrote. Jamie was still having a problem with wetting the bed. Sometimes Bill would hear Ant leading him to the bathroom and then he'd hear the sibilant sound of his youngest son hitting the toilet bowl. "That's good, how you help your brother out during the night," Bill said one morning to Ant when they were alone eating toaster strudels at the table, the little boys brushing their teeth. "It stinks when he pees the bed," said Ant without looking up.

Three boys in one bedroom, it was ridiculous and getting

more so. Ant had a faint fuzz of dark hair on his shins, and his voice was all over the place. Bill remembered going through puberty in that same room. He wouldn't have wanted an audience for his wet dreams and whacking off. His eldest son was about the angriest person he knew at the moment, even angrier than Annemarie, but he still needed to protect Ant's dignity. He'd brought up the idea of turning the garage into another bedroom a couple of years before, and his mother had barked, "That would kill the resale value."

"Oh good," Annie had said. "If you sell we can buy a place."

All his wife had really wanted was a house of her own, and he couldn't get away from the fact that she'd died on the floor of a kitchen she'd always complained was too small. When she took the kids for doctors' and dentists' appointments she was always bringing home pages she'd torn from magazines of kitchens, new kitchens, bright white kitchens. She loved the idea of a white kitchen. Annemarie had a white kitchen, although she didn't use it much. Tom traveled. She was on the road. They ate out, called in. "I love this kitchen," Annie had said the first time they went to Annemarie and Tom's for dinner, running her hands across the glossy unused surfaces. Bill didn't get it. He thought the room looked more like a place where you'd perform surgery than where you'd have a hot meal.

They'd been saving for years, to buy or at least add on, but it felt like every new baby was a little bit of a setback. They'd traded a second bathroom for a third child, and a screened porch for the fourth. Each time Annie said "I'm pregnant" she was ecstatic and he was surprised, and the nest egg got another crack, and a different sort of future ran out of it. Bill was almost glad when it turned out that Jamie would be the last, even though sometimes when Annie was singing Jamie to sleep, after the fifth pregnancy had ended too soon, Bill would see her tears fall onto the cotton candy floss of his drooping head.

He was so lost in thoughts that he hadn't heard someone knocking on the passenger window of the van. Liz Donahue was bent at the waist to look in, which allowed him a straight shot down from the neck of her blouse to the waistband of her pants. She was wearing a pink bra made of lace. For a moment he envisioned her breasts, which he had actually seen twice, once in a basement at an after-prom party in high school, another time in his old Ford pickup when she was home from college. He could feel his face pinking up; he had that kind of skin—pale, freckled, burn, blush.

It made him feel like a perv, his wife gone just three months and looking at some other woman's chest. But it wasn't all on him, not exactly his fault. Out his windshield you could see a trash can at the curb, the cracked macadam drive to a green house, and some patchy lawn. Out his side window you could see the bottom half of Liz's face, her chest, her bra, and a shadowy area where her belly below the bra was concave, the way it was when you've never had kids. He couldn't help seeing unless he looked away. He put his notebook over his lap. It was that damn pink bra.

He let the window down. "Sorry, I'm really early," he said.

"Absolutely no problem!" she said. She'd always been on the perky side, but selling real estate seemed to have increased the perk. Almost everything she said sounded as though it should have either italics or an exclamation point. She always wore what looked to Bill like makeup, although what did he know? Lipstick for sure. He remembered being at a pool party and Liz talking about rush week at college, and the theme events. Hat day, swinging sixties, dress like your mother. She'd loved that last one, shoulder pads and feathered hair. He'd heard Annemarie mutter to Annie, "If I hold her under the water and she drowns, could I call it justifiable homicide?" Annie had started with that burbling laugh, and Liz had said, "Right? That jacket with the shoulder pads was too much!" Bill had felt sorry for Liz. He hadn't really known Annemarie or Annie then, and Liz was still sort of his girlfriend, though with her away at school and him at home it was hard to tell for sure. It was later, some other party, when Annemarie cornered him in the kitchen and said, "I don't know why, but my best friend wants to make you dinner." He'd walked into the hall and there was Annie, leaning against the wall with a wine cooler in her hand, and she saluted him with the bottle.

"I've got coffee for you!" Liz said as he got out of his van at the curb. "Light, two sugars, right?"

He was surprised that one of Liz's FOR SALE signs was on the lawn of this house. He'd heard that she was making a lot of money, selling the bigger houses on the roads out of town, the old places nestled comfortably into the low part of twenty forested acres, the newer sprawling houses on a rise so you couldn't miss the square footage when you came up the drive. He got called a lot to the old places, but more often to the new ones, where the construction was all for show and the plumbing slapdash.

He knew the house Liz had bought for herself, an old farmhouse down a gravel drive, though it had been years since he'd had a service call there. It had been on a downward slide then, but his mother said it looked like *House Beautiful* now—how she knew he couldn't imagine. "That girl is minting money," his mother said, rubbing thumb and index finger together, and Annie had rolled her eyes. Liz had gone away to college, worked, and gotten married, then come back trailing a cloud of rumors about the marriage, her husband was gay, he was sick, he ran off with someone else, she kicked him out, whatever. He'd heard them all, his wife and her best friend, his mother and the neighbors, talking in the kitchen. Annie told him later that it turned out it was just your ordinary starter marriage, a couple of years and eh, meh, why are we here? No one could figure out why Liz had come back to Greengrass after it was over until Annie had run into her with her mother in Giant Food, her mother in one of the mobility scooters with a cart on the front, a scarf wrapped around her head, no eyebrows, no lashes, claw hands on the handlebars, bruises all over the backs of them from the needles. After that Annie had shut down Annemarie's snark on the subject of Liz. Mrs. Donahue died, her husband less than a year later. Bill and Annie had gone to the wake. "I hate these things," Annie had whispered to him. He had remembered that when he walked into Grant's and saw Annie lying there under a blanket of quilted white satin. I hate these things.

"I keep bothering you with suspect toilets," Liz said, leading him up the drive.

"What I do," he said.

There was a coffee maker on the counter, and she poured herself a cup, too. The mug in his hands was warm. The house was like every one of its kind, center stairway with no-color carpeting, living room to one side, dining room to the other, kitchen along the back, windows over the sink, sliding doors to the patio. It smelled of mildew and some kind of air freshener that couldn't kill the mildew smell and somehow made it worse.

"If you're looking, it's priced really well for what it is," she said. "Four bedrooms, two and a half baths. It just needs cosmetics. And maybe the septic pumped."

"That's what I'm thinking," he said. "About the septic. This kind of house, though, it's not really my thing." Sheet-rock instead of plaster, plastic plumbing instead of copper pip-ing. His mother's house was too small for his family and wasn't much to look at, but it had been built just after World War II, when the veterans couldn't afford big but the building trades still built solid.

Liz sighed. "I know," she said. "I think I'll have to do the cosmetics myself and make it look so fabulous that a certain kind of buyer will overlook the cookie-cutter aspect. It's become a real hassle for me."

"The sellers bothering you?" he said. And then suddenly, "Oh, damn, I'm sorry," because it had taken him that long to realize that the house that wasn't really his thing was her fam-ily home. He'd picked her up there any number of times. He was pretty sure it hadn't been green then. Yellow. He thought it had been yellow.

There'd been one night when he thought he could have sex with her in the basement rec room, after he'd slipped his hand under her skirt in the parked truck and she'd started to moan, but her mother had been standing behind the front-door screen, her arms folded across her chest as though she'd known exactly what he was thinking. "She's such a snob, Mrs. Dona-hue," his mother had said. "She wants her daughter to be dat-ing a college boy." Which is what had wound up happening, maybe not because of Mrs. Donahue's feelings but because of Anne Fonzheimer.

"Oh please," Liz said now, waving his words away toward the cement patio, the old rhododendrons at the edge of the yard with their bullet buds still tight, the blue spruce in one corner. "It was a long time ago." Before Annie lifted her drink and gave him that look. Before he got her pregnant in the living room while her mother sobbed upstairs in the master because her husband had taken off.

Just like Mrs. Donahue, he'd never been able to figure out what Liz saw in him. Even when they were kids she'd dressed and talked more like an adult than a girl, most likely to be somebody. She'd done that same waving thing with her hand when he told her that he was getting married. Oh please. No biggie. Congrats! It didn't make him feel any better.

No matter what the girls said, mocking her monogrammed tote bags and her headbands while they sat at the bar, he'd really liked Liz Donahue. But my God, Annie. He sure hadn't planned on getting married when he was only a few years into a real ID to show at the bar instead of his budget fake. He'd had a hard time, the first couple of years, even believing that this was his life, with the matching dishes and the diaper pails and the wreaths on the door, fake yellow flowers for spring, dried branches with red berries for fall, and the evergreen one with the big red bow they picked up when they got the tree right after Thanksgiving. One minute he was a single guy sharing an apartment with two buddies, and the next he was a family man with a joint checking account and sex on order whenever he could manage to stay awake.

And slowly, without realizing it, Annie had become so much a part of him that he felt now like someone paralyzed from the neck down. He just wished his head were numb too, so he could stop thinking of what he'd lost. In the beginning, he had to admit, it was the sex, the sex and the laughter, the sex with the laughter: "Well, look at that," she'd sometimes say with a giggle. "I know what to do with that." He'd learned to love her by inches. I loved her till the day she died, he thought, and then realized that she was dead and he loved her still. Sometimes he turned his head on the pillow, looking for her profile, and that empty space made everything inside him still and freeze. On her nightstand he could see a tiny red star, like a glowing kiss in the dark, the power light on her phone. It was plugged in all the time, his nightlight.

"Are you all right?" he heard Liz say, and he looked up and blinked. "You look so tired, Bill," she said, and she put her hand over his. "Just sit down and drink your coffee. The plumbing can wait."

The foyer to Green View Nursing Home had big color photographs of butterflies along one wall and two couches facing each other to one side of the front desk. One corridor led to assisted living, the other to the nursing home area. Annie had said once that some people practiced walking from one side to the other because they knew that someday they would have to make the transition. Ali and Ant had been there before, to bring Christmas baskets, but the little boys never had. "It's just a ceremony for the family," Bill had said when he told Annemarie about it, and Ali had seen her flinch. "I have no interest in coming along," Annemarie had replied.

It seemed to Ali that every time Annemarie came around now her father said something to hurt her, and Annemarie said something to hurt him back. "Having somebody die makes people mad," she'd said to Miss Cruz at school in their third meeting. "Yes, it does," the counselor said. "But maybe mad is just to cover up the other feelings. Maybe mad is just sad in disguise."

Ali couldn't help it, she liked her. "You only have one more time, right?" Jenny had said the other day. "Then you're done. Then you won't have to talk to her about anything ever again. Did she ask about me?" Jenny asked Ali that every time.

The nursing home director was waiting for them just inside the door. "We're all glad you are here," she said, holding one of their father's hands in both of hers. Something about the way she did that showed that she was used to doing hard things and trying to make them easier.

The common room was at the very end of the hallway overlooking one of those ponds that Ali thought didn't look like a pond at all, a perfect oval ringed with stone, with a whale spout of water in the middle. The pond's surface was pocked with rain, and the daffodils at one end bowed down, their ruffled yellow heads just above the grass. "We were hoping to be outdoors but the weather didn't cooperate," the director said.

The room was full of nurses and old people, some as bent as the daffodils, so that they could barely lift their heads, others standing tall just as they had since they first learned to walk—but face, neck, and hands now creased and pleated as though they needed ironing. It was a little hard to tell the difference between the men and the women. Everyone seemed to be wearing sweatpants and sweatshirts. "I thank God every day for the elastic waistband," Ali remembered her mother saying once, and she realized that she hadn't only been talking about dressing and undressing her kids.

In front were a row of wheelchairs, and the people in them had afghans over themselves covering everything up to their collarbones. Black, purple, orange, red, violet, yellow, pink. No white. "No matter what you do, the white gets dirty," Ali's mother said once when Ali asked why she never used white yarn, even for the things she crocheted as baby gifts.

"My mommy makes those," Benjy said so loudly that it seemed to echo off the dropped ceiling, and the old people started to laugh, and then applaud, but one woman held her afghan to her face and Ali could tell that she was crying. Ali started to cry then too, but she smothered her mouth with her palm because she could feel that if she didn't push it down she might not be able to stop, not with all those afghans like signal flags right in front of her, a message from her mother saying, "I was here once."

"I have to pee," Jamie said.

"I'll take him," said Ant.

Her father walked over to the line of wheelchairs to say hello and shake hands, and Ali followed and started doing the same at the other end. When she got to the woman who was crying, the woman wrapped her hand, which felt like a random collection of bones, around Ali's wrist. "Here's my Annie," she said, nodding. Her eyes were faded to the color of eucalyptus mints and her lips were dotted with dark bruises. "Here's my Annie to the life, just like her." Ali wondered if this always happened, that when your mother died everyone felt obliged to tell you how much you looked like her. No one had ever said it, and then boom, they were at the funeral home and everyone did, and everyone kept on doing it.

"There's a very strong resemblance," said the woman behind the wheelchair, her hands like claws on the bars of a walker. "Are you sweet and kind, too?" Ali couldn't imagine the right answer to a question like that, so she just smiled.

"We have a poem," a man with a mustache said loudly, and

Ali and her father and the boys pulled back and lined up across the front of the room to make themselves an audience. The man cleared his throat and then read:

> *She brought us sunshine every day,*
> *We always wanted her to stay.*
> *She was the best nurse that we knew,*
> *You let us share her with all of you.*
> *When Nurse Anne tucked you in at night*
> *And stood there and turned off the light,*
> *She always said, sleep tight, good night.*
> *We miss her so much every day,*
> *We always wanted her to stay.*
> *She made us laugh, but now we cry,*
> *Because we had to say good-bye.*

The man handed their father the piece of paper. Someone had written the poem in calligraphy and drawn pictures of flowers in each corner.

"Thank you all very much," Bill Brown said. "Annie loved her job here and talked about all of you."

"She talked about you, too," said the woman with the walker.

She pointed at them, Ali, Ant, Benjy, Jamie. "She said you were the smart one, you were the strong one, you were the sensitive one, and you were the sweet one. And she said your father was the love of her life and could fix anything."

Not this, Bill Brown thought. I can't fix this. But he didn't speak because he knew he wouldn't be able to. Even at dinner with Liz the other night he had gone somewhere in his mind, so that she had said softly, "Earth to Bill," and he'd had to shake himself like a dog, his just-trimmed hair flopping on his forehead. "I'm here," Liz had said, reaching across the table.

"We have planted a tree by the pond in Annie's memory," the director said. "It's a little hard to see it because of the rain, but it's a weeping willow. We chose it because it's a symbol of hope. It's also a tree that grows very quickly, and we hope you will come and see it when you all are a little older and it has gotten bigger. Please take some time to meet everyone, especially Annie's colleagues, and to have some refreshments."

There were sandwiches on soft rolls, which one of the nurses whispered was because they were easier on the residents' teeth, and different kinds of salads. The little boys sat down at a table ringed with people in wheelchairs. "I want to sit in your chair," Jamie said to the man next to him, but the man shook his head and said, "Nice strong legs like yours, you don't want this."

"You have big veins like worms on your hands," Jamie said, picking lettuce and tomato out of his sandwich.

"Hey!" his father said from the next table.

"Now, is he telling the truth or is he telling the truth?" said the man. "That was the thing about your wife. You'd say, 'Nurse Anne, this ticker is not going to hold out forever,' and some of the others would say, 'Oh, it's fine, you'll be fine.' But she'd say, 'Well, Walt, I hear you and I know it's giving you a hard time. But it's held up for eighty-eight years now, and that's pretty remarkable.' Perspective. That girl had perspective."

"My mommy is dead," Jamie said.

"I know that, young man, and I can't begin to tell you how sorry I am. She was one of a kind. You just remember that. Most boys don't have a mother who is one of a kind. It's very hard to lose her, but it's really something to have had her. Really something. You just tell yourself that."

"It's okay," Jamie said. "When she comes home from the hospital she won't be dead anymore."

I can't take one more minute of this, Bill thought, and across the room Ali thought the same. The woman with the walker was telling her a long story about her mother giving her a pedicure when she was planning to go to her grandson's engagement party, only the engagement was broken two days before. "She said she wasn't feeling it," the woman said, widening her eyes. "What kind of a thing is that to say? Wasn't feeling it! But your mother said, 'Ruth, better to have the plug pulled before the engagement party than after the wedding, and don't your feet look fine with that Candy Apple Red polish on them?' "

The woman in the wheelchair looked down at her afghan lap. "I miss the hand massage she would give me every week," she said softly, and her fingers moved in a pattern over and over again. "It wasn't part of her job. I told her that. 'Anne,' I said, 'you didn't sign up for this.' She would roll her eyes and say, 'Oh, Miss Evelyn, do you think this is the hard part of my job?' "

"Some of them wear diapers," the woman with the walker hissed, and Miss Evelyn said, "Oh, hush."

"I know who you are," Ali said. "You're the one who plays the piano."

"Played, my dear, played." She flexed her hands. "Not present tense, not with these knuckles and this arthritis."

"My mother told me that you played in the symphony orchestra."

"Correct. The Philadelphia Symphony. Thirty-two years."

"Thirty-two years!" said the woman with the walker. She reminded Ali of Jennifer Lasorda from their class. You couldn't have a conversation or tell a story without Jennifer repeating whatever you said, as though she could make the conversation partly hers.

"Someday you can come here and come to my room and I

will play you recordings of some of my favorite pieces. Do you like classical music, Alexandra?"

"Ali. People call me Ali."

"Well, your mother always referred to you as Alexandra. My daughter, my firstborn, Alexandra." Then, seeing Ali's face, she put out her hand and said, "One need never be ashamed or afraid of grieving. Those who do not grieve cannot feel."

"My mother said you had an amazing life," Ali said.

"Yes," the woman said, and her fingers moved in patterns again across the afghan in her lap.

"She has newspaper clippings," said the woman with the walker, "and a map with stars for all the places she went on tour. She went to Russia and China!"

"Many times," Miss Evelyn said. "Hard to believe for someone of your age, isn't it? I will show you if you come to visit. All of us here, we were all someone else once."

"We've been here longer than anyone else," said the woman with the walker, as though she was proud of the fact. "Some of the time in the assisted living section, some of it here. We've seen it all, haven't we, Evelyn, seen them come and go."

"Indeed," Miss Evelyn said.

"How is your mother's friend, that pretty girl who stayed here?" said the woman with the walker.

"I don't know who that is."

"I said, 'Anne, what in the world is that girl doing in room twenty-one, she can't be more than thirty.' And she said, 'Hmmm, isn't room twenty-one empty since Mrs. Jameson left us for the hospital last week?' So then I knew it was a secret. She was here for a while. She finally came out and watched *Family Feud* one afternoon, and then the next day she was gone. I said, 'Anne, where did that girlfriend of yours go?' and she said, 'What girlfriend?' and she winked at me."

"Which meant," said Miss Evelyn sternly, "that it was supposed to be a big secret."

"Gather round!" called the director.

"Dessert!" said the woman with the walker.

"What did she look like?" Ali asked, but the woman with the walker was gone to the dessert table.

But Ali thought she knew the answer to her own question. Thick, wavy brown hair, hazel eyes, a big smile. "A big secret," Miss Evelyn had said. There was only one person her mother would keep a big secret for.

"The vault," her mother and Annemarie had called it, the place where the things only the two of them knew were kept in the dark forever, pinky swear. Miss Evelyn looked over her shoulder at Ali from the dessert table and gave a small nod, as though she knew what Ali was thinking.

On the table there was a sheet cake with an enormous heart at the center, and inside the heart was a copy of a photograph of their mother taken at work. She was leaning in, wearing her scrubs, a smile on her face, her hair in a ponytail. "Isn't that amazing how the bakeries can do that now," the woman with the walker said. "She was next to Richard's wheelchair in that picture, but the bakery just used the part with her, not Richard."

In the car on their way home Benjy said, "I don't like that place. It smelled really funny."

"Shut up," Ant said.

"No fighting," said their father, but not like he usually said it, not with a lot of push behind his words. Ali thought he looked even more tired than usual.

Their grandmother was in the kitchen when they got home. "How was it?" she asked.

"It smelled," Benjy said, and Ant punched him in the arm,

and Benjy started to cry, and his father grabbed Ant and said, "What the hell do you think you're doing?"

"It was nice," Ant yelled, shaking, breaking, hitting out at his father this time but only punching air. "They made a poem, and they had a tree, and they talked about Mom so much, like she was so great. This man told me she used to cut his hair, and that sometimes if his shaking thing, his tremors, were really bad, she would shave his face." He turned on Benjy, and for just a moment Bill and Ali both could see beneath the soft curves of his face the lines of the grown man he would some-day be. "You're such a baby," he said to Benjy. "Oooh, oooh, oooh, you're sensitive."

"Stop," their father said.

"Well, Bill, you have to admit, he is on the sensitive side," said their grandmother.

"What's wrong with that?" Benjy said.

"What's sensitive?" said Jamie.

"Strong," Ant said. "I'm the strong one."

"Smart," Ali whispered to herself, and then said, "We have to all stick together."

"Shut up," Ant said. "You have your own room."

"The man with the worms on his hands said Mommy was one of a kind," Jamie said.

Their grandmother was opening the box their father had carried in from the car. "They went to a lot of trouble," she said, and she tilted the box so they could see that someone had saved the heart with the photograph of Annie from the cake so they could take it home.

"Can I have another piece?" said Benjy.

"It's not the cake," said their grandmother. "It's just the top part, the decoration. It's something called fondant."

"Can we eat it?"

"We should keep it," Ali said.

We should keep it, Bill thought when his children were finally quiet and watching television in the living room, some movie about kids saving the universe from aliens with bug eyes and claws. Should we keep it? He opened the lid again and looked down at his cake-frosting wife and closed the lid on her smile. How could he throw it away? What could he do with it instead? Everything was a question, every day. "You'll figure it out," Liz had told him. "I know you will."

SUMMER

Her car had become her sanctuary, Annemarie thought, and she wondered how anyone could grieve if they couldn't drive. It was no use at home. Tom hovered, wanted to go places, do things, as though somehow she could outrun her feelings. For their anniversary he had given her a French silk scarf and two first-class tickets to Paris. "Oh, sweetheart, I can't go away right now, I've got too much on my plate," she'd said. He'd been disappointed, verging on angry. He'd picked up the envelope with the tickets in it and said, "Keep the scarf." She was wearing it now.

She was heading west, the sun above her and to one side so that she felt like the highway was a starburst ahead. Driving in the car had always been the place where she let loose, cranked up the radio, sang along loudly, bounced up and down, threw her hair from side to side. Thirty-seven years old now, and as soon as she hit thirty miles an hour she was a teenager again, with Annie next to her, passing the Tic Tacs across the center console so their parents couldn't smell the beer on their breath. Annemarie had never driven drunk, but she'd driven drunk-ish. Which was not to say that she hadn't driven when she was in no condition to do so.

She told Annie at her thirtieth birthday party that if she ever got a tattoo it would say "Lucky to be alive." Annie had four tiny tattoos between her shoulder blades—A, A, B, and J—and the one on her hip of a mermaid that she'd gotten when the two of them went for the weekend to Rehoboth Beach. On the drive home Annemarie had to pull over so Annie could throw up. Annemarie had held her hair. "Oh, shit, no, babe," she'd said.

"Oh chit yes," Annie said when she got back in the car, pulling the pregnancy test from her bag.

"Love Is Here and Now You're Gone" came on the radio, which was set to a Top 40s satellite station since there weren't any Top 40s radio stations anymore. They'd always liked old Motown even though it was their parents' music. The Jackson 5: "Bad guy, great music," Annie always said.

Ali said the event at the nursing home had been nice, and when she said it, she'd searched Annemarie's face as though she was looking for something. She can't know, Annemarie had thought. She can't know I couldn't go there even if Bill had asked me to, couldn't take the chance that some of those old people might have been there long enough to remember me wandering the halls, stashed in that empty room. She can't know I can still smell it, feel it, see it, can feel the fever and the shakes and the cramps and the muscle spasms.

"Every nursing home is the same nursing home." That's what Annie had said at dinner one night. Some have better wallpaper, some have bigger rooms, some have food that doesn't look exactly like what you got in your high school cafeteria. But they all have the same bright entrance area with cheery prints of flowers or birds, long corridors punctuated by heavy swinging doors, that smell combining cleaning products, antiseptics, unwashed bodies, and waste. At night, Annemarie had learned, there are the sounds of people crying out in their sleep, perhaps waking up to black and thinking that between lights-out and daylight they had finally died and that this is what dead looked like, a cottage cheese dropped ceiling and stripes of light and dark where the window used to be.

"God's waiting room," Annie had said at dinner after two people had cardiac arrests in her wing at Green View.

"I think that's what they call Florida," Tom had said, forking up fettuccine, all of them amber in the lights of the restaurant, Annie's amber darker under her eyes because she'd stayed on to call the families. Everyone said she was good at that, although as soon as she said, "This is Anne Brown at Green View," she knew there would be a kind of vibrating silence on the other end of the phone that she could tell by now meant people waiting for bad news they'd been expecting for months, sometimes years. There were a few people at Green View who had come at seventy-five and stayed until they were ninety, families who had known Annie Brown since she had first started working there. Some of them had even come to the funeral home.

"God's waiting room," Annie had repeated. "That's where I work. It's like some weird middle ground between life and death. Like every waiting room I've ever been in, the furniture is cheap and uncomfortable, and everyone is looking around, waiting for their number to be called."

Annemarie would never have gone back to that place, no

matter the occasion. But Bill had wounded her when he said that the tribute at Green View was just for family. She'd always thought of herself as family. Aunt Annemarie, the kids all called her. She'd asked last week to take Ali for the weekend and Bill had said, "I don't know about that. Let's wait a while." He didn't really trust her, and he had reason not to for sure.

But she didn't really trust him either, even after all this time, so many years after wiping the black mascara tears from Annie's face when Annie had told her that she'd given Bill the news that she was pregnant and he'd said, "What are you going to do about it?" Later he'd said, "Let's get married." Later he'd said he was happy. But first he'd asked what she was going to do about it. Annie acted like the other had erased the first, but not for Annemarie.

"Don't Cry Out Loud" came on the radio. Had someone programmed the station to mess with her? She was jonesing, hard to tell for what. She sang along, then beat on the leather steering wheel with one fist. They'd had everything figured out, she and Annie. Annie would finish nursing school and get her certification. Annemarie would finish college and ace the law boards. And then the both of them would press pause and take off for a year, riding the rails through Europe. London, Paris, Rome. Prague, Edinburgh, Vienna. They would have sex and smoke pot and no one would know because they would be away from Greengrass and from everyone who knew them, anonymous, a different version of themselves. But the farthest they got was Rehoboth Beach, Annie spewing into a ditch lined with PBR cans and some burger wrappers and Annemarie thinking, There goes Vienna. Annie got pregnant and got married. Annemarie spent two hours in the oral surgeon's chair, and the dental assistant gave her a prescription for thirty Percocet. And everything changed for both of them.

Jesus, she was jonesing.

But it had been Annie who wouldn't let the vacation plan go. There had been a new plan, firmed up when Annie finally stopped worrying about Annemarie, when Annie had had the late miscarriage, blood all over the kitchen and the car, and then the hysterectomy. "That's that," Annie had said sadly in the hospital, but then she threw an old copy of *Cosmo* across the white sheets and said, "There's a piece in there about Mallorca. There's a ferry from Barcelona." And they'd started spitballing the future again: Ali and Ant at college, Benjy ready to go himself, just Bill and Jamie knocking around the house while Annie and Annemarie went to Europe. Not for a year— that wouldn't fly anymore. But a month? Madrid, Barcelona, Mallorca. The guys could take care of themselves. Frozen pizza. Toaster waffles. Come to think of it, their plan had been for Annie's husband and son to live pretty much the way they were living now.

Annemarie's phone rang. "Just wanted to check in and see how you're doing today," said Tom.

"I'm good. I'm almost there." Scene of the crime: the village of Paschal Flowers. Sometimes people would ask how Annemarie's business had begun, and she would tell a story about seeing a beautiful burl wood bowl on a table and wanting to touch it, to stroke it, to own it, and realizing that there must be others like her. She didn't tell the part about being half conscious in the living room of strangers who had found her shivering on their front porch in the middle of the night. She could still see their faces looking down at her, a combination of pity and censure. She could still feel them helping her to her feet. "I'm fine," she kept repeating. "I'm fine," she told Annie when Annemarie called and asked her to pick her up, and again when Annie pulled up at the house. "Get in the car," Annie had said to Annemarie between clenched teeth, and, turning to the women on the porch, "Thank you for taking care of my friend." But she'd said the word *friend* in a way that didn't sound friendly.

"That was right, right, what I said to her, that they were taking care of you?" Annie asked, turning onto the road. "I assume you didn't score smack from the Amish."

Annemarie had said, "I've never done smack, and that woman said they were Mennonites. I think there's a difference."

She had fallen asleep in the car that morning, woken when Annie was pulling her into a wheelchair at the bottom of the ramp at the back of the nursing home. When she tried to stand, Annie said, "You're going to do exactly what I say for ten days after what you put me through the last couple of years."

"Put you through what?"

"Jesus, do you think I'm blind, or stupid?" Annie said.

"I'm fine," Annemarie had said again.

"If you say that one more time I'm going to hit you, swear to God."

Paschal Flowers, she'd discovered the place was called afterward, although not really. On the map the town was East Remington, but the little Mennonite village on the south end, dairy farms and cornfields and old-growth forest, had been named Paschal Flowers by the families who settled there. Annemarie put Paschal Flowers on the labels of things the Mennonite women knitted and she brought to boutiques to sell, and she was certain it was one of the little details that made the items so popular. They were nicely done, too, in bright but not aggressive colors, and for some reason they smelled like the outdoors on a spring day. A woman named Maude oversaw the Mennonite operation, if you could call it that, a couple of living rooms filled with women quietly knitting away while one read from the Bible. There was a quote on the back of the Paschal Flowers tags: "Joy comes with the morning." The women who paid eight hundred dollars for a butter-colored sweater in a shop on the Main Line of Philadelphia might not know or care that the line was from the Psalms. They didn't know, thank God, that it was on there because a younger Annemarie, blinking hard to focus, had seen it ten years before on a sampler as she woke up with dry mouth and the shakes.

"Dinner tonight?" Tom said.

"Maybe on the late side?"

"I'll grill some steaks."

Annemarie pulled down a gravel road and felt the branches of trees overhead touching the roof of her car, felt them in memory tearing at her hair and face. She shivered.

She always wore a dress when she came here. The Mennonites were not as strict as the Amish, whose wooden bowls and utensils now accounted for nearly a third of her commissions, but who still spoke in front of her in their own language to make absolutely clear that she was not one of them, nor were they fooled by her midi skirts and flat shoes, her bright hair wrestled into a bun. On the other hand, Annemarie sometimes thought Maude was only one good *Forbes* article away from figuring out she could get a laptop and sell direct online. For now, the women in both groups were happier having someone like Annemarie do what she couldn't help feeling they thought of as dirty work. Knitting, godly. Retail, seamy.

"Good day," Maude said while Annemarie leaned across the split-rail fence on one side of the house and felt the sweet velvety noses of the two piebald horses. Something about the softness made her suddenly weak with exhaustion, and she leaned her head against one and felt the propulsive warm air from its big nostrils, in out in out, like standing as a small girl in front of the heat vent in her parents' house. Maybe she would bring Ali with her on one of these visits if Bill would let her. If Bill would trust her. She usually brought carrots to feed the horses, but she'd forgotten them this morning.

"We are all sorry for your troubles and are offering prayers for your friend and her family," Maude said from behind her, and Annemarie remembered the shop owner at Peddler's Village who had said to her a month ago, "You look like you lost your best friend," and then had taken two steps back when she saw the look on Annemarie's face. The incessant drumbeat of women talking to other women. It never ended, except when one of them died, and then the silence left by that one woman was as big as the sky.

Inside, the women looked up and smiled, but they did not stop knitting. Annemarie always thought they could knit watching a movie if they ever watched movies, the way Annie could with crocheting afghans. Maude had laid some new things out on the wooden table—a longish cardigan, a child's patterned sweater, a beanie hat. They would all be easy to sell. Maude's mother-in-law had made another quilt, a star quilt in shades of yellow and blue. No matter how high the quilts were priced, they always sold quickly. Annemarie would take orders for the sweater and hat and take the quilt to the place in Peddler's Village.

"Join us for a cup of tea," Maude said, pulling a rocking chair into the circle.

"I'm so sorry, but I have a lot to do today."

"You can take fifteen minutes to sit and empty your mind," Maude said, as though she was Annemarie's yoga teacher. Or her sponsor. Maude knew. She was one of the women who had found Annemarie passed out on the porch.

The big mug Maude handed her was homemade too, and Annemarie turned it in her hands. She looked at Maude, who nodded, Yes, we can provide those too, if you can sell them. She leaned back with the mug warm against her palms as the youngest woman in the group, her fair hair tucked under a white cap, used her finger to guide her as she read. " 'For I know the plans I have for you,' declares the Lord, 'plans to prosper you and not harm you, plans to give you hope and a future.' " Annemarie wondered if Maude had chosen this intentionally, knowing that she was coming, but then she recalled that the readings were systematically arranged throughout the Bible, only to circle back to Genesis again, to Adam and Eve, when they'd come to the end. Fatigue wrapped itself around her, or maybe it was peace, she couldn't tell the difference, and she thought, Oh, to live like this, with no decisions, no deviations. The faint smell of woodsmoke and something bready baking in the kitchen. The books of the Bible, the order of the day, the same clothes, the same furniture. If she lived like this she would be comforted by the notion of Annie in heaven waiting for her so they could put their heads together and make gossipy comments about the angels. She wished she could live like this. She would go out of her mind, but she'd done that once already, under less pleasant conditions.

The words fell softly over her like a blanket, and she wondered why she always felt so peaceful at this house, given her introduction to it in the first place. The porch, the fireplace, the smell of woodsmoke, the smell of herbal tea: It should be a scar, not a solace. She looked down at the palm of her right hand, where a narrow pink line shone like a ribbon, a little older than her time with these women. She'd grabbed a knife from a kitchen counter by the blade, not the handle. Fourteen stitches and the loss of her hand for anything but clumsy mitten movements for a month. The upside was that they handed you meds without thinking twice, yes they did.

Her hand had been healed when Annie finally saw it, ran one of her short square fingernails from one end to another, sighed and then gave her that look, that I-love-you-you-enrage-me look. It was at the beginning of the end of Annemarie's bad years, when their friendship had fractured, going from Annie saying, "Hey babe, it's me, leaving another message, get back to me when you can" to "Am I wrong or were we supposed to spend the afternoon together, because I got a sitter and I need a manicure" to, finally, "This is ridiculous, Annemarie," and the sound of empty black air afterward, like the sky on a cloudy night—no light, no stars, no Annie. The way Annie felt, the way she lived, the way there was usually a baby crying in the background of those messages, it had gotten easier and easier to ignore them. Annie so far removed from Annemarie's daily life, from the streets of the city with their incessant clang as the cars bounced over the metal plates put down for the construction that never seemed to end, the babble of people talking, all of it somehow softened and made pleasing by the cotton-wool feeling between Annemarie's ears that the pills brought.

"I know how busy you are with the kids," she said one of the few times she called back.

"Don't make my kids an excuse for your no-show," Annie said, biting at her words like an angry dog.

And then that one night Annemarie found herself on another planet, on the porch of this peaceful house, where she'd fallen asleep or unconscious, take your pick, all the same, and woken to the sound of wood doves cooing, what seemed like a cacophony.

"God grant me the serenity," Annie had muttered when she arrived, words Annemarie would recognize in the months to come.

"You fell asleep," Maude said gently now as the mug fell from Annemarie's hands to the floor.

She backed out of the drive, the mug wrapped in a square of tan linen on the passenger seat, drove past the horses, who raised their heads to watch. Usually she made a left turn out of the drive, but today she went right, and just past the woods that belonged to the Mennonites she slowed next to a ranch house with grimy white siding. A decade had passed, and her adrenaline still rose looking at it, so that her heart felt as though it was trying to bust out of her throat and into her lap. A decade ago, and she'd been working as a paralegal at a Center City firm, getting over on smarts and charm because half the time she was out of the office visiting doctors, persuading them that she needed painkillers. The friend from college who was a sports medicine specialist and prescribed for a good year before he cut her off, even when she offered to blow him in one of the exam rooms. The guy she saw for a bad back, and then the other guy she saw for a bad back. The ERs. The medicine cabinets at parties. After almost four years she ran out of possibilities and wound up with an artist—one she'd met in, of course, a doctor's waiting room—at a house where they sold heroin, which was cheaper than Oxy and easier to get, and it was fine to tell yourself that you would never go there but you would go there if you needed to, and she needed to. She'd circled back around to the sports medicine doctor and he'd said, "Annemarie, I love you, but you need help."

"I have a herniated disc," she'd spat at him, outraged that she could not persuade him to accept her cover story, and he shook his head sadly. She'd gone back to her office and stolen six Percocets from the top drawer of a real estate associate. They would all think one of the janitorial staff had done it, not Annemarie, with her big smile and her musical "Good morning"s and the boxes of donuts for everyone on one corner of her desk because my God, did she need the sugar. It was remarkable how normal you could be so much of the time that you were high. She'd been afraid someone would notice and she would have to keep her job by sleeping with the managing partner, who liked to say that he went out with staff for drinks on Friday nights to keep his fingers on the pulse of the firm. His fingers actually went elsewhere, up the skirt of one of Annemarie's coworkers who smoked so much pot that her purse smelled like a bong. When she'd gotten the invitation to their beach wedding, Annemarie had laughed and wondered what the first wife thought of it all. She hoped the first wife had gotten a piece of the firm.

She looked out the window as her car idled and wondered whether the guy who had lived in the ranch house still lived there, and whether he still sold, and whether he would sell to her now, painkillers, because she was in so much pain. He had had a sandy soul patch, and a wet mouth, and two buddies in the living room who had looked at each other when the artist she'd come with went into the back with the dealer, and when they both stood up at the same time Annemarie had whirled around and run for the door. They'd chased her down the drive—"Come on, baby, it's cool"—but she'd run track in high school and they were heavier and higher than she was, and she made it to the road, no streetlights, no car lights, her purse back in the artist's car, the car keys in his pocket. She'd run through the woods and cut her face and legs up pretty good with brambles, so that in the half moonlight it looked as though she were speckled and striped black. When she came upon a big house with a wraparound porch, she thought, I need to sit down for just a moment.

That was how she'd first met the Mennonite women, and then gotten clean.

She looked at the grimy house again and prayed that it was abandoned, because if it wasn't, she wasn't sure what she would do, wasn't sure she wouldn't pull into the rutted drive-way and knock, hold out a handful of twenties as an entrée. But it wasn't abandoned. The door opened and a woman came out with two little girls, all three wearing flowered dresses, so obviously going to some sort of party. Annemarie noticed a swing set to one side of the house and curtains in the win-dows. The woman stopped and said, "Can I help you?"

"No, it's fine," Annemarie said. "I'm lost."

"Where are you trying to get to?" the woman asked, but Annemarie pulled away. When she got to the highway and stopped shaking she realized she would be late to her next stop. "Call Ansonia," she said to the dash, but her voice must have been shaking, because as she made the turn off the ramp, she heard the robotic voice say, "Calling Annie." The Men-nonites weren't as strict as the Amish; they'd had a phone, and that's what she had done when they found her on the porch the next morning—called Annie. "I'll be there in an hour," Annie had said to Maude. "If you have to tie her up, don't let her leave. I'm on my way."

Annemarie scrabbled around in her tote bag for the familiar plastic container, and when she found it she shook it, pounded it against the wheel, and dry swallowed a half-dozen Tic Tacs. She still remembered how to do that. "If you need to speak to me, leave a message here," said Annie's voice from the dash-board. "End call," Annemarie said. No message, except for this: It's broken me, babe, I'm not going to make it this time, as she called the office of the back doctor she'd canceled on twice before and made an appointment for the next day.

Jenny told Ali the very first time they met that she didn't have to take PE. There was a note from a doctor that she said had arrived at school even before she did, and from the beginning she went to the library and did homework while the rest of the class was in the gym. Ali didn't understand why Jenny didn't mind that more. Ali liked gym. Volleyball, basketball, soccer, softball: She liked them all. Her mother and father said it was hereditary. Bill Brown had played football for the high school and was catcher on the baseball team, which is why he said his knees were shot, though Ali's mother always rolled her eyes when he said that since half his work was on his knees, underneath a boiler or a kitchen sink. Her mother and Annemarie had been the stars of the girls' soccer team, and both of them had run track and played softball. Even as adults they were contemptuous of the girls who had been cheerleaders.

"I have exercise-induced asthma," Jenny had said as though it was a sentence she had memorized and delivered before.

"So do I," Ali said. "I just use an inhaler."

Jenny said she had an inhaler too, but she'd left it home, or couldn't find it, or had lost it. If Ali had ever lost her inhaler, there would, in her grandmother's words, be hell to pay. Their mother never let them forget how expensive it was to give them the things they needed. Ant's mitt, Ali's retainer. Ali had once left her retainer balled up in a napkin at the diner, because she didn't like other people to see it, or even to see it herself, the translucent pink plastic, the metal prongs, like something out of a monster mouth. Her mother had marched her back to the diner and made her go through the trash. There had been so much ketchup. It was disgusting. When they got home Ali had washed her hands over and over again and then gone into her room and slammed the door. When her father got home she heard him say, "Don't you think that was an overreaction," and at first she thought he meant the door slam. "Do you know how much that damn thing costs?" her mother had said, and then Ali realized by overreaction her father had meant digging through the diner trash. Ali did. She'd heard it often enough before. Four hundred dollars. "And I don't have another four hundred to spare," her mother had said at the diner, marching her into the dark area behind the kitchen that smelled like fried food and ammonia. At least the waitress gave her gloves.

The thing was, Jenny did plenty of the things that made Ali a little breathless, and Jenny didn't seem to feel a thing. Last year she'd walked home with Jenny when a snowstorm hit hard in the middle of the day and they called school off right after lunch. There was no bus, and plenty of hills, but Jenny didn't get out of breath at all. Jenny's driveway and road weren't plowed, and she was allowed, for once, to stay at Ali's house until nightfall. They'd gone over to the golf course and sledded over and over, with no sign of wheezing from either one of them. Sometimes they would shoot hoops in Ali's driveway, and Jenny seemed fine. She hung around the edge of the soccer field, sitting cross-legged in the grass, watching while Ali practiced. The coach had even asked her if she wanted to play. "I can't," Jenny said. "I'm not allowed." She said that a lot. There were so many things she wasn't allowed to do. "I don't know why, really," Ali had said one day to her mother.

"Sometimes parents of only children are overprotective," Ali's mother said, but Ali was pretty sure she wasn't saying it to excuse Jenny's parents. Her mother had never even met Mr. Mason, and the two times she and Ali had run into Mrs. Mason, once at the supermarket, once at school, her mother had been cool to her in a way that wasn't like her. Ali wondered if her mother thought it was only their house, where Jenny couldn't often eat dinner, couldn't ever sleep over, had to leave before dark and be picked up by her own mother, not driven by Ali's. Jenny lived in a big house with five bathrooms and a fire pit in the backyard. Ali hoped her mother didn't think that Jenny would be able to spend more time at the Browns' house if they had more money.

"When you have more than one child, you relax after the first and stop worrying about every little thing. You let out the line," her mother had added.

"So when Jamie's my age, he'll be able to do anything he wants?" Ali had said.

"Yes, Al, anything. When Jamie is thirteen he'll be able to smoke and drink and swear like a sailor."

"Smoking is bad," Benjy said.

"Shut up, stupid," Ant had said.

"Honey, I've got a plan," their mother had said. "Every time you call someone stupid I'm going to give you a chore, because I am so damn sick of it. The refrigerator could use a good cleaning, and the bathroom, too. So keep it up, and you'll be wearing rubber gloves and spraying Windex."

"I wish I was an only child sometimes," Ali had said to her mother.

"Everyone who has sisters and brothers says that. You wouldn't like it. You think you would, but you wouldn't."

"Do you wish you had brothers and sisters?" Ali had asked Jenny the next day, walking to the library for community service book shelving.

"Why?" Jenny said, narrowing her eyes.

"Just asking."

"Whatever," Jenny said.

So it had been a big deal when Jenny's mother said that Ali and Jenny could have a sleepover on a Friday night just before school let out for the summer. "I can't believe she said yes," Jenny said, doing a little hop from one leg to the other. "I think it's because she feels sorry for you." Ali wished Jenny hadn't said that. She hoped Jenny's mother wouldn't have the sorry face on the entire time she was there.

It was the most excited Ali had ever seen her. Saying "I can't" all the time seemed pretty depressing. Ali remembered when they were first getting to be friends and her mother had asked Jenny if she wanted to go to the Tastee-Freez for ice cream after school, and Jenny had said, "I can't." She had sounded so sad.

"I won't tell if you won't," Ali's mother had said, and Jenny said slowly, "All right," almost as though she thought it was a trick.

"My mother says there's already enough people sleeping at

your house," Jenny had said once about sleepovers, which Ali thought was somehow insulting. But at Jenny's house it was the opposite. It felt almost empty. Her parents' room was at one end, Jenny's at the other. There were two other bedrooms in what Jenny called her wing, but they always looked like they were waiting for someone else to show up, and no one ever did. There was a bathroom between the two with a Jacuzzi tub, but the bar of soap in the dish was still in its wrapper. Jenny's room was on the first floor, with French doors leading to a little stone terrace and then the side yard. When Ali had told her mother about the French doors, her mother had looked at Annemarie and said, "That would have come in handy," and even Ali knew she meant for sneaking out late at night and wondered if Jenny would ever dare. Jenny had a TV in her room, so she never had to leave except to go to the kitchen, where they made popcorn in the microwave. They could hear another TV somewhere, and Jenny said, "My mom is in her room." It was almost like they were alone in the house.

"You're so lucky," Ali said, looking at the big four-poster canopy bed with its flowered quilt and phalanx of pillows, and the walk-in closet, which had a beanbag chair at the back where Jenny said she liked to read with the door closed. "It's like my cave," she told Ali. Ali wasn't sure why Jenny always wanted to come to her house, with her tiny bedroom and twin bed and no TV and tumbleweeds of dust and whatever else rolling around in the corners.

Jenny's bathroom had little canisters filled with different kinds of bath salts, and a pink loofah, and a big white towel with her name in pink embroidery. Ali put on her pajamas in the middle of the bedroom, but Jenny changed in the bathroom with the door closed. She'd wanted to get changed in the bathroom at Ali's one day when they'd gotten wet playing with the hose, but there was only the one, and Ali's father was taking a shower. "You can change in my room," Ali had said, but her mother hadn't known and had walked in. Ali heard her say to Jenny, "No worries, hon, we're all girls here." Later her mother said to Ali, "Poor Jenny. That psoriasis is terrible. I hope her mother is taking her to a good doctor."

Jenny always wore long sleeves and long pants, even in pajamas. She was wearing them now. Ali wondered if the psoriasis was the reason, the reason for that and for no PE. She didn't do swim class at the Y, either. Ali didn't want to tell her mother she hadn't known there was anything wrong.

"I wish I had my own bathroom," Ali said, looking at Jenny's monogrammed towel.

"You get to have hamsters," Jenny said.

"I bet you could get them to let you have hamsters. Or maybe a cat."

"My father says animals belong outside."

"You do have to keep cleaning out the hamster cage."

"Do your brothers do it, too?"

Ali exhaled loudly. "They don't help with anything."

After a while Jenny said, "My mother said that talking about your mother would just make you feel sad."

"I guess," Ali said. "I guess everybody thinks that, which is pretty stupid. No offense. The only person who talks to me about my mother is Miss Cruz."

"But you're done with that, right?"

"I go one more time," Ali said, licking butter off her fingers from the popcorn.

"My mother says that making people go should be against the law," Jenny said.

They were halfway through the second movie, *Beauty and*

the Beast, both of them singing along and wiping their butter hands on the pink carpet, when Jenny's mother knocked at the bedroom door. "Change of plans!" she said, trying to make it sound like a good thing, that way adults did sometimes: Dinner at Grandma's! Trip to the drugstore! Things that had to be sold when no one was buying.

"Oh no," Jenny said as though she'd heard this before. Her voice was quavering, then cracking, and she started to sob. "No, no, no, no," she cried.

"I'll drive Ali home," her mother said.

"I hate this!" Jenny said. "Please, no, Mommy."

"Am I in trouble?" Ali said. "Is my dad okay?"

"Oh, honey, I'm so sorry, I didn't think, I'm sure he's fine. It just turns out this isn't a good night for a sleepover after all. I thought Jenny's father was going to be gone all weekend but he's coming home early and doesn't like strangers in the house."

"She's not a stranger," Jenny said. "She's not. I hate this. I hate this so much. Please, Mommy, don't make me. Please."

"Jennifer," her mother said.

"I hate you," Jenny said, and ran into the bathroom and slammed the door.

"Don't you lock that door again," her mother cried. "We'll take it off the hinges!" Then she turned back to Ali with what looked like a completely different face on, the kind of face that the people who seated you in restaurants usually wore. From behind the door of the bathroom Ali could hear Jenny sobbing. "Please," she wailed. "Please." Ali thought she could still hear it following her as she went out to the car.

It was almost ten o'clock by the time Ali walked through the back door of her house, because Jenny's mother kept getting lost and muttering to herself. Ali didn't say anything except thank you when Mrs. Mason pulled up. "Maybe some other time," Jenny's mother said, and then she sighed.

"Tell Jenny I'll see her Monday," Ali said. "Tell her I had a good time." Which had been true for most of the night. Her stomach hurt from seeing Jenny so upset. We'll take the door off the hinges. That was upsetting, too.

Ali's house was dark except for a lamp on the end table in the living room and the geometric shadow of the windows that laid slantwise across the carpet. The couch had its back to the kitchen now. Her father said his friend Liz, who staged houses, whatever that meant, thought it would look better that way. Ali sat down on it and felt sadness surge through her body, the way a fever had that time she got up to 103 and her mother put her in a cold bath. That's what happened when she stopped whatever she was doing. It all came on her like a fever.

"So keeping busy is the answer," Miss Cruz had said during their session.

"I guess," Ali had said, but she thought keeping busy was the distraction. You couldn't keep busy all the time, or at night in bed.

She heard the sound outside of a car pulling up and looked out the living room window and noticed that there was a full moon, hanging right there in front of her like an enormous glowing coin, worth a fortune. The clouds that had covered it earlier had scudded away like curtains opened to reveal the light. It was so big and bright, picking the entire block out in steel and silver, the daylight of deep night. And there was her father, under one of her mother's moons, standing next to a car with Liz Donahue. It was much nicer than their car, dark blue, more like the one Jenny's mother drove, or Aunt Annemarie. "You should call me Liz," she'd said when Ali had found her in the kitchen one day. "Your father and I are old friends."

There had always been a basket on the little table by the back door, a basket that had come filled with cheese and crackers and some tasteless cookies from the children of a patient their mother had taken care of, and every night their father had dumped his receipts in there. They were crumpled and flimsy, from the kind of pad the diner waitresses used, and they said things like "new toilet Irving house parts 564 labor 220."

"We would starve if it were up to you," their mother always said, smoothing the pieces of paper out and tapping numbers into the spreadsheet she had set up on the computer. She sent out the bills, and if someone was more than ninety days late she wouldn't let her husband go out on a call to that house and he would have to sneak around and do it anyway.

The first week that there were no little crumpled squibs in there, Ali was worried, and by the next she finally said to her father, "Are you doing the bills yourself?"

"Why would you be worried about the bills?" he said, smiling. The smile was worth all the worry. At first.

"I was just wondering."

"I have a whole new system right on my phone," he said. A whole new system. "A friend set it up for me." A friend. Ali thought she could guess who the friend was.

Out on the sidewalk Liz Donahue had her arms around Ali's father's neck, the two of them pressed together, kissing. The silver light picked out the lighter streaks in Liz's hair, from the salon in Belmont that Annemarie had said did something called double process, not like her mother, massaging what came out of a drugstore box into her head while she bent her knees at the sink. "Who knows what it'll look like," she always said. From the bright street outside, mica glittering on the sidewalk in the light of the moon, Ali heard Liz give a little laugh. Oh, what Sally Lankford next door, peering from between her vertical blinds, must be thinking.

Ali looked into the back bedroom and there were the little boys, curled into commas, their backs to her, and Ant by the window, flat on his back, one arm and one leg outside the cowboy quilt. Her father had left her brothers alone to go someplace with Liz and then come home to their house and stand out on the street, kissing, under what she knew was called the strawberry moon. Her mother and father had told her just a year ago that they had finally decided she was old enough to babysit for an entire evening, but they'd left her a list of instructions two pages long, including how to get out of the house in case it caught on fire. What were the boys supposed to do if that happened, and their father was out wherever with Call-Me-Liz?

As Ali watched, Liz got back in the car. She rolled down the window and said something, and Ali's father laughed, a real laugh, and Ali slipped out the back door and through the backyard without making a sound because she didn't want to see her father or talk to him or even think about him. Nothing had made her feel so much like her mother was really dead as watching her father kiss somebody else right in front of their house, and then laugh like that.

She had the fever feeling again, but this time it was anger, knowing that her father could find something new in only a few months but that she couldn't, Ant couldn't, Benjy couldn't, Jamie couldn't, not with Call-Me-Liz, although she remembered Jamie's head in Liz's lap with its black skirt at the funeral home. Liz had been wearing bracelets on both wrists that night and rings on almost every finger, jewelry like Ali's mother had never worn because she had to bathe and dress the patients and she didn't want to tear their tender aged skin. Ali's hand was in a fist in the pocket of her pajama pants. She hadn't even had time to change before she got into Jenny's mother's car. "Maybe some other time," Jenny's mother had said. Maybe some other time Ali's father would leave the boys alone and laugh like nothing bad had ever happened to him, like a man with a new billing system on his phone and a couch in a better spot in the living room. Ali's tears were fever tears, hot and salty, as she ran away from the house and him.

By car it was a little bit of a drive from her street, which was closer to town, to Jenny's big house outside it, but if you walked there the back way it wasn't that far. Ali remembered those French doors to Jenny's room as she cut through the creek, the part where it was shallow and narrow and you could jump over, before you got to the deeper pools where the crayfish lived. The moon was her friend, following her through the reeds and brush, making it easier to see where there were rocks and prickly bushes. Annemarie had given her mother a platter a while ago, bands of blue and yellow with a quote in gold: "The moon is a friend for the lonesome."

Her parents talked all the time about how the town had changed since they were kids, how the place with the big corn-fields was now the place with just a corn maze at Halloween, how there used to be a hardware store on Front Street instead of a Home Depot, how the high school used to be just the one redbrick building instead of the new gym towering over one end and the trailers they'd lined up in the back lot to handle the overflow. The golf course Ali was skirting used to be full of forest before they clear-cut it, her father always said, and so was the area where Jenny's house stood down a steep, long drive, white and shiny in the moonlight, the black glass reflecting back the stars.

Ali figured that if somebody could sneak out, somebody

could sneak in, stay in Jenny's room without Jenny's parents finding out. Somebody could sneak in and come home in the morning and hope her father was out on an emergency call or maybe shopping for groceries, which he'd started doing again. The French doors had a kind of curtain on them, some kind of filmy fabric, so Ali could see that Jenny was still up, watching *The Little Mermaid* now so that Ali could hear her singing ". . . wish I could be, part of that world." Ali wondered how long Jenny had stayed in the bathroom, how long she had cried after her mother made Ali leave. It would make her happy, to have Ali beside her in the big four-poster, whispering about nothing at all. It would make Ali happy, too, to forget what she'd seen outside her own house.

She didn't want to scare Jenny so she leaned in to knock at the glass, her hand looking strange in the moonlight, a white glove with silver nails, not part of her. As though Jenny had heard her, she suddenly turned the television off and leapt in one motion into her bed with its flowered quilt. Ali couldn't see all of the bed through the doors, just the footboard and the edge of the rippling bedclothes. The room went dark, the bedside lamp shaped like a ballerina with a net skirt turned off with a faint click, and then it was light again when the door to the hallway opened.

Ali stood still and watched as Jenny's father, backlit, wearing just boxer shorts, came in and closed the door. She could barely make out his outline, dark in the dark room, and for some reason he seemed enormous, more like a shape or a shadow than a man, and then as he came closer, into a divot of moonlight knifing through the bottom panes of the French doors, she saw only his bare feet, and they seemed monstrous, misshapen. Ali waited for him to walk right up to the glass and stare out at her, sure that she must be a smear of white against the pale darkness, but instead she watched him walk to the bed and disappear. The quilt rippled again and she heard a sound like a groan.

She ran up the driveway wishing she had her inhaler, and retraced her steps, running and thinking to herself, I have nowhere to go, where can I go? and thinking when she pushed through the line of trees to her backyard that she had never longed for her mother more. "What happened, what was it?" her mother would say, holding her close so she could feel her mother's beating heart through her scrubs, and, "I don't know," Ali would say, pleading, "Mommy, tell me, please, I need to know, tell me what it was."

"My name is Annemarie, and I'm an addict."

"Hi, Annemarie."

She had hated meetings in the beginning. "Dirtbag pill poppers," she'd said to Annie, who was keeping track of how often she went. "You mean like you?" Annie said. Tough love from Annie from the very beginning, when Annie had pulled up in front of that house in Paschal Flowers with two little kids in the back seat and that hard, mean look on her face. When they drove past it, Annemarie had turned her head away from the ranch house just past the forest, the artist's car gone now, with her purse and her apartment keys and her phone and credit cards all in it where she'd left them. She knew he'd use those to get the money to score. Maybe she could prevail upon his sense of fair play to use what he stole from her to help her out.

"It smells terrible in here," she'd said.

"Ali gets carsick," Annie had said.

"I threw up," Ali said. "A lot. In a Tupperware."

"Take me home," Annemarie said.

"My ass, Annemarie. You're done."

Annemarie still told that story at meetings, not the shabby house with drugs in the back bedroom, the two guys with the predatory look in their eyes, the porch and the Mennonite women covering her with a log cabin quilt and making her herbal tea. She always started the story with Annie.

"My best friend saved me," she liked to say. She said it now in the basement of an Episcopal church in a suburb halfway between a Main Line clothing store that stocked her stuff and the house she shared with Tom, a basement that smelled of burnt coffee and something sharp that was maybe cheese from the sandwiches probably served in the same room during fellowship potlucks.

Every time Annemarie told the story she figured she was the only person in the circle of addicts, maybe in any circle of addicts, who had done early withdrawal in a nursing home under the strict and secret supervision of her best friend. What Ali had done in the car, vomiting in a Tupperware, was nothing compared to what Annemarie did at the nursing home. She'd lost seven pounds from throwing up, and the body aches were so bad that she cried on and off for a day. "Shut up," Annie said. She gave her meds, although they weren't what Annemarie was used to, and wrapped her in damp, cold sheets and then dry, warm sheets, and gave her foot and hand massages. One morning Annemarie woke up and a tiny woman in a wheelchair was sitting by her bed, an afghan over her lap. One of Annie's people for sure.

"I'm certain you've looked better, dear, but you don't look half as bad as you did three days ago. Don't try to get up.

Nurse Anne says if you try to get up I'm to push you back down." She'd raised a cane in the air. "With this."

"She saved me," Annemarie repeated, looking around the circle of chairs. "There was an empty room in the nursing home where she worked, and they were waiting for the woman who was going to fill it to get out of the rehab section. Physical rehab, for a broken hip, not our kind of rehab. It was empty for ten days and she didn't let the director know, and she put me in it." Several of the people in the church basement nodded, and one man laughed a little. Annemarie had given the story a pleasing shape over the years. She didn't mention the day she trolled the rooms of the patients in the assisted living section while most of them were in the dining room, just in case one of them had meds a doctor had prescribed for the bad pain from a hip or a tooth. Annie caught her and shook her head, disgusted. "You want some stool softener, honey?" she'd said. "You want some blood pressure meds? Because that's all they've got here. We keep the high-octane stuff locked up. Jesus, Annemarie, you are pathetic."

Actually she didn't need stool softener. She had been carrying it in her purse for more than a year. Opiates made you constipated, but worth it, oh, worth it. That week in the nursing home all she could think about was taking them again. She knew Annie must be giving her some, smaller and smaller doses, just to keep her from going berserk, but it wasn't enough. Where, when, how soon, she could almost taste it, feeling them going down, and then the softness. When she'd seen Ali's crib for the first time, the rails were wrapped in padding, dove-gray strips that felt like suede. That's what the pills did, padding on the rails of life. One minute you were wondering what you were going to do and how you were going to wind up, and then in an instant it didn't matter. So, so soft.

"I can walk out of here anytime I want," she said when Annie brought her a fresh pair of pajamas on day three and a Three Musketeers bar because my God, her body was craving sugar, and if she couldn't get it from wine or tequila she would have to settle for chocolate.

"You don't have a car," Annie said.

"I'll call a cab."

"You have no money."

"I'll tell the driver I'll pay him when we get there."

"Yeah, I can see that. A woman who looks like death warmed over with wild frizzy hair wearing pajamas calls you to a nursing home and says she'll pay you later. Any cab driver would be a fool not to take that deal. I mean, that's a no-brainer."

"You are such a bitch."

"Someday you'll thank me. Bran flakes or Grape-Nuts for breakfast?" But Annemarie was already unwrapping the Three Musketeers.

By day six she had stopped throwing up and the body aches were less bad and she was wondering whether she still had the number of the new orthopedic surgeon someone had recommended, when the woman with the wheelchair came through the doorway again.

"Have you showered, dear?" she said.

"Do I smell?"

"It's hard to say. Everyone here has some sort of body odor. But the room is a bit ripe. I'm surprised Nurse Anne hasn't changed your bedding."

Annemarie had laughed. "Nurse Anne is pissed at me," she said. "She probably thinks funky sheets are what I deserve."

"She's probably busy," the woman said, folding her hands over the afghan covering her lap. "I just arrived here, but it's plain to see that she works very hard. Everyone seems to rely on her. It seems that you do, too."

"This whole thing was her idea," Annemarie had said. "Not mine."

"My great niece is an addict," the woman added conversationally.

"Excuse me?"

"She's been in and out of so many places, but she never seems to get any better. She denies it, of course. It's hard because when she was a little girl I imagined she would have such a wonderful life. I'm not sure I believe that anymore. The last time she came to see me she took my watch and my opal ring. Then she said the staff had stolen them, but I knew." She sighed.

Annemarie had a lot of front, wouldn't have made it through almost four years as a paralegal punting on files that were supposed to get done, papering things over with a smile and an apology, always ready to help out with a ride home if someone had been in a car accident or slipped on the ice, because it was easy to palm half the contents of a pill vial while you were making a cup of tea in the kitchen. But she didn't have it in her to say to this woman, with her eyes like little shards of onyx against the spun silver of her hair, "You're mistaken. I'm not like your great niece." Every once in a while you came across a lie that was like ground glass in your throat.

Instead she murmured, "I'm sure your great niece really loves you."

"I'm sure she does, dear. But sometimes love isn't really enough, is it?"

When she went to meetings, Annemarie liked to tell the story about how her best friend had saved her by sneaking her into a room in a nursing home, and she figured Annie thought the same, thought she had bullied and threatened and cared for Annemarie and brought her back from the brink.

But sometimes she wondered whether it was that woman talking about her great niece swiping her jewelry that also put Annemarie over the edge. Because two days later she went to a residential treatment center in New Hampshire for two months. She had a million excuses for being a person who took pills—two, four, six, eventually so many in a day that she lost count, maybe thirty or forty. She'd even managed to put that ranch house mostly out of her mind. But she couldn't stomach thinking of herself in the same conversation as someone who stole an old woman's watch and ring and then blamed people like Annie, working for next to nothing taking care of that old woman.

It was one of the reasons she'd stopped going to meetings, why when she went she always told that same story. She couldn't compete with the guys who'd started shooting up after they got out of jail, the women who'd lost their kids because they nodded off and left them locked in the car instead of dropping them at daycare. She'd held a job, managed to pay her rent, had never taken her mother's Limoges or her father's old Cadillac. She'd siphoned money from her law school savings and maxed out some credit cards, but that couldn't compare to the wife whose husband left her when he found out she'd been doing outcalls as an escort.

"I'm an amateur at Nar-Anon," she'd told Annie.

"Don't get cocky," her friend had said. "I know you."

I know you. How many times had she said that to Annemarie? That was the hole in her heart now, not just that Annie was gone, but that there was no one in the world who knew her, not really. She remembered that first night, shaking and shivering and sweating through her clothes in that narrow bed, and Annie saying she was off for the night and would be back in the morning. "Do I need to tie you down?" she'd said matter-of-factly, and then she'd sat on the edge of the bed and taken her hand. "You have to stop this, because if you don't, you are going to die, and you can't die, because it will kill me. It will kill me if I lose you." Sometimes now Annemarie heard those words in her head, and she would get up and go into the kitchen and nurse a cup of tea in one of her beautiful hand-thrown Amish mugs until either she managed to ease herself past the determination to see a doctor in the morning for whatever ailment she thought she could sell, or the sun came up outside the windows.

She'd stopped going to meetings regularly after she'd been clean a couple of years, though the feeling that she wanted to use was always there, like a tickle in the back of her throat. "The Tic Tac people should enlist you to endorse their product," Tom had said when they were first dating. Yeah, sure: Tic Tacs, perfect for when you want Oxy but know your best friend will kill you if you ever relapse. She'd told Tom before they were married that she'd had a problem, and it had touched her when, instead of asking a lot of questions the way people did—what, how many, how often—he'd held her hand and said, "And yet look where you are today."

Look where she was today, back in one of those dim brown church basements, why were they always dim and brown, telling the same stories over and over to what always seemed like the same people, whether she was in Center City or Lancaster, never in the town where she grew up. She did not want to say "I'm an addict" in the basement of the First Presbyterian in Greengrass and see one of the Ballmer brothers looking back at her. It had been bad enough seeing them at the funeral home, one bald, the other fat, the former stars of the high school gridiron. Wasn't it always the way?

"She saved me," Annemarie repeated again to the circle of people in chairs at the meeting, "and now she's gone." She held her purse tightly on her lap, her expensive Italian purse that Tom had gotten for her last year in Florence. All the time she was sightseeing with her husband she was thinking about how the younger Annemarie and Annie would have loved the Duomo, the Uffizi, the Italian men. "Oh, my God, it's so expensive," she had said to Tom when she looked at the tag on the purse, and he had handed his credit card to the woman in the store.

Now she held it tight, like a comfort object, and she thought of what was inside, of how the others listening to her talk would respond if she'd pulled out the vial of pills nestled in one of the leather pockets, already half empty. She thought of how, the week before, she had bitten into something at breakfast, a piece of walnut shell in the granola that shouldn't have been there, and felt alongside it another hard nugget, a piece of a molar. "You really cracked this tooth," the oral surgeon had said. "Are you under a lot of stress?" And she'd laughed and laughed and then put her head in her hands.

"We can give you something for the pain," the oral surgeon said when she had stopped laughing, and Annemarie heard the voice in her head saying, I will cut you loose, I won't be your friend anymore, it will kill me if I lose you.

"That would be good," Annemarie had said. "I could really use something for the pain."

Yes, yes, your private parts, your permission, but for most of them, Ali and her friends and all the other kids, it was all still murky. She remembered that day her mother had said that she and Annemarie were so naïve that one believed her parents had had sex twice and the other three times because of the number of children in their family. Sex education had started when Ali was in third grade, and yet Annie had taken one look at her daughter's face and realized that Ali had thought more or less the same thing. Ali wasn't stupid; she'd figured out that her parents' wedding anniversary and her birthday were a little too close to each other. But listening to Ms. McMaster talking about ovulation and intercourse while half the class giggled was different from applying those lessons to the daily life of your own mother and father.

She remembered when a rumor had made the rounds that

one of the eighth-grade girls had been captured on the video on a boy's phone giving him a blow job on the jungle gym at the elementary school playground; you could only see the top of her head, but everyone knew who it was because she was the only redhead in the middle school. It took Ali's mother three taps on her phone to find it, make a strangled noise deep in her throat, and pass it to Annemarie, who shut it down. "Do not ever do this," Annemarie had said to Ali. "The internet is forever."

"She would never," Annie had said.

"Ever," Ali said. "Ugh. Ew."

All the adults acted like if you'd been told about something you understood what it was, what it was like. It was like someone saying if you described what mustard was you'd know how it would taste on your hot dog. See something, say something. Good touch, bad touch. But no one told you what to do if you weren't sure what you'd seen, whether you'd seen the good touch, the kind that her father did when he was tucking her in at night, or the other kind, the kind that the adults all pretended they were telling you about without really telling you what it consisted of. Unimaginable things in a four-poster bed, or just her imagination because of all the dangers she'd been warned about.

"I came back to your house that night," Ali said when they were walking together the last day of school.

"When?" Jenny said.

"After your mother drove me home that night we were supposed to have the sleepover."

Did Jenny flick back her hair, or did she flinch? It was like watching a horror movie, when every closet door seemed as though it would have a guy in a mask with a knife behind it. Except in a horror movie one of them always did.

"No you didn't."

"I did, but the light was out in your room. I looked but the light was out."

"I was asleep," said Jenny.

"I saw your father," Ali said.

"Doing what?"

"Like, coming into your room."

"Doing what?" Jenny repeated, her voice rising.

"I don't know. I couldn't really see."

"So nothing. You didn't see anything."

Ali looked down. "What?" Jenny said.

"Did he hurt you?" Ali asked.

"Did the counselor tell you to ask me that?"

"No. No. I just saw him, and your mother made me leave because he was coming home and it was weird. It felt weird."

"I was asleep," Jenny said, and walked away.

The more Ali tried to remember what she'd seen through the scrim of those curtains, the less certain she became of what it was, so that sometimes Jenny's father was enormous, a giant, a monster, and sometimes she could faintly see him smiling. But what kind of a smile was it? After she'd heard her mother and Annemarie talking about that video, Annemarie had said with disgust, "Did you see the shit-eating grin on his face?" She remembered when they'd talked about the video at school—"He's not even really cute," Melinda Buxbaum had said about the boy involved, which seemed beside the point to Ali—and Ali had said to Jenny afterward, "When I think about what she did, I want to barf." Jenny had said nothing. Did nothing mean something?

There was no adult she could talk to, and she'd learned over the last long months how squishy they could be anyway. When she was younger she had heard the women in the kitchen talking about Mr. Bessemer, and later she'd asked if he was a bad man, and her father had said, "He's had a rough life." But her mother said, "Oh come on. He's a class-A jerk. Stay away from him, Ali."

Her mother would have helped her understand what she'd seen. Her mother would have known what to do. But even her knowledge of her mother now felt like she was seeing her through a filmy curtain. Sometimes Annemarie would mention something they'd done in high school, or her father would make a comment about something her mother had said years ago, and Ali would feel as though there were holes, as though she only knew parts of her mother, with some of the pieces missing and no way to tell how important the missing pieces were.

She was glad that Jenny had gone away for the month to a beach house somewhere in Virginia, where she said they went every year. When she got back Ali could just pretend nothing had happened, or at least she hoped she could. She'd felt a little crazy when she snuck over to Jenny's house to look in the French doors again, but with only the hall light on there was nothing but black inside, even in the daytime. She was glad that school was out, even though she liked school, liked the order and predictability of it, especially now. She had gotten a bad haircut at the Cut-n-Curl—"It looks great!" Liz Donahue had said. "So sophisticated!"—and Melinda Buxbaum had said "wow" when she came to school the next day. Just "wow," so that you couldn't even say exactly why it was mean, except that you knew it was.

"Beth Landsman's daughter is the class queen bee," her mother had said to Annemarie last year, and Annemarie said, "Well, of course she is. Apple, tree." The code. Ali had never really cracked the code.

She'd called Annemarie, who was supposed to come for the weekend but hadn't. Maybe, as close as the two Annes were, Annemarie could tell her what her mother would have said about Jenny and Jenny's father. She'd left a message and Annemarie hadn't called her back. Then she'd left another message, and Ali thought maybe Annemarie was too busy with work, with the Amish and the Mennonites and the stores. Finally Annemarie called and said she would pick Ali up a week from Saturday. "An adventure!" she'd said, in a funny high voice.

With school out she missed the meetings with the counselor. It wasn't that Miss Cruz said anything particularly useful, but she was a good listener, still and attentive, and Ali realized that adults rarely listened to what kids had to say, were always waiting to jump in and say yes, no, but only, and also you're wrong, you're late, you're in trouble. Her father didn't do that kind of thing much, but he didn't really seem to listen, either. Ali thought her mother had probably done the listening for both of them. She wasn't sure whether Miss Cruz listened so much because she was really interested, or because that's what counselors were taught to do. She wasn't even sure that she was "Miss" Cruz, but it seemed too late to ask whether she really preferred "Ms." She had never corrected her, not like Ms. McMaster. If anyone called her Miss or Mrs., she corrected them. She sounded like she was making a mosquito sound when she did it.

"Why isn't she a doctor?" Jenny had asked once about the counselor. "Aren't they supposed to be doctors? Maybe she's not good enough to be a doctor."

"The old one was a doctor," one of the other girls said, "and look what happened to him."

But Ali thought the advice not to talk to the counselor was

because of the counselor who had left, and not because of Miss Cruz. Ali liked talking to her because Miss Cruz let her talk about her mother. She couldn't do that at home. She couldn't do it with Annemarie, who nowadays seemed as far away as her father once had, but in a different, stranger way, like someone listening for sounds from outside the room or the house, her head a little canted to one side.

But Miss Cruz just sat back and smiled as Ali talked about the ceremony at the nursing home, the waffles and pancakes her mother made some mornings, the times her mother sat at her left hand and talked her through long division. "It just clicked," Ali said. "What a wonderful moment that must have been for your mother!" Miss Cruz said. Ali even thought about telling her about the Advil and the ponytail and the spoon and the meatloaf and her mother on the kitchen floor, but she got as far as "That night," and then it was like when she needed her inhaler, her throat a tunnel with the sides caved in.

"There will come a time when you can talk about some of the harder things," Miss Cruz had said, almost as if she could read Ali's mind.

"That was your last time with the counselor, right?" Jenny had said after. "Like, you never have to talk to her again, ever."

Now Ali wondered why Jenny didn't like the counselor, didn't like Ali talking to the counselor. And thinking about Jenny, about what she'd seen and whether it was just what she thought she'd seen, made Ali wonder whether she could go to the counselor even though school was over and she'd finished the number of sessions required. Miss Cruz said she had a private office, too, where she talked to people. It was on Front Street, on the second floor, over the Duane Insurance Agency. There was a Pilates studio on the third floor, and Ali wondered if sometimes people talking to Miss Cruz could hear people rolling around. They'd had the Pilates instructor come to career day at school last year, and she had made them all get on the floor and try something called a teaser. It was harder than it sounded.

Ali was a junior counselor in training at the Y day camp, and Jamie and Benjy were in the camp's elementary group. The three of them all walked over together in the morning, Ali pushing the little boys to go faster, keep up, and they all came home at the same time, and most of the time their father was already there.

"Is that lady coming to dinner again?" said Jamie. He liked Liz Donahue. She called him "little man."

"Well, you can't say she hasn't been waiting patiently," Annemarie had said about Liz when she finally picked Ali up for what she called a girl trip. Ali didn't think a couple of months was long to wait, but then she thought that maybe Annemarie was thinking back to high school, and Liz being her father's girlfriend then, which Grandma Dora mentioned every time she saw her.

Her father seemed better than he had before, more awake, more alive. Her sad father had made her sad because he reminded her every day of what was different, what was lost. Her happy father made her sad because it seemed like he'd forgotten all that. He'd driven Ant to sleepaway camp, a camp way up in the mountains, and when he came home he'd slammed his beer bottle on the kitchen table and said, "Two hours in the car, and I couldn't get a word out of him." Everything was like that writing they'd learned about in fourth-grade history, hieroglyphics. Was her father mad because he couldn't get Ant to talk, or because he remembered who could, and he didn't like being reminded?

"That's just how he is," Ali had said.

An hour in the car, and Annemarie never stopped talking, about the people they were going to see, about the businesses she was selling to, about how her mother and father were going to spend the winter in Florida, about how her two older brothers were thinking of going down there too. It was like if she filled the space inside the car with words she wouldn't notice it was empty, or at least empty of the person she and Ali really wanted there. Once, she looked over at Ali in the seat next to her and blinked, as though she was surprised to see her.

"How's school?" she finally asked, the adult fallback question.

"Fine," Ali said, the kid fallback answer. They didn't really want to hear, did they, any of them, except maybe for Miss Cruz. "I see your grades are remaining good," Miss Cruz had said the last time they met, looking down at a file.

It was Ant who was failing. After he got back from sports camp he would be spending a month in summer school. Ali thought some of her teachers were cutting her a break, but Ant wasn't the kind of kid you cut breaks for. She bet the whole way to camp he was hating their father for Liz Donahue. Ant would get up for breakfast and raise his head in the living room, like a hunting dog, and sniff the air. Liz Donahue wore some perfume called Perfect. Ali knew because she'd seen a little spray bottle in her open purse on the kitchen table one night.

"Why do you not like her?" Ali said suddenly.

"Who?" Annemarie said.

"Liz."

"Do you like her?"

"I asked you first."

Annemarie sighed and beat a hand on the steering wheel. "I

don't dislike her," she finally said, which even Ali knew was what you said when you didn't really like someone.

"She told me she was friends with my mom."

"Well, that's not true," Annemarie said. "So totally not true."

Ali wondered if it was something about driving in the car, that Annemarie couldn't see her, couldn't see that she needed help here, some way of thinking about all this, of living with it. But it couldn't just be the car. Ali and her mother had had some really good conversations in the car. It was during a car ride that her mother had told her about getting her period, and about what it meant to be gay, and about how she had felt when her parents split up. It seemed as though it was easier to talk about hard things if you didn't need to look the other person in the face. But with Annemarie it seemed like not having to look at her almost meant that Ali wasn't even there. It seemed like Annemarie was always talking to herself now.

They were driving on a gravel road with only an occasional driveway on either side, no houses, no people. Then they passed a little ranch house with paint peeling so it looked to Ali like Jenny's skin must look, psoriasis paint. There were two girls out front blowing bubbles into each other's faces and laughing, and Ali thought, That's how I once felt. Annemarie was drumming her fingers on the wheel, and then she dug around in her purse and tossed something into her mouth. "Tic Tacs," she said to Ali, but she didn't offer her any the way she usually did.

"Here we are," Annemarie said as she turned into a tunnel of trees that ended in an enormous sunny, open space, a big house and a paddock with horses and a barn to one side.

"Welcome," the woman standing on the porch said.

"This is Maude," Annemarie said.

When they left, back the way they'd come, into the dark of

the trees, Ali realized that for that afternoon she'd forgotten to be sad. Annemarie had gone inside the house and the woman had sent Ali out back to where there was a long metal building with a sliding door. The yard and the building were full of girls wearing long gray dresses and white caps. Ali was wearing a T-shirt and blue shorts, and she was aware of her knees and her elbows in some strange and uncomfortable way, but the girls smiled and one said, "Come help." Ali saw that they were pouring honey from buckets into glass jars, the honey running slow and golden through big funnels. One of the girls took her by the hand in a way no one she knew would ever do at school, had done only when they were little, and brought her behind the barn. Boys were there turning a big wheel with honey-combs clipped into it so that the enormous metal bowl beneath the wheel filled with honey. The girl gave her a piece of the comb, and Ali chewed on it until the honey flavor was gone.

"Leave it," the girl said. "The bees will come and take it back home." Both of them put their mangled ends of wax, the points of their teeth sharp valleys in it here and there, on a stump to one side of the barn.

"They told me your mother died," the girl said.

"So you would be nice to me?" Ali said.

The girl thought for a moment, squinting. "I don't think so," she said.

"No one I know talks about it because they say it will upset me," Ali said, thinking about all the sentences, situations, photographs, stories, that people assumed should be kept hidden. She had overheard her grandmother say, "I think seeing Annemarie upsets them," one day to her father in the kitchen. "I think seeing Annemarie upsets you," her father said. "You're not yourself these days," their grandmother had said, gathering her things together to leave.

"Does it upset you?" the Mennonite girl said, the smell of

honey in the air all around them, and a few stray bees, too. "Should I not have spoken of it?"

"It actually makes it worse, not talking about it. Like they're all pretending nothing happened," Ali said.

"My mother died also," the girl said, handing Ali another piece of honeycomb. "I was very little so I don't remember her very well, except that she had long hair at night, when she let it down, and it smelled like mint leaves."

"My mother always put cream on her hands that smelled like coconut."

"That's nice," said the girl. "I like that smell."

"I like the smell of mint," Ali said.

"Prudence," called an older girl from the back doorway of the building, "we are here to help, not to gossip." Ali wanted to say, This isn't gossip, this is important, but she thought it wasn't her place to argue with the older girl.

She spent an hour helping to fill jars with honey, and she was sad when one of the girls said, "They're calling for you from the house." She looked around at all of them and thought that if she lived here she would never be sad or lonely. And then suddenly, as though she'd been flying and bumped back to earth, she remembered that Jenny had once said something like that about living in Ali's house, with her three brothers, and she wondered how many people it would take to make you feel not alone in the world.

"Is that your mother?" said one of the girls, seeing Annemarie waving from the porch.

"No," said Ali.

"You should come back sometime," another said. "It's good to meet new people."

Annemarie was standing on the porch with Maude. "Did you enjoy yourself?" she asked Ali, smiling.

"A lot. They were all so nice to me."

"Bring her back," Maude said to Annemarie. "Come back soon yourself. I am concerned for you."

"I'm fine," Annemarie said.

"I am concerned," Maude repeated, and she touched Annemarie's arm.

"Why is she concerned?" Ali said in the car.

"I'm fine," Annemarie said again. "Don't you worry about me, babe. I'm fine."

Two weeks of sports camp, two calls from the director about Anthony Brown. The first time, fighting. The second, bad language. "I'm not going to repeat what he said over the phone," said the camp director. "I'll just put him on."

When Ant said hello it was so formless and deep in his throat that it sounded more like phlegm than language. In the background Bill could hear kids yelling at one another, and he pictured them dribbling between their legs, giving a hip to someone guarding them, shooting around. Kids who weren't fighting, using bad language, kids who still had both parents. Maybe it hadn't been the best idea to send a boy to the sleepaway camp his mother had signed him up for in January when she was gone a month later.

"Do you want to get sent home?" Bill said between clenched teeth, and then he thought maybe that was exactly what Ant wanted.

"It's three strikes you're out, even in basketball, Mr. Brown," the director had said.

Bill had gone to baseball camp when he was sixteen. The school sent four of them to a half-assed place in Virginia somewhere. It was free or he would never have been able to go—there was zero chance that his mother would ever write a check so someone could tell him he had the angle a little bit wrong on his batting stance. There were two things he remembered about the two weeks: that on the weekend they'd bused them to some town nearby and he'd had a Reuben sandwich for the first time, and that he'd been unable to eat most of it because he was so nauseous with homesickness, had felt that way since halfway through the state of Delaware. It was the strangest feeling, and at first he thought he had the flu or something, but the camp nurse was a big warm woman with hands like baseball mitts, and she'd wrapped one around his bony shoulders and said, "I'm guessing this is your first time away from home, son." It didn't make sense to him because it really wasn't that he missed his mother and father. His father was a dim figure always in the shadow of the certainty of his wife, and his mother's idea of love seemed to be to sit at his games and yell at opposing players, then walk him through his shortcomings at dinner while his grandmother, who still lived with them then, patted his hand and said, "Next time. Next time."

But the homesickness was just like what they said about getting seasick. The moment his feet touched the ground of the high school parking lot it evaporated, and that night in bed he stared at the ceiling, already bored, and wondered what all that had been about. Years later he'd told Annie about it. "Have you ever gotten homesick?" he said. "I've never gone anywhere, really," she said. Neither had he, just Virginia, and Orlando for their honeymoon.

Maybe grief was like homesickness, something that wasn't just about a specific person, but about losing that feeling that you were where you belonged, even if where you belonged seemed as everyday as brushing your teeth. Sometimes he felt like that was what was missing, that he'd had a life and a family and it had been a wheel and then the hub of the wheel was gone and it was just a collection of spokes, and a collection of spokes didn't spin, didn't take you anywhere. He wondered sometimes if he missed the Annieness of Annie, or just that feeling of home. But maybe that was the Annieness of Annie. Or maybe he was doing this all wrong. He was afraid sometimes that what he missed was the shape of their lost life, and that he'd lost sight of her amid the empty kitchen cupboards, the full laundry hampers. He didn't want Annie reduced to a full hamper.

"There's no right way to grieve," the counselor had said when he went back because he couldn't sleep without a couple of shots of bourbon and then he felt terrible in the morning, and looked it. "Everyone does it in their own way." He could tell she thought that was helpful, but it was the opposite. There was a right way to put a new washer in a leaky faucet, a right way to clean a furnace so on the first cold night you'd hear that soothing, satisfying whir and tremble beneath your feet, beneath the floor, and know that the house would soon be warm. He wanted to know the right way. He wanted the ordinariness of everyday. Before this happened he would leave in the morning and there'd be a family-sized package of chicken thighs and a box of wild rice on the kitchen counter, and when he stopped for lunch at the diner he would get a cheese steak or the meatloaf special because he would know that for dinner he was having chicken and rice. That was how his life used to be, before.

Annie had been sure of things, not in a way that was obnoxious most of the time, in a way that was soothing. There was a plan, but it ran in the background, like the tech guy said when his work laptop was acting up. "You've got a lot of stuff running in the background," the guy had said, but Bill hadn't even known it was there. Now he knew what Annie had been running in the background: meals, doctors' appointments, story hour at the library, swim classes at the Y. But that wasn't really what was missing now. It was the other thing, the thing that meant you didn't feel homesick.

"She had so much personality," Liz had said one night at dinner when the waitress told them that she remembered Annie on the soccer field, being thrown out of the game because she argued what was obviously a ham-handed call.

Bill hated it when Liz talked about Annie, but he didn't know how to tell her that. He could tell when he upset her because she would get very quiet and breathe audibly through her nostrils. "That's just stupid, babe," Annie would say if she didn't like his opinion, which was a lot better than nostril breathing.

It was especially notable because the rest of the time Liz was so different. "Always upbeat," it had said under her yearbook picture, which was about right. (It also said "Where's Bill?," which had made him feel bad whenever Annie and Annemarie brought it up, giving him a hard time.) Maybe he hated to hear Liz talk about Annie because he felt guilty, the two of them in one sentence. He was a different guy with Liz, that guy he'd imagined sometimes in the bar, a guy who hadn't been with Annie Fonzheimer, who didn't have four kids who needed backpacks and underwear and haircuts. When he first slept with Liz he thought he'd feel bad afterward, about cheating on his dead wife, about having sex without any pretense of love. He was worried that he would think of Annie when he was with Liz, but thinking didn't seem to come into it. His head might be a mess, but everything below it worked just fine, apparently, even given his lack of experience. "Oh, Billy," Liz had whispered at the end the first time, and he knew there was something pathetic about it, but just for a little while he felt like high school Bill.

There was nothing high school about Liz, even when she was in high school. That wasn't where she wanted to lead him. The Bill he looked at through the long end of the telescope sometimes, the Bill with no responsibilities and no worries, that wasn't the Bill Liz imagined. She was like the CEO of her own life, with a schedule and a website, and she was trying to be the CEO of his. She liked a project, and he had become one.

She'd done the research and figured out that there was no plumbing supply place within thirty miles after he told her he'd spent a couple of hours one day driving to pick up parts. She had the kind of enthusiasm about things that made you feel not that they were going to happen, but that they already had. She had drawn up a spreadsheet about a plumbing supply company with the start-up costs and the possible profits. "It's such an undeniable opportunity," she'd said, standing in the kitchen handing around food from the burger joint, Benjy and Jamie with eyes alight as they poured ketchup on fries without anyone reminding them that ketchup cost money and half of what they had there would go to waste.

"What is?" said Ali, who was picking pickles and onion out of her burger.

"You haven't told her, Bill?"

"I haven't decided what I'm doing yet," he'd said.

"I love french fries," Jamie said.

"Me too," said Benjy. Ant was still at camp, hadn't had his

third strike, or Bill was sure he would have said, "Everybody likes french fries, stupid." Liz had wondered if Ant should go to the private school in West Belmont. "You don't want him to fall between the cracks, Bill," she said.

"Making sure that doesn't happen is my job," he'd said, maybe with a bit of an edge, because Liz started breathing audibly. "Just a thought," she finally said.

His mother was always talking about Liz, the houses she'd just sold, the dresses she wore, the car she drove. He knew it was because she'd never really liked Annie, had felt that her son was destined for better things and had been unfairly saddled with too many children and too few prospects. She was always calling Liz a go-getter, which was apt but showed surprising ignorance about how that would work for Dora Brown going forward. Private school was not in Dora's plans. Neither were the houses for sale that Liz kept sending him pictures of.

"You don't need to be stuck with a mortgage, son," his mother always liked to say.

"I need to look for a bigger place," he'd told his mother the last time she'd said that, when she stopped by for dinner and asked him if he'd lost weight, which he had, because he was nauseous, because he was this new version of homesick. "You need to do a better job feeding your father," she'd told Ali, and Bill had said, "Mom, shut up," which had shocked them all into silence because Annie had always said, "No one in this house will use that term to anyone else in this house." Bill could see his mother riffling through her mind for a comeback that would be more persuasive than the millstone of a mortgage or the alleged bargain of his rent, and he had to hand it to her—she got it in one.

"Those poor children have had enough change in their lives," she said. "The last thing you want to do is uproot them."

"I can't uproot my kids now," he told Liz the next time she sent him a description of a brick center hall colonial, circa 1952, with five bedrooms, two baths, and a screened porch. Although he had to admit the place looked good, and he'd serviced the heating system in that house himself, so he knew that it was a cream puff: good, solid construction and systems that would last for years.

He was afraid Liz would start breathing, but instead she put her hand over his and said, "That's so insightful." Which sounded good except that he had zero insight. If insight was an eye exam, he wouldn't get any further than that big E at the very top.

Six months in, and he was tired of the sympathy, tired of hearing people tell him that if there was anything they could do all you have to do is ask, Bill, really, just ask. What would that be, he always wondered, sometimes with more of an edge if he'd had a couple of shots, which he hadn't done until recently. The thing about sympathy was that it separated you. You could never be one of the guys when the guys, who were loud and profane and wisecracking, suddenly went serious, went silent, when you were around. And he felt like this was going to last forever. That was the thing about losing someone when you were young. Mr. Jenkins was a widower but he was right on time, eighty-three, the wife eighty-two and gone, to no one's surprise, after a three-year bout of some kind of cancer that made it painful to look at her. But a guy whose wife had died suddenly before he was even forty was going to have to carry the weight of sympathy forever, and yet still move on. No one was expecting Mr. Jenkins to find a mother for his children, who were all older than Bill was and were scattered all over the state.

He was so grateful one night at the bar when one of the

guys he'd gone to high school with, a guy named Brian Dunphy, who was a contractor, had heard someone tell Bill that they were there for him, all he had to do was say the word, and Brian had erupted. "What, you're going to bring his wife back to life?" he said savagely. "Because that seems like the only thing that anyone could do to make things better."

"Hey, chill," said the bartender. "People are just trying to be nice."

"People are just trying to say shit," Brian had said, and suddenly Bill remembered that the Dunphys had had a kid who died, drowned in a backyard pool about ten years before. A party, some drinking, the adults talking a little too loud, the kids wandering away, and then the screaming. He remembered Annie in their backyard right afterward, at the picnic table, drinking iced tea and watching Ali and Ant pulling clover out of the grass, saying, "There's no coming back from that." Looking at Brian, seeing the way a sneer had settled into the lines around his mouth, Bill thought about how, years ago, when he was just learning the trade, his old boss Ed Martin had told him there was a river that ran under the whole town. Bill had never heard of it, could hardly believe it, and then one day they were pulling up a storm grate behind the dry cleaner and from beneath a deep, deep hole he had heard the sound of water running. Underneath the whole town was something most of them didn't know about. But it was there.

He thought, looking across the shiny expanse of bar to a guy who would see that little body floating, white on blue, for the rest of his life, that there was some kind of river of loss underneath them all. There was no way to know how to move on, which everyone insisted you should do, without leaving the person behind, so that the further you got into this new, different, strange, impossible existence, the fainter they got, like a ghost in a movie that at first had clear edges and a discernible face and then was a cloud, and then smoke, and then nothing. Who could he ask? Annie had been good at these things. "My wife the philosopher," he would say in bed sometimes when she was puzzling out why Kathy had never married or whether Annemarie's business was a substitute for a domestic life.

Annemarie seemed to have disappeared, and without Annie between them they had less and less to say to each other and more and more grievances. The last time she'd been at the house it was like her mind was elsewhere, and she hadn't stayed long. He was sure she would say he'd moved on too fast; he didn't know how women seemed to almost mystically know things, but he would bet she knew that he had had a couple of dinners with Liz Donahue, and then more than that. "Stay," Liz said after the first time, but he'd already left his kids alone for hours, and he was pretty sure Ali would be awake and waiting for the sound of his car.

He would never understand women, never, not in that fuck-'em way that the guys at the bar had, what the hell, crazy bitches. They just came with something he didn't have, some way of being with one another and in the world as though they were born with antennae and he was not. The best he figured a man could hope for was not to understand them, but to find one who understood you. He'd had one. They'd married too fast and too young, and there had been days, even weeks, when life eddied around them like they were stones in the old creek by the golf course, so that they scarcely touched each other. But over time he'd realized that Annie not only saw him as he was—she liked what she saw. How many men could say the same about their wives?

Driving Ant back from camp, he wondered if he understood

men any better, or at least boys. There was that moment somewhere between the ages of his two little boys and where his big
one was heading, when it seemed they got the memo that real
guys talked about jump shots and team standings and which
girl had a nice set on her, that it was time to put the lid on
everything else, everything that meant anything. Even watching them all trudge from the cabins to their parents' cars, with
their duffel bags and their ball caps, was like watching people
who knew that real feeling was forbidden. To say goodbye,
the most effusive bumped into one another, shoulder ricochet-
ing off its opposite, not hugging like the girls. How could they
possibly comfort one another if something bad happened?
Becoming a man seemed to mean becoming a person who
would be poisoned by loss and heartbreak and still pretend
that neither existed. As his son walked toward him, his head
down, Bill had tried to grab him, but he slid past to put his bag
in the back of the van.

Lord knows he'd tried, hadn't asked the questions that
came naturally to him but tried to think of the ones Annie
would have asked. Walk me through your day. Which guys
did you like hanging out with? What new skills did you pick
up? Open-ended, Bill thought.

Close-mouthed was what he got in return: like, normal
stuff. A couple of them. Nothing, really. Halfway home there
was a hornet in the van, and Bill rolled down the windows and
Ant's baseball cap blew out. They pulled over but it had rolled
down into a culvert and Bill slid down a gravel highway slope
while cars whooshed by, and then scrambled up again, his
hands taking a hit so that there was blood on his palm when
he handed the hat over.

"I don't really like that one anyhow," Ant said without
looking up.

Bill pulled out, driving too fast, wild with rage and adrenaline, his hand bleeding harder now so that he wadded up a tissue beneath it on the wheel and finally said, "Son, I'm doing the best I can here. I'm really confused about everything and I feel like I don't know what I'm doing most of the time, and it would help me a lot if you would cut me a little bit of a break. Just a little bit."

He thought Ant sneezed, then coughed, but when he looked over he could see that he was crying, sobbing really, his hand over his face like he was embarrassed to be seen that way. Bill put on the hazards and pulled over to the shoulder again, and he wrapped his arms around his son, who fell against him like a sack of something, heavy and formless, like giving in, finally giving in.

"I want my mom," he heard Ant whisper, and Bill started to cry himself. "I know, Ant, I know," he said. "I'm with you. I want her too. I miss her so much. I'm going to miss her forever." Then he thought maybe that wasn't so useful, and he added, sounding more like the grief counselor than himself, "But it will get better."

Ant reared back, pale tracks on his grubby cheeks. "When? When will it get better?"

"I don't know," Bill said.

Ant turned away and looked down again. "Are you getting married?" he said.

"What? What?"

"There was this kid at camp, his mother died, and his father got married. Like, really fast. He said they all do. All the dads get married again. He said you would for sure."

"Some kid from camp that I don't know and doesn't know me told you I'm getting married? That's crazy."

"Are you going to marry her?"

Bill wasn't good at any of this, but he knew not to ask who. "I'm not getting married," he said.

"She thinks you are," Ant said, turning his head and drilling his father with his dark eyes that looked so like Annie's.

"Son, I'm telling you right now. I am not getting married." Ant's head dropped again. "Let's get you home," his father said.

It was so quiet in the van for so long that Bill could tell his carburetor needed a little adjustment. Finally Ant cleared his throat, rolled down the window and spit out. It wasn't the time to tell him that his mother always said he wasn't allowed to do that.

"The food sucked," Ant finally said.

"Don't use that word, okay?" Annie never let them use that word.

"The food blew."

Bill started to laugh. "Do you think blew is any better than sucked?" he said. And Ant finally, finally smiled.

"There's mac and cheese with your name on it in the fridge," Bill said.

"Good," said Ant.

AUTUMN

The Gift Show in New York City, and Annemarie needs to be on top of her game. Last year, her little booth parked between teak furniture and silk flowers, she'd picked up dozens of accounts, almost without trying, stores in California and Oregon, even one in Amsterdam that ordered so incessantly now that she had to turn them down for some things and jacked her prices way up for others. This year could be bigger, better. The sand-colored bowls to match the mugs. The sweaters with the fanciful Fair Isle patterns. She had asked Maude to come with her. "You could wear pants! You could drink margaritas!" she'd said, a little too loud. "Thank you, no," Maude said, holding Annemarie's hands in hers. "I will be right here waiting." She was finding Maude irritating nowadays, passing judgment from her little Eden among the trees. She was like Annie without the fun, reading Annemarie's face, listening to the timbre of her voice, making assumptions. "I hope you find peace," she had said the last time Annemarie was there, as though she were one of those little signs that people hang in their kitchens. Although, come to think of it, maybe the men could make those signs for some of the accounts.

The Gift Show, and feeling as though the edges were a little too soft, would not do. She needed to feel sharp, energized. Luckily she was prepared. She and Tom had had dinner at the home of one of his biggest customers outside of Philadelphia the month before, and Annemarie remembered the conversation they'd had a year ago with the couple about their son, who was starting boarding school after flaming out at a local private school. "He has really profound issues with focus," the wife had said.

Annemarie had only been half listening that night, distracted: Why in the world had they chosen that chandelier over the table? How late did she and Tom need to stay? But that had been a year ago, when Annie was still sending her memes on her phone, when Annemarie thought she was done with using forever and for always because what would Annie say if she could tell she was using again, because she could tell—it turned out she'd always been able to tell. Annie said she had been afraid of losing Annemarie. She'd never considered the vice versa, but Annemarie lived with it now every day. And apparently some recurring pain from her dental work, which Annemarie made as convincing in the retelling as possible. Her mouth actually felt fine, but her pill vial was running low. "This darn thing just won't resolve," the oral surgeon had said thoughtfully, maybe even a little suspiciously. Annemarie was going to have to find a gynecologist. Could they tell if you didn't really have endometriosis, just said you did?

"I will kill you and dismember you," Annie had said once when Annemarie was complaining that her back was bothering her.

"You have nothing to worry about," she had said, snapping the elastic on her wrist so that Annie would see her do it. Nothing to worry about except dying. There was that. But they hadn't factored that in.

Standing at the back of her tables on the first floor of the convention center, smiling at two women rhapsodizing over the sweaters, she could hear Annie's accusatory voice: Don't use me as an excuse. Ali had told her what Bill told the kids, about how they would be forever hearing their mother's voice in their heads. Annemarie heard it too, but sometimes she wished she didn't. She looked at her phone. Ali had left her another message. She had to remember to call her back.

"They're beautiful sweaters, aren't they?" she said to the women. "I watched them being knitted. I work with Mennonite and Amish women."

"I wouldn't even be able to keep them in stock," said one woman, and Annemarie felt herself smile. It was as though her mouth had a life of its own, first for loss, now for faux happy. She was so grateful for that unknown schoolboy and his lack of focus. His lack-of-focus pills had been right there in his medicine cabinet. The artist who had taken her to that ranch house that had changed her life had told her once that it was called speedballing, when you mixed the up and the down, but it was only speedballing if you used a needle or your nose. She was just settling things down a little bit, a little of this, a little of that.

She felt good. Or as good as she felt these days. Tom sat her down one night and leaned toward her and she thought, Oh no, here we go, but he wanted to know if she was having an affair. She'd laughed. "You seem so distant," he said. He wasn't Annie. He couldn't tell. And she wasn't in too deep yet. She kept telling herself that. She had it under control. Not like last time. That's why he didn't suspect. Or maybe he didn't suspect because he'd never really known her that well, known her the way Annie had.

"I am not having an affair," she said. "Cross my heart and hope to die." No backsies, Annie said in her head. Except that it had planted an idea in her head, the idea of feeling some-thing, someone, inside her. Tom was what they called a gentle and considerate lover. She didn't want force, exactly, but she didn't want gentle and considerate either. She didn't want love, or connection. Those were the things that got you in trouble. She had just wanted sensation, maybe even a little pain, of a different sort.

So there had been the lawyer she'd run into in the shopping district who was a young associate at the firm and whose apartment was not far from the restaurant where he had taken her to lunch; and the man she had met in the waiting room at the hospital who had taken her number and called her the next day. And there were two people from meetings. You weren't supposed to get involved with people you met at meet-ings, but she didn't consider it involvement, not just one time, fast and dirty and done.

She'd planned to go to a meeting at the end of the second day of the Gift Show. There was a Nar-Anon meeting every day at a Catholic church a few blocks north of the convention center. She'd gone there the last two years. She had been pretty sure that the others in the circle were actors. They were not insincere, but there was a certain performative quality to their stories that had made them more entertaining than most. One had even described playing Laertes while high at a theater in the Berkshires and how he still thought it was his finest Shakespeare. The way he said it, with such fervor and a certain glitter in his blue eyes, made her think that he was still using. At the more suburban meetings she attended, most people were painfully, tediously sober. Five months, five years, Annemarie still saying nine years until she'd done a meeting a month ago downtown in Philadelphia. A beautiful girl with wild tight curls, leather skirt, and T-shirt with WTF in red on white had walked past her as they were leaving and muttered, "Nine years my ass." Took one to know one.

She'd always imagined, on the rare occasions when she thought things might go all to hell again, that it would be dramatic, intense, one of those moments that lived inside you, like the moment when she'd stood in the kitchen, phone in hand, listening to Bill sob so that she could barely understand what he was saying, and when she could understand, could not believe. Tom had taken the phone from her hand and she had fallen into a chair and begun to scream. No, no, no, no, no. Yes.

But the fall, when it came, hadn't been like that at all. It had happened slowly but surely, step-by-step. The nutshell in the granola and the oral surgeon. The orthopedist so sympathetic to her shoulder. The boys who had put the hand-carved rocker into the back of her SUV; one of them had angled it so it wouldn't shift and scratch the maple, and when she was taking it out it had fallen on her finger, hard, pinning it between the back of the chair and the hatch of the car.

"You have to have someone look at this," Tom had said, staring at the blackened nail and puffy knuckle. "You have to have someone look at this right away," he insisted, as Annemarie thought, Of course, you're right, I definitely will.

"You've broken this for sure, but it's a clean break and you won't need a cast," said the ER doctor. "I can just tape it up."

"It really hurts." Her motto, retired now for so long. Like riding a bicycle. Take some Advil, said Annie's voice in her head, but she could scarcely hear it over the voice of the doctor, who looked as though he'd barely graduated from med school or started to shave. So sweet, so concerned, nodding his head: "Are you allergic to any medications? Have you ever taken opiates?"

"Years ago, when they took my wisdom teeth out, they prescribed them," she said. Which was true. She hadn't even been able to remember it, she was so zonked on whatever they'd used to remove her teeth. "They give you Versed," Annie said. "It's an amnesiac. They used to give it to women who thought they were asleep during childbirth, but they were wide awake. They just couldn't remember anything."

"Jesus God."

"Yep. Apparently nurses used to have a field day talking about what they heard."

She hadn't even remembered getting the pills that first time, though she remembered going back, saying her mouth hurt. "Dry socket," the oral surgeon had said then knowingly, nodding, so that with her cracked tooth a decade later and the eventual removal, she had known exactly what to claim. That first time, after her wisdom teeth, when she said it was still painful, they had doubled the prescription and added a refill option. And so it all began.

"Be careful with the opiates," the young doctor who had looked at her finger in the ER said. "Don't take them any longer than you need to."

"Promise."

Liar, Annie said.

"You should see a real orthopedic guy," said Tom when he saw the splint.

"I will," she said.

Her finger stopped hurting and the tape came off, but she found an orthopedist and said she could scarcely stand the pain, although the pain she was talking about had nothing to do with her finger. Annie was still alive in her mind, and though she was scoldy, at least she wasn't a pink-cheeked mannequin beneath a satin quilt, silent forever.

Annemarie kept going to meetings as though they were the antidote, and she'd intended to go to the one at the church near the convention center. But a woman she'd met while setting up who worked at one of the big publishing houses and was part of a clutch of people tending their enormous spread of journals, note cards, and coffee table books, had told her that a group was getting dinner at the Thai place on Tenth Avenue, and she went along for the ride, telling stories about the Amish that were mostly true, listening to one of the women dish about a bestselling writer who apparently was so mean they called her T. rex. Everyone was younger than she was. It was amazing, how fast you could get old, or older. The years between twenty-two and thirty-seven made a universe. She and Annie tried to be hip, but they were baffled by the girls who let their bra straps show through the armholes of their dresses or to one side of their tank tops when they'd worked so hard to hide theirs when they were young.

The Thai beer didn't mix so well with the pills, but she felt better when she got back to her hotel and took some more and had a brandy at the bar, and that's where she met Greg. Was that his name? She'd told him her name was Leslie. They talked for a long time, about business, about politics, about the city. It didn't amount to much, but it served the purpose.

"You have a rubber band around your wrist," he finally said, taking her hand in his and turning it over.

"I do," she said with a little laugh. "It's like tying a string around your finger so you'll remember something."

"Can you remember it?" he said, running his finger up and down her palm.

"Not at the moment," she said, and ordered another drink.

"My place or yours?" he'd said, and she'd laughed again. They were judicious in the elevator. Both of them knew that there were security cameras, that they were not interested in putting on a show for the two minimum-wage guys eking out their hours in front of the computer monitors. Greg, or whatever his name really was, was in a room two floors above hers.

Not gentle and considerate, and probably on meds himself, the other kind, the kind that guys took now as a matter of course, so that they went so hard and for so long that she wondered if she would be sore in the morning. When she left his room a little before three, her mouth so dry that her tongue stuck to her gums and made a gross clicking noise when she tried to unstick it, she ran into a room service waiter in the hallway pushing one of those tables she'd left outside her own door a dozen times, the gristly parts of the steak, blood congealed on the plate with little islands of fat floating, a basket of rolls still wrapped in a kitchen origami napkin, all of it somehow disgusting. The waiter dropped his eyes when he saw her. She dropped her shoes to the hall carpet and pushed her feet into them, happy it hurt.

The elevator had mirrored walls, and she saw herself: mascara raccoon eyes, a red area to one side of her mouth that was probably mirrored on her thighs. Greg had fashionable stubble. "I am not this person," she said to herself. "I am not." She lay down on her hotel room bed in her clothes. "I am not," she said, dry swallowing two pills. She remembered that she had to call Ali, and she picked up her phone and hit the button and too late realized that it was the middle of the night. She fumbled to cut off the call, dropped the phone on the floor, and heard faintly, from far away, "Hi, you've reached Annie Brown. If you need to speak to me, leave a message here."

"Oh my God," she said, rolling over to pick up the phone. "Just—oh Jesus." Finally she managed to cut the connection.

Her head hurt when she woke up, still in the dark, the heavy drapes shutting out the sunshine glinting off the windows of a hundred buildings ranged around the hotel. The message light on the phone blinked red in the dim corner of the bedside table, and there were seven missed calls from Tom.

"My phone died," she said when he answered.

"Did the phone in your room die too?"

"I was out with some people from the Gift Show. You know how hard I work this thing."

"Annemarie, you're in New York City. When I call your cell at two in the morning and get voicemail, and then call your room and get no answer, I assume you've been mugged and you're in the morgue."

"I'm sorry," she said.

"We'll talk when you get home," he said, and hung up. There was a universe in the silence when a cell connection was cut, a kind of enormous soundless sound. She fell back to sleep to its emptiness after taking two more pills.

Bill was walking around the old farm supply store, his hands in the pockets of his work pants, when the principal called. The warehouse building had been empty for three years, since Dan Reider decided that the addition of snowblowers and rider mowers for the newcomers to the usual tractors and balers that had once been of use to the farmers wasn't really cutting it. He'd retired to someplace in the South where his kids were and where, he had told them all in the bar before he left, there was no state income tax. "Damn," one of the guys had said softly. "Plus, no snow," Dan said, although Bill had remembered that he'd seen on the news last year that they'd gotten three inches down there one day in February. "Climate change," Annie had said flatly, unloading the dishwasher. "I bet Dan wishes he had one of those snow blowers now."

Liz had the listing for the empty warehouse, even though she usually didn't handle commercial, and she kept saying it would be perfect for him to set up a plumbing supply business. There wasn't much to look at. It was your standard cinderblock and sheet metal industrial building. Bill recalled it being cold in the winter, when he'd bought a Weedwacker on sale. But Liz was right, she was always right about things like this, it would be perfect with some aisles of wire shelves installed. She'd already sent him the paperwork for a small-business loan, and he would need some permits that he was sure to get because they would pass through his mother's hands. "Everybody wins!" said Liz, who would get the commission on the sale of the building. He lived in a conspiracy of women—he always had—but at least Annie had been a double agent, circling back to fill him in.

"Hold up," Bill said, on his phone, nodding, his face getting tighter and tighter, like the fist he'd be making if he didn't have his keys in one hand and the phone in the other.

"I can assure you I will take care of this right now," he said into the phone.

From across the warehouse Liz sighed. "Can't people wait?"

"It's Ant. He missed school today. I'm going to look for him."

"I'll come."

"No," Bill said.

Ant was at the middle school now, which was only because of the kindness of some guy named Horton who had called Bill in August about summer school. "Bottom line, Mr. Brown, is that I'm going to pass him as a little bit of a gift," he'd said. "He didn't hand in half the assignments, and he skipped a couple of classes. But he's bright, very bright. I think he's got a math head, and I can't say that about most of these kids. When he comes out of his fugue state he gets things like—" There was a faint click in the background, and then he said, "Sorry, that was me snapping my fingers."

"What the hell is the matter with you?" Bill had asked Ant at dinner the night before as the whole table paused, mouths a little open, forks raised.

"That's swearing," Benjy said.

"Hell isn't swearing," Ant said. "Hell is a place." Bill knew what place he was referring to.

"This teacher says you're very bright," Bill said.

"Mr. Horton?" Ali said. "He's really hard." She looked at Ant. "Wow," she finally said. "Mr. Horton says you're bright?"

"Don't sound so surprised," Ant said.

Ali was standing in front of the middle school as Bill drove up, and maybe because he so rarely saw her from a distance he was able to see her, really see her, and see how much like a grown woman she looked, with her long tanned legs and her features sharpened now, less baby fat, more bone. She was hunched beneath her backpack; Bill remembered how he had remarked to Annie that the weight was making her back bow like an old woman's, and how his wife had said girls Ali's age stood that way not because of their backpacks but because they were embarrassed by their breasts. He'd shut right up, embarrassed by the mention of his daughter's embarrassment over her breasts, and Annie had patted his arm. "I'm not going to send you out to buy tampons," she'd said. He guessed Ali must be buying her own now.

Ali was standing with a woman, short, brown-skinned, with her black hair in a braid down her broad back, wearing an orange dress and dangly earrings. Together they walked to the window of the van.

"Miss Cruz, this is my father. Daddy, this is Miss Cruz, the counselor. She thinks she might know where Ant went." Bill narrowed his eyes and the woman said in a soft voice, "I had a session yesterday with your son, Mr. Brown. I was told you'd agreed for me to meet with him as I did last year with your daughter."

"What did he say when you met with him?"

Miss Cruz looked up with her enormous dark eyes as though in consultation with some higher power, and Bill wondered if she was a religious person. Finally she said, "He is struggling."

He never would have found Ant without this woman, Ali sandwiched between the two of them in the front of the van. He'd told the counselor she didn't need to come with them, but she said she thought perhaps she could help when they found Ant. "We talked quite a bit yesterday," she said. Don't talk to the counselor. Even Bill had heard that that's what everyone said. Either Ant was too new to know, or he'd disobeyed unwritten middle school kid rules the same way he was disobeying the written adult ones.

When they got to Green View he pulled the van around to the side of the building. Ant was sitting on a bench that was next to the young weeping willow tree near the far edge of the perfectly oval, obviously man-made pond, with its aerator plume watering the sky above and then dropping to dapple the surface of the greenish water. "May I speak to him, Mr. Brown?" Miss Cruz said.

He watched her walk slowly across the back lawn to the pond the way he used to walk toward a deer in the yard when he was young enough to think that if he came in peace the animal would let him advance, even touch its muzzle. Whatever he said to his son himself now would be wrong, he knew.

After that moment on the way home from camp, Ant had turned back to stone, like one of those monoliths Bill had seen in pictures pulled upright by long-dead tribes, a standing stone boy. His father had been careful not to bring Liz around unless he knew Ant was elsewhere.

"You like this woman?" he asked Ali.

"Yes. She's a really good person to talk to." She turned to him. "You might want to talk to her sometime."

"Uh, I'm not in middle school anymore, Al."

"She sees private patients," Ali said coolly, as though sitting there watching her brother, his elbows on his knees, his head in his hands, had suddenly turned her into a forty-year-old, full of judgment. Bill looked at her face, the sharp little nose, the dark eyes, the broad brow, and realized that that was what had happened, that she not only looked like her mother, but had taken on her burdens, and he'd tried to ignore it because it suited him to do so.

"I'm sorry," he said.

"I know," Ali said, and that almost made it worse, that she wasn't confused or ignorant about why her father would apologize to her.

It was like watching a scene in a play, the two of them with their front-row seats, the boy folded in on himself, the counselor turned toward him with one hand on his back. Even at this distance Bill could tell by the way her hand quivered in the soft autumn air that Ant was crying.

"I don't know what to do with him," he said.

"I know."

"I guess it will just take time."

"You know, one thing I like about Miss Cruz," Ali said. "She never says that. It's like she knows that time can pass, and things can get better, or things can get worse, or maybe they'll just stay the same. People act like time will fix things so everything will be the same again, everything will be all right, but sometimes it's the opposite. Ant can get harder and meaner until that's the person he is, for all time."

"That's a terrible thought," Bill said.

"I know," Ali said.

Both he and Ali jumped when there was a pounding sound from the side of the van. It was a woman in a wheelchair holding a cane in her left hand. Bill thought it seemed a little bit much, a wheelchair and a cane.

"Hello again, Alexandra," she said, peering up at the passenger-side window.

"Hi, Miss Evelyn," Ali said. "We came to get my brother."

Bill looked at Ali. Was everyone he loved a mystery to him? Did they all know people and things that he did not? He remembered how he would go to someone's house to install an outside hose, to disassemble the disposal to get the baby spoon out, and have a woman say to him, "Oh, your wife is just wonderful, she gave me your old stroller when we first moved in." He would think to himself, Did Annie tell me about this? Was I even listening?

The woman in the wheelchair nodded at his daughter. "We suspect he's been here all day, although we didn't notice him until we went into the common room for lunch. It's the best vantage point for seeing the pond."

"Didn't anybody think to call and tell me he was here?" Bill said.

"I suppose most of us assumed you knew where your boy was, Mr. Brown. Didn't you know where he was?"

"He missed school," Ali said.

Miss Evelyn looked toward the bench. "Maybe there are occasionally more important things than school," she said.

Then, raising the cane again, she turned to Ali and said, "That was not a piece of advice for you, Alexandra. Nose to the grindstone. That is what your mother expects of you." His daughter being given advice by a woman in a wheelchair wielding a cane like a cudgel, whom Ali seemed to know and he did not recognize, and who was channeling his wife. His son being comforted, found by a person he had never met when he himself would have driven fruitlessly from arcade to pizza parlor to ball field. He was a visitor in his own life, without a map or a guidebook.

"I never had children, Mr. Brown," Miss Evelyn added. "I played the piano. But that taught me that practice makes perfect, and every key is different and distinct. Here's your young man."

"He wants to sit in the back," Miss Cruz said, her hand still on Ant's back, his head still bowed. "I'll sit with him."

"It's not comfortable back there," Bill said.

"We will be fine," she said.

"You come back, Alexandra," said Miss Evelyn. "But on a Saturday, so you don't have to miss school." She turned to Bill. "You will prevail, Mr. Brown. You have no choice."

"Prevail is a good word," Miss Cruz said as they drew away, her arm around Ant's shoulder.

"Who is that woman?" Bill said.

"A friend of Mommy's," Ali said.

So it turned out that if you had to go to the counselor it was easy, but if you wanted to go it was hard. Ant had barely figured out how to open his locker before they had him in to see Miss Cruz. "How is it?" Ali asked him. "It's okay," he said. "It's a little boring." Which for Ant was a compliment. It also seemed that he had stopped calling Benjy stupid, although Ali didn't know whether that was because of his counseling sessions or because his father had told him that each time he did it there would be an additional chore on the whiteboard.

But when Ali decided she wanted to talk to Miss Cruz, the principal's secretary had handed her a form to fill out. Was she self-harming? Did she have issues around eating or excessive exercising? Did she have suicidal ideation? She was pretty sure that most of the kids, even in her grade, would not know what that last question meant.

And how were you supposed to answer? It reminded her of when her father had been called for jury duty and her parents had discussed how you might answer questions so that they would excuse you. "I mean, obviously, with a murder case, you would say you were opposed to the death penalty and then the prosecutors wouldn't want you," her mother had said. If you wanted to see the counselor, should you say yes to the suicide question, or would that land you in the hospital instead of across the desk from Miss Cruz, with her big happy bead necklaces, her patterned dresses, and her horizontal smile?

Ali folded the paper, put it in her backpack, and left. The secretary was on the phone arguing about a delivery of rippled printer paper and didn't even look up.

"Always have a plan B," her mother said, and Ali knew what it was. She maybe wouldn't have thought about it a year ago, but a year ago she didn't know to take the meat out of the freezer the night before to thaw, or how you could throw a bunch of stuff in the slow cooker in the morning and have a dinner that not only tasted good but whose parts were so hard to identify that even Benjy didn't know to say he didn't like tomatoes. Although she wouldn't make the mistake of putting a bay leaf in anything again, no matter what the recipe said.

"Well, this is a pleasant surprise," Miss Cruz said when Ali sat down across from her in her office on Front Street. "I would have seen you at school if you'd wanted." When Ali told her about the questionnaire, Miss Cruz shook her head and sighed loudly. "Thank you for telling me," she said to Ali. "I did not know. I will take care of that."

"I don't mind coming here," Ali said. "I didn't know if you took insurance so I brought money." She pulled a hundred-dollar bill from her pocket and laid it on the desk.

"I can't remember the last time I saw a hundred-dollar bill," Miss Cruz said.

"I'd never seen one!" Ali said. "I got it for my birthday. And I got a cellphone. My mother said I couldn't have a phone until I was fourteen so my father got me one. Finally."

"Happy birthday! How was your birthday?"

Ali had no idea how to answer. She had not wanted a party, but her father had insisted, and so had Liz Donahue. "Can I come?" she'd asked Ali breathlessly, and what did Liz think she could say but, "Yes, of course, sure"? Liz had hung a big banner in the living room, and when she saw it, Annemarie had rolled her eyes and taken the bunch of balloons she brought—because Tom's company did party supplies, too—and parked them in the corner next to the banner. "There are fourteen of them because, you know, you're fourteen today," she said, exhaling loudly. Her grandmother brought the cake from the Italian bakery, and it had a plastic Pooh Bear stuck in the center, as though Ali were still a little girl.

"Can I have that?" Jamie said, and Ali had nodded, not speaking, because her grandmother had just said that the cake had lemon filling, and Ali hated lemon filling. "Ali hates lemon filling," her mother always said, and even though Annemarie seemed exhausted and gray-faced and in a mood—Hurricane Annemarie, Ali suddenly thought—she'd said, "Ali hates lemon filling," because obviously she had heard it before, and Ali knew just where she'd heard it, and her eyes filled and her tears fell on the cake. Because it was that bakery's buttercream that her mother always complained was mainly made of Crisco, her tears sat like iridescent bubbles on the white surface. Her mother always made her birthday cake, chocolate with chocolate frosting. Ant got red velvet, even though Ali told him it was nothing but vanilla cake with food coloring, and Benjy got chocolate cake with vanilla frosting. So far Jamie had changed his mind every year.

"Oh no," Liz said. "Maybe you can eat around the filling?"

"Everybody likes lemon filling," her grandmother said, cutting up the cake.

"Oh, be quiet, Dora," Annemarie said, and the room got very still.

"Let's bring down the level," their father said quietly.

"I don't know what this girl has to complain about," Ali's grandmother said.

"I wasn't complaining," Ali said, wiping her eyes.

"Her mother died," Annemarie said, and Ali started to cry again, harder this time.

"My mother died too, and you don't hear me going on about it."

"Jesus, you are such a cold bitch."

"What? What did you say to me? Bill, did you hear what she said to me?"

"He heard me. He knows it's true."

"I don't know what I expected from a junkie," their grandmother said. "I can't believe my daughter-in-law even let you around her children."

Ali looked from Annemarie to her grandmother, and back again, and then Benjy ran into the room. "Ali, something's wrong with the hamsters," he said. "I gave them cake and they won't come out and eat it."

Annemarie laughed a mean laugh, the kind you never wanted to hear in the locker room after gym. "I guess the hamsters don't like lemon filling either," she said.

Ali and Ant went into Ali's room. Jamie hung over the cage, poking with his finger. The little boys had moved the cardboard box that Ali had put in the cage for the hamsters to sleep in and, eventually, to chew to bits. Beneath were what looked like two tiny grimy fur pelts, flat, unmoving, a piece of cake between them.

"They're dead," Ant said. "They look like they've been dead for a couple of days." He turned to Ali. "Didn't they smell?"

"No worse than usual," said Ali, and the two little boys started to wail, and Ali cried too, not only because the hamsters were dead, but because she hadn't even noticed.

"Oh, for pity's sake, they're hamsters," their grandmother said. "They never live that long. You can get some at the pet store tomorrow. I'll buy them for your birthday. Quit the crying. You kids, you're spoiled. You don't know how good you've got it. And you," she turned to Ali. "You should say thank you for the birthday cake and not be complaining about lemon filling."

And finally Ali's father, who had been silent through it all, said quietly, "Mom, I'd like you to leave. I'd like you to leave right now."

"This is my house."

"Is it? Great, then I'm giving you thirty days' notice that we're moving out."

"Score!" Annemarie said in a very loud whisper, raising her arms in the air.

"Oh ho," their grandmother said, turning to Liz Donahue, who had not uttered a word. "Oh, you're going to regret this, Liz. Your life won't be the same with this crew jumping on your nice furniture."

"What?" said Ali.

"What?" said Ant.

"I loved the hamsters," Benjy cried.

"What the hell are you talking about?" their father said. And then he looked at Liz, and so did Ali.

"You all would be welcome in my home," Liz said, smiling. "Absolutely. It would be wonderful to share my home with all of you."

"I'm buying a place of our own," their father said, and the smile disappeared, and everyone was silent.

"I can help with that," Liz finally said with a fake smile this time, and Ali felt sorry for her.

"What a shit show," Annemarie said as she stood by her car, and that's when she handed Ali the card with the hundred-dollar bill inside.

Ali didn't think she should tell Miss Cruz that her birthday party was a shit show, so she just said, "Our hamsters died."

"Oh, I'm so sorry. That's sad." Ali's eyes filled, and Miss Cruz added, "But that's not why you're here. Although sometimes a pet is more than a pet, if you get my meaning."

Ali nodded. "It's that I keep having these bad thoughts. I have bad thoughts about everything," she said.

"Tell me about that."

"Not just bad, like, the worst. Like, there's this girl in my class that I've known since we were little kids, Carrie Fessenden? She's really nice, I mean, we're not really good friends but, like, we talk and sometimes we sit together on the bus. But I looked at her when school started and I could see her collarbone in the neck of her T-shirt, and right away I thought, Carrie's anorexic. And then last week Teddy Young came into the Y with a black eye and he said he got it because he fell against the fence post in his backyard, but I kept looking at him and thinking maybe his dad hit him. But his dad doesn't seem like the kind of person who would hit his son, but how do you know? How do you really know what's going on anywhere? My grandmother said my aunt Annemarie, who was my mother's best friend, is a junkie. Now I keep remembering things my mom said about Annemarie, things she said to my dad, that seemed like she was worried about her, so maybe it's true. Could Annemarie do all the things she does if she took drugs? And my father has this kind-of girlfriend, I guess she is, and she's nice and she tries really hard to make us like her and I keep thinking that maybe she's just pretending to be nice."

"Are you afraid that these things are really happening? Or are you afraid that you're simply imagining the worst?"

"Both. It's like, since February, everything is flipped, and instead of seeing the good things all I can see are the bad."

"Since your mother died."

"No offense to you, but I wish I could talk to her about all of this. Except if I could talk to her, maybe I wouldn't believe any of it, or see everything as the scariest version of itself. Like Jenny's father."

"Your friend Jenny."

Her best friend, she'd thought, even though she hadn't heard from her all summer, which at first she kept telling herself made sense since Jenny wasn't allowed to have a cellphone or email. Ali had made a new friend when she was working at the day camp over the summer, a girl in the grade above her named Ciara. Ali had heard about her, even seen her sometimes at the mall or in the diner sitting with her sisters, whose names were Ariadne and Bella. They had arrived in Greengrass three years before, when their mother had been made head of the county library system, had moved into one of the big old Victorian houses on a rise overlooking the town, overlooking their street. "I love those houses," her mother always said when they drove past them.

The three sisters had had the usual period of being side-eyed by everyone at school, but it had been shorter than usual because it turned out they all three could sing, really sing. The music director at the high school, who for years had had to give solos to baritones who sang through their noses and sopranos who thought falsetto conveyed deep emotion, now had the real deal, one after another. Ciara had gone to an arts camp in Michigan for the second half of the summer, but for the first half she'd been stuck teaching little kids to sing "Frère Jacques" while they banged away on xylophones, although she didn't seem to mind. When she'd walk home with Ali and the boys, they all sang "Row Your Boat" in rounds. "She's nice," Jamie said. "She's pretty," said Benjy. Both were true, but Ali was realistic. Ali was going into her last year at the middle school, Ciara into her first year at the high school. It wouldn't last, not in any bad way, the way Melinda Buxbaum would make someone her best friend for two months and then drop them over the weekend for someone else. She would just be a victim of circumstances.

But it had still made Ali feel guilty about Jenny, and when she was helping with the pottery class she'd made a plaque for her, pink with white letters: TRUE FRIENDS ARE ALWAYS TOGETHER IN SPIRIT. She walked over to Jenny's house on a Saturday morning to put it in the mailbox, but when she'd gotten there Liz Donahue had been standing out front, wearing a purple dress, the kind of dress her mother would have worn to a party or a wedding. She was holding a folder.

"Fancy meeting you here, Alexandra Brown!" she said. Ali wondered if she would be like that even if she'd been hanging around all of them for years, like what her mother called company manners, that went away when people weren't company anymore.

"My friend Jenny lives here," Ali said.

"The Masons? Oh, they're long gone, hon. They've moved. I don't even know if I have a forwarding. They were renting, and we don't always get forwardings for renters." Car doors slammed behind Ali, and Liz stood up a little straighter and smiled. "You must be the McMenamins!" she'd called, and turned aside.

Ali looked across the desk at Miss Cruz. "She's gone," she said, and saying it made it finally completely real. "Jenny is just gone."

"What did you want to say about her father?" Miss Cruz said, picking up a pen and opening her notebook, and Ali took a deep breath.

When she was done talking about that night at Jenny's, about what she'd seen or not seen, about all the things Jenny couldn't do and places she wasn't allowed to go, she sighed and looked down at her hands in her lap. "I don't know what to think," Ali said. "Like, if you look at it one way it's nothing, and if you look at it the way I've been looking at everything else, then Jenny's father is, you know, doing stuff to her. She said no, but how do you really know? And now I can't even ask her again because she's completely gone. Without saying anything to me about leaving."

Miss Cruz wrote for a moment, then looked up. "What can I do to help you with all this? Because it's a lot."

"Just tell me what you think. Like, oh, Ali, you're just imagining things."

"Is that what you want me to say? Because I can't do that. It's true that sometimes what we imagine is real and sometimes it's not. I once had a patient who every time she drove thought the car was going to crash, hit a tree, a truck, the car in front of her. What she was really worried about was something else, something completely different, but she turned it into a car crash. But sometimes what we think we're seeing is what we are seeing. There's a prayer that I love that says, 'God grant me the serenity to accept the things I cannot change, the courage to change the things I can, and the wisdom to know the difference.'"

"My aunt Annemarie has that on a plaque in her home office."

"The woman your grandmother says is a junkie."

Ali nodded. "But I don't think she is. She's really successful. And my mother loved her. Like, they were so close. So close. But maybe it's true. She's been weird lately."

Miss Cruz slid the hundred-dollar bill back across the desk. "Do you have your new phone with you?"

Ali pulled it from the front pocket of her backpack and handed it to Miss Cruz. She still handled it carefully, couldn't believe that her father had given it to her. "Your mother promised," he'd said. When she had looked at the screen for the first time she'd seen that two numbers had already been entered into Ali's Contacts. They were labeled "Mom" and "Dad."

Now there was a third. "That's my cell number," said Miss Cruz. "You can text me anytime. We can arrange to meet here or at school. This money is yours. You should save it, or use it. Maybe you want to get new hamsters."

"That's what my grandmother said. But I hate that idea. It's like the hamsters we had didn't matter, like things can just be replaced."

"How did you get to be so wise?" Miss Cruz said.

"I'm going to be moving," Annemarie said to Ali as they pulled into the driveway of Annemarie's house, the curved lines making the place look as though it were a boat docked to one side of the turnaround. That's what it had always looked like to Annemarie, a yacht. The SS *Tom and Annemarie,* although she believed it had always been more Tom than her.

When she walked through the place with the real estate agent, it had occurred to her for the first time that all those pink and purple binders, all those boxes of big chunky crayons in red and blue, might have made Tom enamored of a blank page, a white sheet of paper, walls of no color, carpeting that showed everything, so that he was always stooping to pick up some little piece of dark lint. She'd gone along to get along, which she sometimes thought was the linchpin of marriage. All the beautiful quilts the Amish and Mennonite women made, the log cabin in deep red and forest green, the double wedding quilt with the pink-and-gold background, and she had chosen one that was white on white for their bedroom. It had an elaborate pattern of vines and flowers, but you really had to squint to make it out.

"My mother always said how much she liked your house," Ali said.

"Yeah, I know," said Annemarie, but she didn't really think it was true. With Annie gone she was somehow able to see her friend more clearly, more as she really was and less how Annemarie wanted or needed her to be. It was probably an oversimplification to put it that way, but their friendship was based on the fact that one wanted to be special and one didn't really care. Annemarie had been one of those little girls whose parents were always asking her to sing to the people in the living room or show off her ballet moves at the picnic table in the backyard, and that had morphed into her having a kind of flashy quicksilver personality. At a certain point, she'd realized that high school would end, and then there would be college, and a job, and a house, and a husband and kids, but nothing much would really happen after that, and she had been troubled by the idea.

But when she talked to Annie about it she could tell by the look in her eyes that Annie understood what Annemarie was saying but couldn't feel a bit of it, that that's what Annie really wanted, a lovely reliable life that went on day to day with the occasional occasion, a party, a new baby, dinner out, vacations. That was enough. And that was exactly what Annie had had. When she talked about how much she loved Annemarie's house, when she ran her hand over the marble countertops as though she were petting them, purring, it was because they were pristine, no smears of chocolate milk or peanut butter illuminated by the glass pendant lights over the breakfast bar. It was so clean, and for a woman with four kids, that was the dream. But Annie always held on to her wineglass tight when they sat in the living room, her knuckles betraying her fear that she would spill on the carpet. No matter how many times Annemarie asked, Annie never spent the night. "It'll be like old times," Annemarie said, but Annie didn't want old times, not really. She'd liked the times she had right then.

Annemarie looked over at the girl next to her in the car balancing a cardboard pizza box on her lap. Ali had had that growth spurt that Annemarie and Annie had had together, thank God, in eighth grade. Ali was still lanky, but there was a curve to her hips now, and to her breasts, and her fine caramel-colored hair had a bit of summer shine. Sometimes it was like having Annie ride shotgun again, and then Ali would turn to Annemarie and she would see the look in Ali's eyes. Annie had been joyful, while her daughter was thoughtful. Annie had been funny, while her daughter was serious. Everything was in the eyes. If you had identical twins, one with eyes of caution, the other with eyes carefree, you would be able to tell them apart easily. That's how Annie had known what Annemarie had hidden from everyone else. She might have been able to pull together a case file, to go to a firm meeting, to help at a court hearing. But Annie could see that the old Annemarie was gone by looking at the eyes pixelated at the end by twenty, thirty, forty pills a day.

Everything now was in Ali's eyes. Annemarie was ashamed that she couldn't remember whether they had been that way a year ago. The girl had been a satellite of her mother then. If Annemarie was being honest, she'd always resented Ali a little, the thing that had first opened the gap between Annie and Annemarie that had gotten bigger every year. Annemarie would call to talk, and there would be a bleat, then a wail, and Annie would be gone again, something more important to do. Annie wondered if Ali was jealous of Annemarie's place in her mother's life, though she wouldn't admit it, but Annemarie had been jealous of Ali as well. When they were young she and Annie had played a game about who they would rescue in their lifeboat if they were ever in a shipwreck, and the answer had been simple and easy and symmetrical. Then Ali came along, and Annemarie knew she was swimming alone.

The thing that had shaped Ali for all time would make her different, maybe stronger, harder, even smarter. It was too soon to tell. What had shaped Annie, the horrible weekend when she'd discovered that her father had been sleeping with, of all people, one of the lunch ladies at school—"she wears a hairnet," Annemarie remembered her crying at one point in that long night—had drawn a line between the two of them that Annemarie had taken years to figure out. Annie wanted a home she could rely on, a place full of people who would be beloved and who would stay because of it, unwavering dedication. She wanted something she could count on forever. She just hadn't counted on forever being so short. None of them ever did, ever had.

Ali put the pizza on the breakfast bar, and Annemarie pulled out the plates and the paper napkins. She was happy to see Ali rip wordlessly through one piece. Her hand, with its bitten nails and frazzled cuticles, hovered over the box. "Can I have another slice?" she said.

"Are you kidding? We got eight slices in that sucker. You can have four if you want, although four slices is a lot of pizza even for a growing girl. Woman. Growing woman."

"Girl's fine. You guys worry too much about stuff like that. It's just that at our house, one pizza is one slice for each of us, except Ant and my dad. I usually get the cheese from Benjy's. He only eats the crust."

"He's always been a picky eater."

"The doctor says he might have lactose intolerance. I don't know. Maybe he's just a picky eater. That's what my grandmother says. She says she doesn't believe in all that other stuff."

Annemarie put her hand over Ali's. "I shouldn't have talked to your grandmother the way I did at your birthday party. It was wrong, and I regret it. I sent her a note a couple of weeks ago and told her so."

"I know," Ali said.

Annemarie chuckled. "And she said?"

Ali thought for a moment. That was another thing. Annie always said the first thing that came into her head. Ali was a thinker. Finally she said, "There's this girl at school? Melinda Buxbaum?"

"I knew her parents."

"It's like, if anyone else has anything, it makes things less for her. Does that make sense? Like, if you have a new hoodie she has to make some comment about how nobody wears hoodies anymore because she doesn't have one. Or she has one but she wants hers to be the best one. Sorry, this all sounds really stupid."

"No it doesn't," said Annemarie, who thought back to their ten-year reunion, when Skipper Buxbaum, who had started dating Beth Landsman when they were both sixteen, prom king and queen, and had married her the week after they graduated from college, had pulled Annemarie into the walk-in fridge in the back of the cafeteria kitchen, pushed her back against a shelf of frozen hot dogs and buns, and whispered in her ear, "I can't remember a time when I didn't want to do this."

When Annemarie had told Annie, next morning, Annie had said, "Oh, babe, I don't want to burst your bubble, but he has slept with half the women I know at this point. Poor Beth put some tracker on his phone and wound up going into Duane Insurance and screaming at their receptionist and it wasn't even her, it was the Pilates teacher two floors above. Bill told me that at some town council meeting Skipper was talking about how I hadn't lost my figure even after having all those kids."

"And Bill said?"

"'Dude, I will cut it off. I will cut it off and put it in the pocket of your polo shirt.'"

"It doesn't sound like Melinda Buxbaum is a very happy girl," Annemarie said to Ali now. Which was sad. Beth Landsman had been a happy girl, before. Annemarie had been tormented by the idea of a quiet, uneventful future, and Annie had been contented with the same idea. But Beth Landsman, once upon a time, had just been happy with the present, being half of the Cutest Couple in the yearbook.

"I guess, but what I mean is that my grandmother is kind of the same way. I think it always bothered her, that she wanted to be able to tell all her friends that she and my mother were really close, went shopping together and all that, and everyone would know she was lying. So I think it bothered her that my mother was so close to you."

Annemarie didn't want to say, It bothered your father, too. No man ever likes his wife's best friend, because that friend knows her in a way he never will, and because he will never have that kind of friendship with his own friends, even his oldest ones. Tom had a bunch of what he called buddies. They played golf together and went on a trip once a year to some exotic fishing camp where a chef cooked whatever they'd caught that day and the wine list was similar to one at a white-tablecloth restaurant. From what Annemarie could tell, they talked a lot about the stock market and professional sports. One of them had a wife who'd been going through chemo-therapy two years ago, and when they got back from Panama or the Virgin Islands or wherever it was, Annemarie had asked Tom how the chemo was going. "What chemo?" Tom said.

The bond between Annie and Annemarie had been hard for Bill in the beginning, but he had really gone sour on her for-ever after Annie had called in sick to work one day and gone out to fetch her friend from her Mennonite caretakers, snuck her into one of the rooms at Green View, and fed her meds to get her through the worst of the first few days, meds she had had to account for on patient charts. Annemarie had been walking around the home one afternoon when she'd run into the woman whose badge identified her as the director. She'd looked down at Annemarie's bedroom slippers and said, "Can I help you?"

The great thing about addiction was that you became a flu-ent liar. Over the years Annemarie had perfected all kinds of excuses when she had made plans with Annie and then can-celed, or showed up looking bad or acting blurry. ("Not excuses! Lies! They were lies, babe!" Annie had said after-ward, still angry.) So without hesitation Annemarie had said to the director, with a big empty-eyed smile, "I'm visiting my aunt." And as though she'd conjured her, the woman in the wheelchair appeared at her elbow, pinching it hard.

"My niece," she said to the director. "Her shoes got wet and are drying on my radiator. Let's go back to my room, dear."

"Billy," she had heard Annie whisper that evening on the phone, sobbing. "I'm going to lose my job and it's all my own fault."

Six months later they had been sitting in the backyard after the nursing home, after the rehab, Annemarie with the elastic band on her wrist. Annie had gone inside for more mustard for the hot dogs, and Bill had said to Annemarie between gritted teeth, no eye contact, looking straight ahead, "If you ever hurt my wife I will make sure she never comes near you again. Swear to God." And when Annemarie had tried to reply, he had raised his hand, palm out, and added, "Don't even talk to me."

Time, and Tom, and her professional success, and her sobriety, had softened him a little bit, but ever since the funeral he had been looking at her as though he was waiting for her to prove once and for all that she was unworthy of Annie's faith, hope, and love. When she finally had, she wondered whether he hadn't said anything because Annie wasn't around to be hurt anymore. At the birthday party he must have known, or suspected. And maybe, her inhibitions trashed, she had only said to his mother what he knew his wife always wished she had, and what he wished he could say himself.

"I know that your grandmother is tough," she said, still with her hand on Ali's, "but I shouldn't have said that to her. And what she said about me was the truth, although I wouldn't put it the way she did. I used to be an addict, and then I wasn't. Your mother made me stop. She helped me stop, and she told me that if I started again she wouldn't be my friend anymore. It was probably the only thing anyone could have said to me that would have made me stop."

"But then you started again, didn't you?" Ali said. "I sort of knew because you weren't around as much, and when you were around you were different. But you didn't seem really weird or anything."

"People who do what I do? What I did? We seem kind of normal most of the time, but we're not ourselves. So we can fool people who don't really know us, but not the ones who do."

"Like my mom."

"Like your mom."

"And you started again because you were sad."

"I guess that's what I told myself. I had a relapse, and if anyone had asked why, I would have said it was because of that. But your mother would have said that's just an excuse." She could almost hear Annie saying it. It was like somehow she was more alive now that she was dead.

"But now you seem okay. You seem better."

"I started, and then I stopped again. I stopped the day after your birthday party." I stopped, Annie, I stopped, because I went to that new doctor, the one someone at Nar-Anon told me about because if you don't think twelve-step meetings are a good source of information about where to score pills, you've never been to one. Except that his nurse practitioner said that before they'd prescribe for my back they wanted to do blood work, and when she came back into the room, me with my butt all goose pimpled from the chilly air from the vents, she said they wouldn't give me Oxy or Vicodin or Percocet or anything.

Not again, Annemarie had thought, and she'd started in on how the nerve pain ran right down her leg, because the other thing addiction taught you was all the symptoms of all the ailments that someone will give you meds for. And the nurse held up her hand, just that same way Bill had when he told her off in the backyard.

"No way," the nurse said.

God bless that nurse. God bless that doctor, who knew another doctor to send her to, to give her a way to slowly, surely, get healthy and completely clean, and another doctor to do the sonograms so she could see what she was fighting for.

"I'm pregnant, honey," she said. "That's why I stopped."

"For real?" Ali said.

"For real."

That cool skeptical look softened, and suddenly it was like having Annie in front of her, jumping up, coming around to her stool, putting her arms around her, squeezing hard. "My mom would be so, so happy," Ali said, and then she started to cry, and Annemarie did, too.

When they finally stopped and wiped their faces with paper napkins and took another slice of pizza, they both started to laugh. "So this is what happy looks like?" Annemarie said. "Two women crying their eyes out?"

"Are you sure this time? Like, it's not going to go away, like the other times?"

"It seems like this time it will stick," Annemarie said. "That's what they tell me. They say everything looks fine." She was trying hard to believe them, trying not to think of what the pills might have done to the funny little fishy in the pictures before she had known that it was there, although the truth was, she thought about it all the time. She would worry until she gave birth and could count fingers and toes, would surely worry even after that. But then Annie had always worried, with far less reason. Was this one finally babbling? Did that one walk with a peculiar gait? Annemarie had had no patience for any of it at the time, but now she understood that Annie had watched and worried simply because that was what a mother did. That was what Annemarie would do.

"I think you'll be a good mom," Ali said.

"Thanks, hon," Annemarie said, and then, her voice shaking slightly, "I learned from the best."

Ali stared down at two lone slices of cold pizza. They looked like yellow-and-red linoleum in a pool of oily cardboard. "Should we save this for Tom?" she said. "Oh, he must be so happy."

"He's gone," Annemarie said. He was a wiz at math, Tom, one reason he'd been so successful. They hadn't had sex more than a handful of times since Annie died. He'd figured out it wasn't his baby. "I don't believe you ever really loved me," he'd said. "I don't know if you're capable of love."

He was wrong. She'd had one real true unshakeable love in her life, but it wasn't her husband. It was Annie. And now there would be another. She'd been in a shipwreck, and she would make sure she never was again, that instead she was prepared to dive in and save her daughter. At least that's what she told herself.

"You know what really bothers me," Ali said in the car, looking straight ahead through the windshield. "That my father can have another wife, but we can't ever have another mother."

"I get that," Annemarie said. "That can happen. Men need women."

"What about women?"

"Women need women, too. Not the way you're thinking though."

"I know what you meant."

"Your mother loved you so much," Annemarie said.

"I know," Ali said. "I'm not really sure if that makes things better or worse."

He didn't recognize the number on his phone. "Mr. Brown," said a soft voice, "this is Philomena Cruz. I wonder if I could have an hour of your time."

"Sure," Bill said. "Want to fill me in on the problem?"

"It's complicated," the woman said.

"Ah, don't worry, we'll sort it out. Do you live in a house or an apartment?"

A silence, and then softly, "An apartment."

"Rent or own?"

"Rent."

"Have you checked in with your landlord? He might be the one footing the bill."

There was another silence. "I think we are talking at cross-purposes," she'd finally said. "I'm the psychologist at the middle school. We met that day that Anthony went missing. I wanted to see if we could speak about your children. About Alexandra and Anthony. Ali and Ant."

He'd pulled the van to the side of the road so fast that the Sentra that had been riding his back bumper veered and hit the horn hard, the driver shouting something from behind the glass of the car window.

"Are they okay?" he said.

"I'm sorry, I didn't mean to alarm you. I merely thought we should talk about how they're getting on. Could you come by tomorrow around six? Not to the school. They all get so agitated, the kids, when a parent shows up at school to see me, and then there's always a lot of chatter afterward. Come to my office. It's on Front Street. One twenty-one Front."

"I try to have dinner with the kids at six," he said. He was trying to be better, trying to be more, trying to be two instead of one. Emphasis on the word *try*. If he didn't have a four o'clock that was more time-consuming than it looked. If he didn't get an emergency call about a burst boiler. Throw one of those trays of lasagna in the oven, Ali. Or maybe two. Again.

"I'll be there," he told the psychologist. "And apologies for the confusion." He'd remembered her face from that day at the nursing home. He'd forgotten her name.

There was so much to remember. The obvious things he had mastered now—the school calendar on the side of the refrigerator, the house as clean as a house could be with four kids in it, the new sweatpants and T-shirts. "They grow like weeds," he could hear his wife saying. But he didn't really anticipate. He realized that Annie had had a gift for anticipation. Maybe it was why she seemed happy most of the time, because she could envision an orderly tomorrow, next week, next year. Or maybe it was just that she got ahead of the small stuff, so that halfway through a roll of toilet paper another would be sitting on the tank and everyone could avoid that fool-making moment he'd had the other morning, sitting there with one fragile sheet in his hand and an empty cardboard roll mocking him. Who knew toilet paper could wreck your day or make it?

He hadn't had that knack for planning ahead. His mother did, but in a different way. She liked to have something to say about him, so for years she would tell people, "Oh, Bill, he's going to go to the state police, been talking about it since he was a kid, taking the test as soon as they give it again." He figured that she was never going to be able to say he was a lawyer, never be able to say he'd gone to California and invented some computer chip that would change everything, so she'd fastened on to the state police. "He likes to help people," she told the guys she knew applying for permits, when if it had been about him and not about how he made her feel about herself, she would have said, "Do you need a good plumber?"

The fact was, he liked his job, because it didn't require him to think much past the end of each day, and because he was good at it, because it amounted to something real, unlike the jobs of other people he knew. It might sound crazy, but he always thought of it as helping people. If you turned on your dishwasher and it spewed water all over the floor, you thought it was a big help if someone made sure that didn't happen, wasn't ever going to happen again. Hell, he'd had women open the back door and cry when their toilet wasn't working and he showed up.

Annie knew that and appreciated it. One night at dinner she'd said, "I was at that new coffee place with Annemarie's mother, and there were two women at the table next to us. The tables were really close together so you could hear everything the people next to you were saying, these two women, expensive haircuts, expensive purses, cashmere this and that"—sometimes Bill felt like she was speaking a foreign language—"and the one starts talking about how cute the plumber is and how she's going to have a couple of leaky faucets turn up just to get him to come back."

"Oh, gross," Ali had said at the time, eleven years old maybe, but starting to figure out how things worked.

"Your mother is making this up because she thinks it'll make me feel like a dude," he'd said.

"First of all, you are a dude. Second of all, I would make it up if I thought it would make you feel like a dude, but I'm not making it up. Ask Annemarie's mother, she choked on a scone."

He'd worked on a big job about five years ago, an older couple who had a second home, an old stone place with six bedrooms and a summer kitchen out back that they'd decided to turn into a guesthouse. They'd had a housewarming and, along with their friends, had also invited all the guys who had worked on the guesthouse—the construction crew, the electrician, the roofer, the plumber. It was one of those things that sounded like a good idea but wasn't really, like those edible arrangements of fruit that Annie said were stupid because why would you pay for pineapple cut up into flowers when you could just buy pineapple? The crew guys and their wives all wound up standing at one edge of the flagstone patio nursing drinks. "Come have something to eat," the woman who owned the house told them, and they straggled over to the buffet table, lobster rolls and tiny salmon sandwiches and three kinds of salads.

"To the craftsmen who made this possible," said their host, raising a glass of white wine, and the other guests applauded.

"So you're a craftsman," Annie had said in the car on the way home.

"Weird food."

"Are you nuts? I could eat lobster rolls all day."

"You'd like that, wouldn't you? All that." The guesthouse with an antique copper tub, the beamed living room with two enormous couches, the mahogany bookshelves in the den covering an entire wall, the kitchen with two stoves and two sinks and backsplash tiles with pictures of animals. That house, it was all money.

"Would I like a house like that? Sure, who wouldn't? Do I want more room someday? You know I do. Do I want a different life than the one I have? No. If I want lobster rolls you can take me on a weekend trip to Cape Cod."

"Who's going to take care of the kids?"

"We'll just leave a twenty on the table and some food in the fridge and let them go feral for a couple of days." He thought about that sometimes now, how the kids had gone feral for sure, and how she had been able to picture a future so close she could see the lobster rolls on the restaurant table facing the wild gray ocean of the cape, a future that had been a mirage. She'd anticipated, and for what? What was left?

Her voice was in his head, that was for sure, just like he'd told the kids that night driving home from the wake, before he'd known it was even true.

The week before, he'd been driving down a narrow country road, bare limbs scratching at the hood of his truck, and he'd seen a sign at the head of a gravel drive: GOLDEN RETRIEVER PUPPIES FOR SALE. It was like the truck turned in all by itself. He got to an old farmhouse that had once been red but had since faded to rust, same as blood did. He could hear barking from the back. A woman wearing overalls came out a side door wiping her hands on a plaid dishtowel.

There were seven puppies, maybe not so much golden retrievers as retrieverish, the mother's coat not quite as rich and lush as others he'd seen, her face a little too pointed, ears a little too cocked. But the puppies were what puppies always were, little nuggets of warm, soft possibility. He'd held one to his chest and could feel the wet of nose and tongue tickling his neck, and then the warmth as it peed in his palm. The overall woman held out the dishtowel. "It is what it is," she said, and she laughed, and then gulped back the sound as she saw that he was crying, the soft pale fur darkening and forming itself into spikes.

He'd never had a dog as a kid. "Of course you didn't," said Annie, who had grown up with one beloved and nasty Scottie after another. But his friends all seemed to have them, for some reason with western names, Bandit and Maverick and Duke. Duke had torn the skirt off the sofa in Andy Szach's living room, and the next Saturday Duke had gone to that farm they always talked about, where he'd have more room to run around. When your friends were nice guys, the farm fiction prevailed because none of you were going to say, Man, I think they're going to kill your dog for messing up the furniture, and none of them were going to say to their moms, What farm, where?

The overall woman was talking about how the puppies wouldn't be ready to leave for another three weeks and how important it was to crate train and how she had papers, they all had papers. He kept his head down, just trying to make this fit, make it work, be that thing that would pull them all together again, get Ant out of his room and off the computer, make Ali's face go soft and sweet once more, give the little boys something they'd be excited to come home to, all of them sitting on the floor while the puppy gnawed on their out-stretched fingers with needle teeth, rolled extravagantly onto its back for a belly rub, fell asleep at the foot of someone's bed. Tried to push aside the notion of the little pile of poop in the middle of the hallway, the chewed chair leg, the cold winter nights when no one wanted to go outside at midnight, the long days when the house was empty and what the hell did people do with puppies when they went to work?

"Do you have a fenced yard?" the woman said, and it broke the spell. He put the puppy down. Its mother licked his tears from the tawny fur, and the puppy pushed past into the folds of her slack underside and began to nurse.

"It's a lot to think about," he'd said.

"I thought about getting a dog yesterday," he said when he was finally sitting opposite Miss Cruz the next day. He'd looked up and down Front Street before he pulled open the door. He finally figured that if it went around town that he was seeing a therapist or taking a Pilates class, he could make up a story about the plumbing in the building.

"My mother raised dogs," she said. "German shepherds."

"I'm probably all wrong, but I always think of them as guard dogs. Police dogs."

"That's exactly what she raised."

"Doing what you do is a long way from raising guard dogs," he said, rubbing his hands on his pants. He hadn't been this nervous since childbirth classes. He'd needed oxygen that first time, when Ali was born, just at the critical moment. "We're losing the father," a nurse had said.

"We're losing the father," Annie said from time to time, laughing.

"They've lost their mother," everyone said about his kids. Or whispered. Mainly whispered, as though death were an obscenity. Which he supposed it was. It was obscene that Annie Fonzheimer, that wine cooler in her hand, that Annie Brown, that warm, willing presence in his bed, was lying in the cemetery now.

"Does your mother still raise dogs?" he said, because he couldn't think of anything else ordinary to say and because he was so nervous about what this woman might tell him about his kids and so ashamed at the idea that what she said might surprise him.

"My mother's gone now. But she had three sons who were police officers and one who was in the Marines, so maybe raising guard dogs rubbed off on some of us. What did you decide about getting a dog? I assume it was for your children."

"It was a foolish idea," he said.

"Why do you say that?"

It was that easy. Were they magicians, these people, burrowing into your mind with just a simple question? He began to speak, about how hard Ali had become sometimes, about Ant's problems at school and sleepaway camp, about how Benjy was afraid of so many things now, bugs and birds, about how Jamie had stopped wetting the bed but now sucked his thumb and his teacher said he would drop his head below his desk so he could suck it in school. He talked about the ceremony at the nursing home and how much he had dreaded Christmas. He talked about how people's sympathy was well meant but made him feel freakish and set apart, and how bothered he was by that because he had always loved being one of the guys, being ordinary. Wasn't that weird? Most people wanted to be special and he missed being ordinary.

He stopped when he realized he'd been talking for a long time. He'd felt good while he was doing it and felt foolish now. It reminded him of Liz. She liked to fill space. There was a wall in her living room and another in the hall filled with framed pictures, ten or twelve, in what was a nice geometric arrangement but didn't invite you to really look at any of them. It was the same with her bed. The first time they slept together it had taken them more time to get all the pillows and quilts and throws off the bed than to get undressed. And that was the way she talked, too, as though silence were an empty wall or a bare bed and it had to be filled with something. This was the most he'd talked for a long, long time. Or talked to someone who was actually there. In the truck he talked to Annie. He tried not to move his lips when he did, but it was so real, she was so real, that it was hard not to speak aloud.

"I need to stop talking," he said. "You're supposed to be telling me something or you wouldn't have asked me to come here."

"It's fine," she said. "I'm happy to have you talk. But there's something I'd like you to think about. You've talked for more than thirty minutes, and you haven't truly talked once about your wife."

"Well, I'm worried about my kids. What's wrong with that?"

"Nothing. I'm worried about your kids too, or at least the two that I know. We've had some good conversations, and I hope we have more. But it's not enough. Ali is carrying a lot, some that you know about, some that you don't. Ant is depressed, I believe, but I think I can help him work through that. But they share a problem that I can't fix, or maybe I'm trying to fix now. I think they both feel that you disappeared your wife—not that she's dead but that she has vanished, which is different and much worse."

"I didn't disappear anybody," he said, digging his nails into his palms. "An aneurysm did that."

"You know that's not what I mean. Let me ask, when is the last time you talked to your children about their mother? Not a serious sit-down talk, but a casual mention of her in conversation?"

He opened his mouth because something about her question had created a moment so big it was black, ready to burst, and all he wanted to do was avoid it. Yesterday, last week, in the car, in the yard, at breakfast, at dinner. Not true.

"It's been a while," he finally said.

"They believe you have moved on."

"Goddamn it to hell, I wish I could," he said, and she pushed a box of tissues across her desk.

"I would be happy to do this again anytime, Mr. Brown," she said when he had blown his nose. "But sometimes at the school I give my kids what we call emotional homework, and here's my homework for you. You need to bring your wife back to life for her children. You need to let them know that you will never forget her, and that you will help them never forget her, too. You need to let them know that sadness shouldn't lead to silence. You need to find a way to do that every day. Also, dogs are a lot of work. Just saying."

"I don't know how to do this," he said, pushing himself up from the chair.

"No one does," she said. "I promise you, no one does. But we all have to do our best."

When he came in through the kitchen door he could see that Ali had made grilled cheese sandwiches and some kind of soup, and when she saw him she went to the stove.

"You don't need to cook for me," he said. "I'll eat what's left on everyone's plates, the way your mother always did." There was that silence again, that he realized had taken over the house too much of the time, and then there was a thump, and another thump, and a third, as he took magnets off the refrigerator and put three pictures he'd found in his office drawer on the front of it. Annie in the hospital holding Benjy with Ali and Ant on either side, Ali smiling at her mother, Ant looking down at his new brother suspiciously. Annie at the picnic table in the backyard, Jamie on her lap, laughing up at the camera while the baby pulls her hair. Annie with her arms around her husband, her head against his chest. He put them up without looking at them because he didn't want to lose it again. And he realized as he turned to the table that what he'd felt when he held that puppy, what it had loosened within him, was the feeling he had always had when they first got the new baby home from the hospital. Each time he had held this warm, boneless, breathing miracle under his chin, careful not to scratch the fragile pink skull skin with the bristles of his beard, and felt as though the heart within it and his own had melded into one and that they were beating together. And damn it, he said to himself, he said to Annie, "I am going to resurrect that feeling if it's the last thing I do."

"You can have my other half of grilled cheese," Jamie said, handing it to him across the table.

"I always said a BLT was the best sandwich, but your mom said a grilled cheese was," Bill said.

"She was right," said Ant.

WINTER

One of those uncommon cheats of a February morning, unseasonably and unreasonably mild, with a whiff of April that the adults knew from experience would turn its back on you a day or two later with a hard freeze and a heavy snow. If it lasted for more than a day or two, the trees would be fooled, too, sending tentative buds from the ends of their finger branches only to have them turn to ice pellets and brown and fall to the hard, unforgiving ground.

All of them were there again a year later, in the cemetery, in a circle: Kathy, Annemarie, Ali, Ant, Benjy, Jamie, and Bill. Filling in the oval of their booted feet was a small gray square of granite, ragged at the top edge:

Anne Fonzheimer Brown
ANNIE
She was so loved.

The ground was partly frozen, partly not, sheets of ice as thin as paper clinging to the grass and then cracking under their feet. Jamie wandered away and was stomping on it, making water shoot up around his rubber boots. "It's okay," Bill said when Ali started to go after him. For the last few months he'd been acting like someone who had been reading books on how to be a parent to your children in difficult situations. When Ali had yelled at Benjy one night after dinner, his math book left in his desk at school yet again so he couldn't get his homework done, her father had said, "I've got this." Later on he'd sat on the side of Ali's bed and said, "You don't have to be the grown-up here." She had only nodded, though she'd wanted to say, Too late. She'd been elected president of her class without even trying. "Congratulations, Brown," Mr. Horton had said. "I'm not surprised. You're the most mature student I've got." Melinda Buxbaum had smirked. Ali liked Mr. Horton, but he wasn't the guy to understand that a fourteen-year-old didn't necessarily see maturity as a virtue.

"I suspect you were like this even before your mother died," Miss Cruz said when she told her how she felt.

"It's hard to remember whether that's true," Ali said.

She was putting her life back together, but a lot of the pieces were different now. The Guatemalan woman who cleaned the house came twice a week, and on one of those days she cooked as well, so there was real food to heat up and eat. Early on, Ali had to tell her that one of her brothers wouldn't eat things that were too spicy. "Caliente," said Ali, who was in her second year of Spanish, but Elina said, with a head tilt and barely an accent, "So you want only cold food? Just kidding you, baby, I know what you are saying." From then on the chili tasted like sloppy joes, so Ali put it on buns. The boys all loved it but she'd liked it better before. There was a good chicken dish, too, and some kind of stew, and so there were only a few nights when Ali called for pizza or their father brought burgers home.

She had a group of new friends, mainly girls on the soccer squad she'd known before but not hung out with. She'd heard nothing from Jenny, nothing at all, and when she went to the school secretary to find out the name of the district that had asked for Jenny's records, she had looked at her over the top of her half-glasses and said, "A student as bright as you should know that that would be a gross violation of policy."

She wondered whether she hadn't been as close to Jenny as she'd imagined, whether she'd offended her by the questions she'd asked about that night, that night that still bothered and puzzled her.

And then everything became clear one day, right after they were back from Christmas break, when Miss Cruz asked Ali to meet her in her office at school. In one of the chairs was an older girl with long blonde hair in a ponytail, and as Ali came in she stood and put out her hand and smiled a little sadly.

"This is Jenny's sister, Elizabeth," Miss Cruz had said.

"Jenny doesn't have a sister," Ali said. "She's an only child." And the sad smile wavered, and then faded and disappeared, and the girl sighed.

"Sit down, Ali," Miss Cruz said.

She talked for a long time, Elizabeth Mason, but Ali was so overcome by her, the fact of her, the story of her, the look of her, which was so much like Jenny, that she felt as though she could only be quiet as the room filled with words. One sentence, over and over again: "My father is not a good man." The first time she'd said it Ali had looked at Miss Cruz, who nodded slightly, as though to say, You were right. Ali had shivered, and Elizabeth stopped speaking. "I'm cold," Ali said, though everyone complained that the heating in the school building was stifling.

"I moved in with my aunt when I was twelve," Elizabeth had said, looking down at her hands in her lap. "She lived in a different town, close enough that I could see Jenny, but not so close that I would see my parents. I didn't tell my aunt the real reason why in the beginning. I just said that my father wouldn't let me do anything. I couldn't play sports, I couldn't go out for the plays, I couldn't go to parties or games or sleepovers or field trips. At first she didn't think that was a good enough reason, but then she talked to my mother, and my mother said it was okay for me to live with her. And then I knew my mother knew."

There were long silences but no one tried to fill them. They seemed full already.

"Jenny was eight. The next year I asked if she wanted to come too, but my mother said no. And then right after that they moved. For his work, my mother said. A promotion. Jenny seemed okay in that place. She said she was okay. She wrote me letters.

"And then they moved again. They moved here, and she wrote me all about you. She said how much fun she had at your house, how she was playing soccer and basketball, how she liked sleeping over because you had brothers. And hamsters. She said our mother got her hamsters because she loved yours so much. She said she was going to go to day camp and be a counselor with you. She was doing things, all the things that I was never allowed to do, and it made me think she was safe."

Miss Cruz passed over the box of tissues. "It made me think it was just me," Elizabeth said. She reached for Ali blindly. "Was it true? Was she making it all up?"

"We had hamsters," Ali whispered, "but they died."

The crying went on, quieted, stopped. "My aunt made a mistake," Elizabeth said. "I was throwing up my food, and she sent me to a doctor. I told the doctor what my father had done, and she said I should tell my aunt, and I did. My aunt called and spoke to the counselor here and told him that she thought Jenny might be being abused."

"The old counselor," Ali said.

"I might have handled it differently," Miss Cruz said. "But Jenny insisted it wasn't true. Jenny's mother insisted it wasn't true."

"I'm sure my mother told them that I was mentally ill," Elizabeth said. Again, Miss Cruz nodded slightly.

"They just left," Ali said. "One day they were here, and then they were gone. Where did they go?"

"I don't know," said Elizabeth. "I turned eighteen in July. I'm getting an apartment and I'm going to college. My plan was always to come and get Jenny and have her live with me. Maybe they knew that. Maybe that's why they moved away."

"It's my fault," said Ali. "I asked her about your father. She acted like I was crazy, but I think she could tell I thought something was weird."

"Weird," said Elizabeth bitterly, with a hard little snort. "That's one way of putting it." Then she looked up and leaned forward to put a hand over Ali's. "I feel like in all this time, you were the only person who saw, who knew, who tried to do anything. Who said anything. Thank you."

"I don't feel like that," Ali said. "I feel like I just made her disappear."

"I bet she misses you. She misses me. I know she does. But she's afraid. He tells you terrible things will happen if you tell anyone." This time Miss Cruz closed her eyes.

"When I find her I'll tell her you miss her," Elizabeth said.

"How will you find her?"

"It's not that hard with the internet," she said. "The first time they left a forwarding address. The second time they didn't. He always finds a good job. They always have a nice house."

"Jenny had a canopy bed," Ali said.

"So did I," Elizabeth said.

At the door of the office she turned and looked at Ali, then at Miss Cruz. "She told me your mother died last year," Elizabeth said. "I'm sorry. I'm sorry you had this, and that too."

"I'm sorry that you had—you know. What you did."

"Was your mother a good mother?" Elizabeth asked. "Did she take good care of you?"

Ali nodded.

"You're lucky," Elizabeth said, and turned away.

"I'm so sorry," Miss Cruz said when she was gone.

"Jenny said there was no use talking to you because you couldn't fix things," Ali said.

"And now you know that she was right."

"Then what's the point of all of you? You just let Jenny leave, and now the terrible things are still happening to her. What's the point of grown-ups if they can't fix things?"

Looking down now at the granite marker with her mother's name on it, Ali thought of what Miss Cruz had said, so sadly. "There's some things you can't fix, no matter how hard you try."

Ali looked over at her father, who had his hand on Benjy's head, and wondered if he knew about Jenny, about what Ali had seen and what she now knew. She had figured out that Miss Cruz hadn't been able to tell her what she'd suspected about Jenny when Ali had first come to her, but she didn't know whether Miss Cruz could tell her father what Elizabeth had said to Ali in her office. Melinda Buxbaum had said at lunch one day, "So is your whole family going to the counselor?" It felt like one end of the room was listening, waiting, and then Ali said, "Your meanness only makes you seem sad and pathetic."

"I'm glad my father doesn't have a girlfriend," Melinda spat back.

"Are you sure?" Ali had said.

"That was a clever thing to say," Annemarie had told her when Ali repeated it. "But I think your mother would say it was beneath you." Annemarie had changed since she got pregnant. Ali had cried that night in bed.

"Are you okay?" Annemarie said at the gravesite, moving to stand behind her so that her rounded belly made a kind of body bridge between them.

"I am," Ali said.

"I'm tired," said Benjy. "And hungry."

Their father had asked each of them to bring something to leave for their mother. There was a small holly bush behind the gravestone in a metal surround that the cemetery had added. In spring there was an azalea bush, in summer daisies, in fall asters, all sent and paid for by their mother's mother in California. "Online mourning," Kathy had said disdainfully, but at least it didn't look bare.

Benjy had put an old copy of *Goodnight Moon* in front of the holly bush. Ali wondered whether they should leave it there. She pictured it sodden, faded, the pages wrinkling up, the binding giving way. Maybe all that didn't really matter.

Jamie came back to the stone, his boots muddy almost to the very top. He had left a little Lego man at the grave, and he squatted down and picked him back up.

"You're supposed to leave it," Benjy said.

"I don't want to."

"It's all right," their father said. "He can take it. Your mother would understand. Sometimes when you were little you would give her things, and then you would take them right back, and she would just laugh. Do you want to take your book back?"

Benjy shook his head no.

Ant squatted down and put the most valuable player medal he'd won at the foot of the stone, the blue-and-gold ribbon bright against the granite. Ali squatted next to him, smoothing the skirt of her dress over her knees. Their father had told the boys they didn't need to dress up, not like last time, but Ali did anyway. She remembered that horrible sack of a dress last year and wondered what had happened to it. It was probably crumpled in the bottom of her closet underneath her softball gear and her skates. This dress was burgundy, wool, a little too short because it had been her mother's and she was taller now than her mother had been. It wasn't the kind of dress her mother usually wore, but she could tell by the look on Annemarie's face that she recognized it. Aunt Kathy had just said, "What a difference a year makes."

Ali took a small enamel box covered with flowers from the pocket of her coat and tilted it over the metal surround that held the holly bush. There was a succession of pinging sounds, tinny and high in the cool air.

"What was that?" Annemarie said.

"Baby teeth," Ali said. "Eleven of them. Which means some are missing, but since they all look the same, who knows whose?"

Ali looked up at her father and then looked away.

"The tooth fairy took our teeth," said Benjy. "She took our teeth and left us money."

"Five dollars," said Jamie.

"Five dollars for each tooth," said Benjy.

"The tooth fairy gave them back to Mommy to remember us by," Ali said. "Mommy kept them in this box, in a drawer."

"So did you give them back to Mommy?"

"Is she still in there?" Jamie said.

"Not really," said Ant.

"She's everywhere," said Annemarie.

"That's right," their father said.

And yet when they went back to the house for sandwiches, it suddenly felt to all of them as though she were everywhere but there. The house felt different somehow. Same shabby brown corduroy couch with throw pillows that looked as though their stuffing had surrendered years ago. Same pine table with its polka dots of water stains that Annie had gotten with six chairs at Goodwill "just for now" twelve years ago and never replaced. It felt like Annemarie figured a house might feel after an exorcism, as though a spirit were gone. Maybe what they'd done that morning at the cemetery had let Annie leave the place where she'd lived and died. Or maybe it was that they were all leaving, that soon this house would be a memory, that Bill had found another place for his family to live.

Or maybe, thought Annemarie, it was her now. Maybe she had turned inward, toward the heart within her that beat in tandem with her own, the way she had realized Annie was doing time after time.

The hardest thing about friendship, she'd sometimes thought, was accepting that your friend wants what you think is not worth having. For years she had soothed herself with the notion that Annie was trapped by accident, that she would never have married Bill Brown, settled for the Green View job, lived among this untidy welter of jackets and shoes and dishes covered with crumbs and carpet crunchy with grit. There had been one disastrous weekend early on when they'd gone together to a spa, Annie on the phone constantly with Bill about Ali's eating, sleeping, dressing, all, Annemarie drinking a mojito by the hot tub, using it to wash down a couple of pills when Annie made one of her trips to the bathroom, and Annemarie describing their future, how now that Annie was going to have two kids she could finally finish school, get a job at the hospital, buy a house instead of moving into her mother-in-law's place.

"It has one bathroom," Annemarie had said. "One." She remembered watching the ceaseless circles Annie made around her belly with her palm, and for some reason it had enraged her. "It's your turn to live your life," she had said, raising her glass so the attendant could see that she needed another, and Annie had said slowly, with a smile, "Babe, this is my life. Stop acting like it's a phase. Stop acting like it's a shitty phase. It makes me mad, and I don't like to be mad at you." She'd rubbed her belly again and looked down. "It upsets the baby."

Annemarie was shamed by her memory of that day. She wished Annie were here so she could tell her so. She remembered a day they'd gone shopping together at a dress store in Belmont, and, stripped down fish-belly white in the punishing fluorescence of the dressing room, she had seen what Annie laughed at and called her baby apron, so different from the flat expanse of tanned flesh that was once above her bikini bottom at Rehoboth Beach. This was a sad little mottled pouch between navel and pubic hair, like a balloon losing its air on the floor of the party venue the morning after. Annemarie looked down now at the curve of her own belly beneath the navy jersey dress and knew that she might complain about her baby apron in the years to come but always bless the way it got there.

"You should sit," Bill said. "You look like you're going to burst."

"A little tact, dear," Kathy said to him.

"He's right," Annemarie said.

"When are you due?" Kathy said.

"The middle of March. Or this afternoon. Pick one. Everyone who sees me seems to think I'm eleven months pregnant. People give me a wide berth when I walk down the street now."

In some ways it had all been easier than Annemarie had expected. The doctor continued to predict that the baby was fine, strong heartbeat, good size, no sign of trouble, despite what she'd done in those early days before she knew. The pregnancy had certainly boosted her business, perhaps made her seem more approachable, more like a pottery and sweater person. The Mennonites had presented her with a beautiful oak cradle carved with ginkgo leaves; she had now commissioned four more for some of the shops and priced them high. Tom had signed over the deed to their house. "I never liked it," he said, which had surprised her. Neither had she. Why had they lived in a house together that neither of them liked, like some version of that O. Henry story? Had they known each other so little? With the money from the sale, Annemarie bought a little row house in Philadelphia, three bedrooms and an attic playroom. The kitchen cabinets were apple green, the floor red linoleum. She had gotten a couch with a geometric pattern and an imitation Oriental rug, and she was keeping the most colorful quilt Maude's crew had made in a long time. She was done with white. "I love this," she could hear Annie say.

"I hear you're class president," Annemarie said to Ali. "You didn't tell me about that the last time we had dinner." Ali shrugged. "I don't know if we ever even had a girl class president. I think we all had to be the secretary." She squinted at Ali. "Did you get your ears pierced?"

"The dentist did it," Ali said.

"Dr. Farrell? He did mine, too. And your mother's. He must be a million years old by now." Annemarie had never gone to Dr. Farrell with a story about an imaginary toothache, a terrible, terrible pain that made it impossible to sleep or eat. Maybe that had been the smart thing to do, given that he'd been her dentist since she was seven.

"I love those earrings," Annemarie added, smiling. "I gave them to your mother for her thirtieth birthday."

Ali turned the garnets round and round. "We're moving right before Easter," she said.

"I know. I'm giving your father some of the furniture from my old house. You're getting the iron bed from the one guest room, I think."

"Is that a double bed?"

"A queen, baby, a queen. You are trading up. Are you okay with the move?"

"It makes getting to school harder. But I get my license in two years."

"Oh my God, do not say that. That's a terrifying thought."

"Stop thinking about the future," Maude had told Annemarie the last time she went to see the Mennonites. "Be present in the moment." She sounded Buddhist, but then Annemarie assumed all religions had more or less the same underpinnings.

"How could anyone expecting a baby not think about the future?" she'd said.

"If you do you will miss so much," Maude said. "I have eight children, and the best times are when I see them as they are now and don't think about someday." Annemarie was automatically dismissive: "Someday" for Maude's boys would be woodworking, farming, marrying a neighbor girl at nineteen. "Someday" for Maude's daughters would be quilting, canning, marrying a neighbor boy at nineteen. But in the car, she was ashamed by that. She had had a someday that had veered into something else. She'd had a few, in fact. Annie had had one, and then none. Or maybe now she knew Annie's real secret, that she would never die because her children lived on in the world, that Annemarie's someday was now the child inside her, one heel pressed hard against a rib.

"Do you have a name yet?" Kathy said.

"Hope," Annemarie said.

"Bill, get me an Advil, my head is killing me." He could still hear it, but it didn't torment him every single night the way it once had. Philomena Cruz had warned him the kids needed his attention, and providing it had shaken something loose in him, so that the edges of the pain were less sharp, more pine needles, less razor blades. The knot in his chest had loosened somehow. Some of the trees were beginning to green again, and it felt not like an outrage as it had the approaching spring before, but like some sense of possibility, even if possibility would always be edged with sadness. The new house felt like that, too. Moving day, with a van and a real moving company. He'd never had that before.

"You can call me Mena," Miss Cruz had said the last time.

"Mena, I wonder if you would have dinner with me some evening," he replied, and he could feel his face reddening.

"I will have to think about that," she had said. "I'm not sure it's ethical."

"I'm not exactly a patient," he'd said. Or at least that's how he liked to think of himself. Not exactly. He was still enough of the old Bill for that.

He'd asked his mother to join them at the cemetery, gone to her office and taken her to lunch at the diner, although she said she could only get away for a half hour. "I don't understand this whole thing," she'd said. "This is what Jewish people do. Somebody told me that at work. They get you in the ground like that"—finger snap, hard nod—"and then a year later they unveil the stone. That's what they call it. Unveiling the stone."

He wasn't going to get into it with her, how he'd postponed picking a stone for months for reasons that he figured Mena would find pretty obvious, how he'd gone to the lot three different times, each time driven away by the behavior of the owner, who acted like he was the solemn and holy cousin of a car salesman trying to interest him in something bigger, showier, a cherub atop, a stone vase below. "My wife would kill me if I got a pink stone," he told him the last time, when the guy was trying to sell him on something mottled pink and black, almost the pattern of the workout pants he'd seen on the women getting out of their cars in front of the gym. He could tell the guy was disappointed by the size of the stone he'd chosen.

"And the inscription?" he'd asked, and when Bill froze, the man had pulled out a catalog of inscriptions, each worse than the other. Another something about the angels. Resting in the arms of God. We will meet again someday, and Bill thought, If only. Live laugh love, which had also been on a trivet in Annemarie's mother's kitchen, and when he saw that one it cheered him up, mainly because he could hear Annie laughing that big laugh she had, that would quiet and then erupt again.

He could hear her: You know, I remember sitting in that kitchen eating French toast and thinking, That's what they should put on my gravestone.

He'd have to tell Annemarie that.

Probably better that his mother had eventually refused to come to the cemetery, given how angry she was at him. One Sunday night at dinner, after the kids had gone into the living room to squabble over what to watch on television, she'd gotten up to clear the table as though she were at war with the plates and silver, and finally she'd said, "That Sally Lankford, she'll say anything. She said at bridge that you were seeing that Puerto Rican girl that they hired as a counselor at the high school. She said people saw her at school getting into your van."

"If you're talking about who I think you're talking about, she's not Puerto Rican."

"I said, 'Sally, if Bill is going to be foolish enough to stop seeing Liz Donahue, which I don't even know if he has, he would at least be with someone who was American.'"

He'd watched Ali pivot around the doorjamb like it was a dance move. "Puerto Ricans are Americans, Grandma. Just like you and me."

"Oh really, miss? When you look at a list of the states, is Puerto Rico in there right after Pennsylvania?"

"It's a territory, not a state."

"Exactly," his mother had said.

"And Miss Cruz is Filipina," Ali said, her voice rising. "And she's one of the best people I've ever known, and she's a woman, not a girl. And you can't talk like that. It's wrong."

Bill had taken a step back, gobsmacked. Annie's daughter for sure.

But if he had to guess, it was the house that finally broke

her. He'd blurted out what he'd said at Ali's birthday party about moving, and like some things he'd blurted out—"Let's get married" to Annie was probably the most memorable—it turned out that while it had been hasty, it was also true. He knew from experience that Liz would help him even if he had disappointed her yet again, finally buckled under the weight of her endless words and plans and expectations and the simple fact that he could not seem to love her. He knew that love sometimes came slowly. People talked all the time about love at first sight, the lightning bolt. Tom had said that sometimes about Annemarie, how she had come up to him at some conference and he had said to himself, "That's the woman I'm going to marry." The first time he'd said it in front of Annie, she had rolled her eyes, and Annemarie had nodded, and said, "Cleavage."

"Well, there was that," Tom said, laughing.

But no one ever talked about slow love, love that maybe didn't even start out that way, started out instead with sex and laughs and accidents that led to situations that led to a life you hadn't counted on but a life that covered you like a second skin. The love and the life inseparable day to day until you looked at a woman lying still as a stone under a cheap satin blanket and thought to yourself, Who am I now? What do I do?

In the beginning, with Liz, when he was feeling the guilt and the glory of having sex with someone, someone new, he had thought that someday love might catch fire. But every time Annie's phone went dead he charged it again, and one night, when he came home from Liz's house and sat down on his side of the bed and listened to the recorded message, he realized that love and a life with Liz were never going to happen. "If you need to speak to me, leave a message here." He figured he would keep this phone until the day he died himself, when it would be some kind of relic of a lost age, of his lost age. Even if Mena agreed to have dinner with him, and then maybe more than dinner.

"That might be strange for your children," she'd said. He wondered if there were guys who were drawn to psychologists because it would be useful to have a person who could analyze problems in the house, though there were probably guys who would feel just the opposite, who would call them head shrinkers and prefer their own heads stay the same size they'd always been. He knew there were women who said they would like a plumber around the house. He'd met them over the years. When he was married, they usually had something fast and dirty in mind, the ones who stood too close and made sure to say they were in the house alone. Once Annie died, it was something else, a yearning that was palpable and made him sad because it made him realize how many lonely people there were in the world. His own loneliness had made him turn to Liz Donahue, but he didn't think it was why he wanted to spend time with Mena. It was something about her small smile, her stillness, her silences. Her kindness.

He'd felt terrible about yet again leaving Liz, but just like the first time, she refused to hold it against him. She'd called the first week in January and asked to stop by, and he'd envisioned tears, maybe yelling, certainly recriminations or maybe an attempt to lure him back, a button unbuttoned here, the touch of a hand there.

But she had a house in foreclosure, an old side-hall farmhouse not far from the center of town, yet still on several acres, with a small pond in the back deep enough to probably have sunnies and maybe even some bass, shallow enough that none of his kids would drown in it. The bank was willing to make a deal that would make it possible for him to buy it now that he had the plumbing supply warehouse up and running. It needed gutters and paint and, according to Liz, a kitchen island, central air, and a screened porch, but it had five bedrooms and two bathrooms and an old canoe at one end of the pond. He'd signed the papers two weeks before they'd gone to the cemetery and then given his mother two months' notice. "Don't come to me if you need approval for a new septic," she'd said, and he laughed. He was laughing for two, and then he stopped because he was struck by sadness, the notion that the new house would have made Annie so happy. Five bedrooms! One for everyone. The kitchen was shabby, but no one had died on its floor.

The move forced him to do some of the things he'd ignored all that long year. On Saturday Kathy, Annemarie, and Ali had gathered in his bedroom and dealt with Annie's bureau and her half of the closet. First they'd argued over who would be most upset by the exercise, and eventually they concluded that each would be more upset by not being part of it. Ali had kept two dresses, two sweaters, and a T-shirt that said "Because I said so" that she said she would sleep in. Kathy wanted a set of scrubs and the old suede jacket Annie had worn in high school, and neither of the other two were willing to suggest that that jacket would be far too small for her to wear. Bill thought that wearing it probably wasn't the point.

Annemarie wanted the birthstone ring she'd given Annie for her twenty-first birthday. Annie had worn it always, except when she was at work, when she'd needed to keep her hands free of jewelry, when she'd needed to wash them constantly. Bill hadn't buried her in it because he thought he would give it to Ali one day, but when he'd seen the look on Annemarie's face, he knew that letting her have it was the right thing to do. He wasn't sure whether it was because of how she felt about the ring, or how she'd felt that day years ago when she had been holding it, looking at it in their bedroom during the darkest times, and Annie had said savagely, "If you were thinking of selling it, I'd rather give you the cash and keep the ring."

The look on Annemarie's face that day had been terrible. Now she just looked weary and a little untidy, and no wonder: Hope was only two weeks old, nursing constantly, spitting up a lot, never sleeping. Bill and Ali had told her to stay home, but Annemarie wouldn't hear of it. "How the hell did she do this four times?" she'd muttered, trying to eat breakfast at the old table and jostle the baby at the same time. "I often wondered that," Bill said, taking Hope away and walking her around the living room while Annemarie had a piece of toast. Tom seemed to have disappeared completely, and he wasn't going to ask why, not yet. Maybe not ever.

In the very back of the closet, inside a dry cleaning bag, was Annie's wedding dress. "Who gets a wedding gown on sale?" Annemarie had said at the time, still sure that all this would come to nothing, that her best friend would wake up one morning and realize that a life as Mrs. Bill Brown was a ticket to nowhere, as Annemarie had said one night when she was drunk and Annie wasn't because now Annie couldn't drink. Very quietly, with only a little edge to her voice, Annie had said, "You need to stop saying things like that."

"It was actually a really pretty dress," Annemarie said, as though she were continuing a conversation the other two hadn't heard.

"It was so her," Kathy said.

"Remember how she picked the date so there'd be a full moon?" Annemarie said.

"And then it was so cloudy that you couldn't see a thing," Kathy said, taking the dress in its plastic shroud from the closet.

"I've only seen it in pictures," Ali said. So they stripped off the plastic and Ali reached out and touched the cotton lace. "It's what's called a Mexican wedding dress," Annemarie said. "A little hippie dippy, you know? Flutter sleeves, tiers."

"We always said she could wear it again," Kathy said.

"Yeah, no one ever does that."

"Maybe Ali can wear it at her wedding."

"It's really pretty," Ali said.

From Ali's bedroom there was a sound like a squeaky door. "Maybe she'll go back to sleep," Annemarie said.

"That doesn't sound like it," Bill said as the squeak increased to squawking.

"Someday I intend to tell her in vivid language what she put me through," Annemarie said, heading for the door and beginning to unbutton her blouse.

"No you won't," said Ali.

"Yes she will," Bill had said. "But Hope won't care. And neither will Annemarie by that time."

"Can I keep the dress?" Ali asked.

"Of course you can," Kathy had said. "Why don't we fold it and put it in the hope chest." It felt final, somehow, Annemarie leaving the room to nurse, Kathy folding the dress carefully as Ali watched. It felt as though Annie, gone, had created a centrifugal force that was sending them all in other directions, to the edges of one another's lives, away from the center. Or maybe Bill was just sad, leaving this house he'd never liked and always lived in and in which so much had happened, everything.

The hope chest was the final thing to go in the van. That last day Bill kept all to himself, the empty rooms, the echo. Jamie and Benjy went to afterschool now, kicking soccer balls around and learning to play chess. Ali had a student council meeting. Ant had basketball practice. Between June and January Ant had grown five inches, so he was taller than Ali and would have towered over his mother. "Growing pains," the doctor said when Bill took him in because his shins ached constantly. He was not yet the star of the middle school team, but he was the best seventh-grade player, which had made him a bit of a school star, which had made him happier, brighter. Counseling had probably helped, too, and glasses. It was Mena who had noticed how Ant squinted when she gave him a pamphlet, and Bill had felt terrible. He remembered a list of Annie's he'd found on the refrigerator more than a year ago and had put away in her bedside table with the death certificate, some photographs, and two old pregnancy tests, both positive.

Tide, the list had said. White vinegar. Dry cleaning. Insoles. Glasses. Maybe the glasses were drinking glasses, or sunglasses. But maybe Annie, like Mena, had noticed the squint. When Ant put his glasses on for the first time he had had a look of wonder that made Bill's eyes fill. "Wow," Ant said. He had a special pair for games that wouldn't go flying if someone fouled him. Bill hadn't missed a game. If he had to put off a call, so be it. There was a new young guy in Belmont who was taking business away from Bessemer, which was fine with Bill. When he couldn't make it to someone's house, he sent them to him. Earlier in the week he'd left a message on his work phone saying he'd be unavailable all day, yesterday and today. Loading. Unloading. Arranging.

The hope chest had been at the foot of their bed from the morning they'd come back from their honeymoon. Annie had shown it to him the day after he proposed, when it was in the room she had lived in growing up. It was red, with a Pennsylvania Dutch insignia Annie said was called a compass rose, though he thought it looked more like a star. Annemarie had the same insignia on some of the things she sold. It was on Kathy's hope chest, too, but hers was green. They'd been bought when the girls were very small from some Amish craftsman—Annemarie said he was long gone, but his sons still did woodworking—and had been filled methodically by their mother with the sorts of things that were once thought a necessary part of married life, although by the time Annie first opened the lid of the chest for Bill, with a whiff of cedar and lavender sachet, almost everything in it had seemed laughable. "We're going to need these tea towels, mister," Annie had said. "Plus four embroidered pillow cases, although my mother calls them pillow slips." Annie had behaved as though they would never use any of those things, and yet somehow over the years they had: a tablecloth for Thanksgiving dinner, some tiny napkins with flowers in each corner for one of the baby showers. Little by little the things in the cedar chest had disappeared, become stained, or become so worn that they had become dust rags and then gone into the trash. At the bottom of the chest now there were only two things left. There was Annie's wedding dress, folded carefully and put to one side. Next to it was the nightgown Annie had worn on their wedding night, a transparent thing she'd called a negligee. "I think when my mother got this she figured it would be the first time the groom would be seeing me naked," she'd said. But even though it wasn't the first time, not even close, seeing her body through that thin veil had left him breathless, and more avid than he thought he should have been with a pregnant woman.

"Can we load that up, Bill?" one of the movers said, and he nodded. The negligee was flat and empty, no hint of a woman inside now or ever. He left it where it lay.

If he had picked it up, he would have seen that there was one more thing at the bottom, beneath the dress for the wedding day and the gown for the wedding night. It was a square of heavy paper with a butterfly at the top. "Bill Brown," it said, "by this time tomorrow I will be your wife. And I know this isn't what you planned, but let me tell you, mister, at this moment I feel like the luckiest woman alive." He would find it and read it someday.

ABOUT THE AUTHOR

ANNA QUINDLEN is a novelist and journalist whose work has appeared on fiction, nonfiction, and self-help bestseller lists. She is the author of many novels: *Object Lessons, One True Thing, Black and Blue, Blessings, Rise and Shine, Every Last One, Still Life with Bread Crumbs,* and *Miller's Valley.* Her memoir *Lots of Candles, Plenty of Cake* was a number one *New York Times* bestseller. Her book *A Short Guide to a Happy Life* has sold more than a million copies. While a columnist at *The New York Times* she won the Pulitzer Prize and published two collections, *Living Out Loud* and *Thinking Out Loud.* Her *Newsweek* columns were collected in *Loud and Clear.*

ABOUT THE TYPE

This book was set in Sabon, a typeface designed by the well-known German typographer Jan Tschichold (1902–74). Sabon's design is based upon the original letter forms of sixteenth-century French type designer Claude Garamond and was created specifically to be used for three sources: foundry type for hand composition, Linotype, and Monotype. Tschichold named his typeface for the famous Frankfurt typefounder Jacques Sabon (c. 1520–80).